Jackson reached for Taylor's hand and brought it to his lips...

Taylor gasped at the pleasure that radiated inward. Then he tenderly kissed the palm of her hand. His touch was suddenly almost unbearable to her in its tenderness.

Gently pulling her closer, Jackson opened his eyes. Pausing, he looked at her speculatively, and for a long moment she looked back at him. He waited.

Taylor's heart jolted and her pulse pounded. Jackson's gaze was as soft as a caress and she slowly leaned forward, her own gaze now frozen on his mouth. Her lips slowly descended to meet his, and she quivered at the tenderness of their first kiss.

FOREVER
ROSE

Janet Wellington

JOVE BOOKS, NEW YORK

TIME PASSAGES is a registered trademark of Penguin Putnam Inc.

FOREVER ROSE

A Jove Book / published by arrangement with
the author

PRINTING HISTORY
Jove edition / March 2000

All rights reserved.
Copyright © 2000 by Janet Wellington.
This book may not be reproduced in whole or in part,
by mimeograph or any other means, without permission.
For information address: The Berkley Publishing Group,
a division of Penguin Putnam Inc.,
375 Hudson Street, New York, New York 10014.

The Penguin Putnam Inc. World Wide Web site address is
http://www.penguinputnam.com

ISBN: 0-515-12782-5

A JOVE BOOK®
Jove Books are published by The Berkley Publishing Group,
a division of Penguin Putnam Inc.,
375 Hudson Street, New York, New York 10014.
JOVE and the ''J'' design
are trademarks belonging to Penguin Putnam Inc.

PRINTED IN THE UNITED STATES OF AMERICA

10 9 8 7 6 5 4 3 2 1

Special thanks to my editor, Cindy Hwang, for shaking up my life in a very good way and enabling this story to come to life. Also, much gratitude to my agent, Linda Kruger, for her hard work, understanding, and for answering all my questions. Lastly, I'd like to recognize Romance Writers of America—a group of professionals who care deeply about teaching aspiring writers what they truly need to know.

Most importantly, praises to my own hero, Jim, for ideas and inspiration, and for assistance with historical research. But especially, he has my undying gratitude for his tolerance of deadlines and writing schedules, and for his endless encouragement and patience.

And to you, dear reader: Always be ready to give true love a new beginning . . . even if you have to wait for the right man, in the right time.

Acknowledgments

Special thanks to my invaluable resources: San Diego Historical Society; Museum of San Diego History; Gaslamp Quarter Association; Ken Cilch, Sr., and the Wyatt Earp Room of the Gaslamp Museum of Historic San Diego; Villa Montezuma/Jesse Shepard House; Horton Grand Hotel; and the *Olde San Diego Gazette*.

Chapter 1

TAYLOR ROSE MARTIN walked into the garden pavilion hoping to escape the sweltering California sun. She breathed deeply, inhaling the essence of thousands of flowers on display in the spacious outbuilding, one of the most popular exhibits at the Del Mar Fair.

She removed her straw hat and fanned herself with it, sending an intoxicating floral breeze against her face. Her forehead was damp from the July heat, and Taylor smoothed her short-cropped mahogany brown hair straight back, fingers moving to the nape of her slender neck where her hair curled in ringlets from the warmth and humidity.

In the immense garden pavilion the temperature was at least ten degrees cooler and the air was refreshing— superoxygenated. Taylor felt instantly rejuvenated.

When he was alive, her father and she had never missed the Del Mar Fair on the Fourth of July. It was a tradition she'd grown up with and an important link to her past. A grin curled up the corners of Taylor's mouth as she recalled how her father had especially loved the county fair, spending hours walking with her through the fragrant and colorful garden pavilion. They would hold hands and read the scientific labels of plants they had never seen before, stumbling over the Latin words, laughing at each other's pronunciations. One of her father's life passions had been gardening and she had grown up sharing that love. She always felt close to him when her fingers were in good, rich soil.

This was her fifth year without him, and Taylor looked forward to the feeling of familiarity as she retraced the path they had followed so often through the gardens.

As she turned the corner at the end of the first aisle, an exhibit captured Taylor's complete attention. Gradually, the ambient noise in the crowded pavilion faded, and the only sounds she heard were the beat of her own heart, slow and steady . . . and a whispering wind.

She walked toward the exhibit and surrendered to the allure of the picture-perfect display—a Victorian backyard, set for afternoon tea. It looked as though the people had just left, perhaps interrupted by someone . . . or something.

On either side of a round table on the lawn were two well-worn wooden chairs. A green leather-bound book was open on one, antique garden shears rested on the other. On the table an old-fashioned china tea set sat next to a plate of delicate-looking cookies. A vase held an enormous bouquet of flowers that seemed freshly picked from the yard, their colors still vibrant. The flower beds that surrounded the exhibit burst with color, every square foot filled with flowering plants and rosebushes.

Now that's where I would like to spend some time, Taylor thought. Such a peaceful place.

"Yes."

Startled, Taylor took a quick, sharp breath, her heart in her throat. She spun around to see who had spoken. Though positive she'd heard a voice, she saw at once that no one was there. Taylor put her hand to her chest in an attempt to calm her palpitating heart.

At the same instant, she realized that the voice had

sounded very familiar. And after a moment of confused concentration, she realized why: it was her father's voice.

Since her father's death, Taylor had periodically experienced the feeling of his presence. Sometimes a familiar song would bring a specific memory of him, and it would seem as though she could almost step back in time and they could be together again. She took a deep breath and closed her eyes, trying to hold on to the feeling of him. "Miss you, Dad," she whispered.

"I know. Miss you too, Taylor Rose. And there's a message coming. . . ."

Taylor gasped, her heart thumping madly. Then, in an instant, the feeling of her father's presence was gone.

She blinked back sudden tears and wished with all her heart that her father was with her again. She missed him terribly. It still amazed her that, somehow, without his humor and encouragement, she had managed to finish college and nursing school, just as they'd planned. She knew he would have been pleased she had settled on becoming a school nurse. He'd been an elementary school teacher, and had passed on to her his love of being surrounded by children. And besides, she was always glad to have the summers off. She loved her job, but had quickly realized she needed the summer break as much as the kids did.

She'd kept busy after her father's death, finishing school, then finding and starting a job. Her busy schedule had helped her get through the years without his support and companionship. Though it still hurt to think of him, the pain had softened with time.

Taylor closed her eyes, desperate to recapture the fleeting feeling of his presence. *He had called her Taylor Rose.*

Her father had chosen her mother's name as her own middle name, so she would have a part of her mother with her forever, he had always said. Though Taylor had never known her mother, she had grown up hearing wonderful, romantic stories—how her mother and father fell in love with their first kiss, how they'd run away to be married, and how they'd dreamed of having a child to cherish. His tales of their adventures had been her favorite bedtime stories, and she'd never tired of hearing them. It was the kind of fairy-tale romance she longed for, but couldn't seem to find.

Throughout her childhood, Taylor and her father had used the symbol of the rose for special messages. He had managed to hide a rose in Taylor's school lunch every once in a while, pretending to be her secret pal. During her teens, he had trailed rose petals to the sink full of dirty dishes to remind her of an afternoon chore. In the end, they had used the rose to let each other know they were okay, that everything was all right between them.

Taylor opened her eyes. Back to reality. She scrutinized the perfect, peaceful garden for several moments, committing it to memory. She wanted to be able to close her eyes and see it, to be able to associate it with the comforting feeling of her father's presence.

Slowly her attention returned to the garden displays, until her gaze finally rested on a nearby rose display—one of her favorite parts of the exhibition. She had her own small rose garden on the patio of her downtown condo, where containers of miniature roses and assorted flowers covered every available spot on her deck. She strolled closer to the display.

Elegant single-stemmed roses of all sizes and colors were presented in simple glass vases. Each blossom was exquisite, and the fragrance in the small area was almost overpowering. She paused to study an array of crimson roses that had been in the morning floral competition, then leaned forward to examine a particularly dark red rose that was sporting a blue ribbon. It was unusually dark red, its edges almost black.

"It's beautiful, isn't it?"

Taylor gasped at the sound of the voice. This time, though, at least it was real.

Only inches from her, an old woman now stood who

barely reached her own shoulder in height. Oddly, she was entirely dressed in black—her blouse and long skirt were tailored to fit her tiny form perfectly. In dramatic contrast, her snowy white hair was intricately twisted into an old-fashioned chignon.

The old woman spoke again, in a low, silvery voice. "The color is quite remarkable, isn't it? That one's an antiquated variety. This rose has been in existence for a very long time—well over a hundred years. Isn't that astonishing?"

Taylor swallowed, her throat suddenly dry. "It certainly deserves first place." She couldn't stop staring at her companion. The old woman's face was dominated by dark eyes that gleamed like volcanic rock and her pallid skin magnified their inky blackness. Fine wrinkles extended from the corners of her eyes, covering her face like a road map.

Each studied the other with curious intensity. And to Taylor, it almost seemed as though the woman was trying to decide if they'd met before. Her stare was analytical, questioning.

"Do you grow roses?" Taylor's voice was breathless.

"I used to . . . a long time ago. Now I find it satisfying to enjoy the efforts of others." The old woman's attention returned to the roses.

Both women stood silently for a few moments until, without a word, the old woman turned and strode toward the exit.

Taylor's gaze followed the woman's shadowy image as she walked away. Just as the tiny figure reached the doorway, the sun came out from behind a cloud with an almost blinding glare. Taylor blinked. When she could see again, the old woman had disappeared.

Feeling slightly dazed, Taylor turned back to the roses. A business card now leaned against the vase of the dark red rose they had admired. She picked up the card and read: *Madame Rosalinda, Clairvoyant. Learn your past and future . . . if you dare.*

The card was handwritten in an elaborate, old-fashioned script; a drawing of a long-stemmed rose bordered the top edge. At the bottom of the card was an added line: *This card may be exchanged for a psychic reading, first ten minutes free—tent located near the Ferris wheel.*

So that's what the old woman was up to, Taylor thought, she was just trying to generate some business. Pretty clever, actually.

Tucking the card into the pocket of her jeans, an uncontrollable wave of apprehension swept through Taylor, sending a shiver up her spine. She shuddered. A thought slammed into place in her head. Was this the message?

Dad? Taylor called out mentally to her father. No response. With trembling hands, she removed the business card from the pocket of her jeans.

Madame Rosalinda . . . tent located near the Ferris wheel.

Nervously, she bit her lip, convinced she knew what her father had meant; she should visit the clairvoyant and have her fortune read.

Taylor turned away from the roses and walked briskly toward the nearest exit.

She had a Ferris wheel to find and a message to hear.

Chapter 2

TAYLOR LEANED BACK to enjoy the spinning of the giant Ferris wheel. The weather had stayed warm, and the ocean breeze smelled fresh and moist. And somehow the air felt different; charged with energy that surged with every revolution of the wheel.

She let her gaze fall on a small canvas tent—Madame Rosalinda's tent, a faded red rose gracing its peaked roof. A sudden chill traveled up her spine, causing an uncontrollable shiver. She rubbed her goose-bumped arms, thankful for the warm sunshine.

The wheel spun more slowly and stopped regularly to allow its riders to disembark. Taylor's gaze locked on the tent as she waited her turn.

On the ground now, she circled the base of the Ferris wheel and looked for the tent she had seen from above. A few minutes later she stood in front of a hand-painted sign at its doorway.

She gazed at the sign and read aloud, "Madame Rosalinda, Clairvoyant. Dare to enter the Astral World and experience the Third Plane of Being. Madame Rosalinda has the power to travel to the Astral Plane to see your future and your past . . . if you dare. Astrology. Tarot Cards. Palmistry. Tea Leaves."

With her hand at her neck, Taylor felt the throb of her heartbeat quicken. *What am I doing here? What if this fortune-teller's message is not what I want to hear?*

She leaned around the sign to peek into the tent, and sniffed the faint aroma of ginger incense, then stepped forward to get a better look. It was pleasantly dim and definitely cooler than the July heat outside. She felt the difference in temperature even at the entrance. Feeling suddenly a little nauseous and breathing uneasily, she took another step forward.

The sides and ceiling of the tent were draped with shimmering, silky cloth of dark green and blue hues that created an exotic ambience. A table stood in the center of the tent, where a candle created a flickering pool of light on the jet black cloth that fell in satiny folds to the floor. Two intricately carved chairs of dark cherrywood sat on opposite sides of the table. Taylor's breath caught in her throat and, her heart still pounding, she walked into the tent.

The floor was covered with a thickly padded rug in a floral design. Taylor's sandaled feet sunk into its cushiness. Dark red roses bordered the carpet and Taylor saw it was shabby and worn, though still elegant. She sat in one of the chairs.

In her peripheral vision, Taylor saw a movement at the back of the tent. When she turned she saw an area was sectioned off by dark, thick drapes. A shadowy figure came out from behind the fabric, and Taylor watched intently as the person stepped into view. She immediately recognized the old woman she had met in the garden pavilion. Noiselessly, the woman approached. Though still dressed in black, she had added a fringed blood-red shawl over her shoulders.

Well, she sure looks like a fortune-teller, Taylor thought. With trembling hands she reached into her pocket for the card the woman had left for her by the rose. She placed it on the table and waited.

"Ah, yes. You have come for a reading, I see." The woman sat in the empty chair, then smiled at Taylor and stared openly into her eyes.

Madame Rosalinda felt a spark of excitement as she stared at the young woman's face. It was a plain face, free of makeup, framed by mahogany-colored hair. Though she did nothing particularly to enhance her looks, she had nice eyes and good bones.

"Let me see your hands." The old woman reached out her own pale, wrinkled hands.

Taylor quickly obeyed and extended her trembling fingers, her palms glistening with perspiration.

Madame Rosalinda gently touched Taylor's fingers. "So tell me, are you interested in palmistry, perchance? Or perhaps we should talk to the Tarot, hmmmm?"

As she held Taylor's hands palms up, Madame Rosalinda carefully inspected the long, artistically slender fingers and the major lines of the young woman's hands. Suddenly, a jolt of heat coursed up her arms and caused her to gasp unexpectedly. It was an omen. She'd been right to leave the card for her.

It was the first sign.

Taylor abruptly pulled back her hands. "Are you all right?"

"Oh, not to worry, now. I just had a bit of a rheumatoid twinge in my old bones. Not to worry." The old woman held out her hands and smiled warmly.

Visibly relieved, Taylor reciprocated with a weak smile, putting her hands back on the table.

Taking Taylor's right hand, Madame Rosalinda turned it gently to examine the area on the side opposite the thumb, more than intrigued at what might be revealed there. Just below the little finger she noted the mount of Mercury, then looked down to the mount of Mars just at the edge of the palm. She saw a great steadiness in Taylor, and the mount of Moon indicated the young woman's great imagination.

The clairvoyant was careful not to react to the design within Taylor's lines of travel. It had been a long time since she'd seen that particular configuration. Her lines of travel delicately crisscrossed into an ethereal star-shape. From the star-shape, a shallow, barely visible line extended all the way to the palm and eventually intersected with the line of destiny.

The second sign.

Could she be the one? The thought made the old woman tremble.

"Do you see anything interesting?" Taylor's voice was quiet, barely audible.

"I see much happiness for you, my dear, in the very near future." Madame Rosalinda released her hands and stared into Taylor's luminous green eyes. *Yes, she could well be the one. The Tarot will tell.* "Would you like to see what the Tarot cards show for you?"

Taylor nodded.

The old woman reached into a pocket of her long black skirt and placed a small deck of cards on the table. "Place your right hand on the cards. Try to empty your mind. Think of nothing."

Waiting for the girl's breathing to become relaxed, Madame Rosalinda observed Taylor carefully. Though mostly hidden under the brimmed straw hat, her dark brown hair was cut short. Wispy curls framed the young face, her complexion creamy and fair. Laugh lines creased the corners of her eyes and there was a hint of a dimple in each cheek. Yes, her first impression had been correct. The young woman was not overtly feminine, but she was attractive in a natural, plain way.

As she squinted at Taylor, Madame Rosalinda guessed the young woman to be no older than twenty-five. Hopefully with enough life experiences to cope with what might come, but young enough to have an open mind, the old woman thought. Slight of build, she appeared to be in good physical condition. And there was a sense of inner and outer strength in her.

"You may open your eyes now, my dear."

The old woman tipped her head back and closed her eyes, then spoke. "May the angels and guardians of all worlds be with us today as we consult the ancient Tarot. May we see clearly and trust that the truth . . . is before us." Madame Rosalinda's head gently dropped forward. She breathed deeply, raised her head, then opened her eyes. "Let us begin."

The breath Taylor had been holding escaped from between tightly pressed lips.

"What is your name, dear?"

"Taylor. Taylor Martin."

"Ah, an unusual given name. Taylor, please mix the cards and choose a number lower than twenty-two, and we will begin our inquiry."

"Eleven," Taylor answered after she shuffled the cards several times.

"Now, take the eleventh card from the deck and place it facedown on the table. Mix the cards again, and choose a number," she said. Taylor obliged, and they repeated the process until five cards were facedown on the table.

As Madame Rosalinda held her hands over them, she felt a distinct vibration rising from the five cards.

The third sign.

Madame Rosalinda closed her eyes for several seconds, silently asking the blue light of protection to surround them during the reading. Finally, she opened her eyes.

Turning each card over one by one, Madame Rosalinda knew she needed to remain calm and reserved.

If she is the one, I must tell her the truth in such a way that she will do as the spirits command without fear or hesitation.

"Taylor," she began, "our inquiry today will be answered from the twenty-two cards of the Major Arcana of the

Tarot. The first card you chose is in a position of the Affirmation. The second is one of Negation. The third, Discussion. The fourth, Solution. And the fifth card,
Synthesis."

Pausing a moment, Madame Rosalinda said dramatically,
"Let us behold the prophecy of the Tarot."

She watched as Taylor set her shoulders in determination, and continued to silently gaze at the five cards on the
table between them, listening, her mouth tight and grim.

"The first card is the card of Judgment, which indicates
change for you. You are about to begin a journey of great
change, Taylor. The change will be significant and will take
a form that will be astonishing to you."

She noticed Taylor's face brighten at the suggestion.

The old woman cleared her throat before she proceeded,
choosing her words carefully. "This journey of change will
be precipitated by a real journey, one by train, it seems."
Having already confirmed the astral signs of travel on Taylor's hand, Madame Rosalinda had also distinctly heard the
rhythmical chugging of a locomotive when she concentrated on the first Tarot card.

When Taylor's stare met the old woman's, a momentary
look of discomfort crossed the girl's face. The woman
could see in Taylor's eyes that already the reading was
accurate.

"Your second choice is the card of the Moon. There will
be danger on your journey. The danger may be physical in
nature or it may manifest in the form of false friends."
Madame Rosalinda paused and briefly glanced at Taylor
for any sign of a reaction. She saw only an expression of
eagerness.

"Ah, the Lovers take the third position. There is passion
for you on this journey, my dear. You must put your faith
in this love, for it will guide you through the danger." Madame Rosalinda paused again to observe Taylor's reaction
to the reading. She still sensed concentration, but also a
degree of disbelief.

This time Taylor blushed, but she still remained silent.

"The fourth card is the Empress. Your journey will place you in a position of importance and you will need to look within for strength. Your actions will be pivotal to you and especially to others." Madame Rosalinda did not mention her strong intuition that the choices Taylor would make would determine life or death.

The old woman allowed her breath to escape in a sigh of relief. "The last card shows us the Stars. The Stars promise hope. You must remember, my dear, to believe in your own power to create a positive outcome."

Both women sat motionless. Only the sound of their breathing and the muffled voices of the crowd passing by the tent disturbed the silence.

Taylor stared at the cards and tried to absorb what she'd heard. The reading sounded mysterious, and the only part that made any sense at the moment was the train trip. The rest sounded too curious, unconnected.

Certainly, the romance part would be a nice change, she thought. She'd welcome the chance to meet a tall, dark, and handsome stranger and hoped the stars had better luck in choosing a mate for her. She had become resigned to the fact that none of the men in southern California were interesting or adventurous enough to compete with her fantasy of the perfect man. She'd grown weary of her pattern of short, shallow relationships. Never enough romance. Never enough spontaneity or devotion.

Madame Rosalinda caught her gaze, and Taylor watched as the old woman gathered the Tarot cards and returned them to the pocket of her skirt.

"Taylor, do you understand what the Tarot has revealed?"

"Well," she began, "in a few days I'm taking the train to Santa Barbara, but the rest seems unrelated. Not much else makes sense, really."

Madame Rosalinda covered Taylor's hands with her pale, wrinkled ones. "You must believe in whatever you feel, my dear. Believe in what you see, and believe in what you might hear." She hesitated for a moment. "Have you ever had an experience of clairaudience—hearing voices from those who have passed on?"

Taylor felt the blood drain from her face and, at the same time, her stomach lurched. *Clairaudience?* Her father's voice in the garden pavilion. She nodded mutely.

"Believe in voices, Taylor. Let them happen. The spirit-world is all around us and is here to assist us. Remember that."

Taylor watched, still speechless, as Madame Rosalinda stood.

"Good-bye, Taylor. I bid you a safe journey. Our reading is finished."

Without another word, Madame Rosalinda walked to the back of the tent and disappeared behind the floor-length black drapes.

Behind the heavy curtains, Madame Rosalinda dropped heavily into a chair, her entire body weary from the reading. She bowed her head, then put both hands over her eyes and said a silent prayer of protection for the young woman.

This one will be fine, she thought. The three signs had been revealed. Better yet, she sensed that the young woman's character was pure, and her determination solid. The journey would undoubtedly be difficult for her to accept at first, she thought, but she knew Taylor had no choice.

She had been chosen.

Chapter 3

Aboard the train at the Santa Barbara depot, Taylor walked down the aisle and found her seat. She got settled and watched the activity outside.

In the dim light of the station, people were finishing their good-byes, scrambling for suitcases, squeezing in one more hug. It had been a nice break, a long weekend in the beautiful, quaint village—a beautiful but *boring* village to someone who had expected a journey filled with passion, danger, and adventure.

As the train pulled away from the station, Taylor closed her eyes and allowed its steady rhythm to comfort her. She snuggled down low in her seat, her cheek against the soothing cool of the window.

Soon the constant rocking of the train made her body feel heavy and relaxed. Blurred images flashed through her mind of long-ago car trips from her childhood, like scenery moving by too fast to see clearly. With Dad driving, Taylor remembered, she always felt safe, protected from whatever was out there in the dark. She felt the same way now.

She was glad to be going home. The trip to Santa Barbara had been basically dull and uneventful—downright disappointing, probably because her expectations had been so high. And it was the clairvoyant's fault, Taylor decided.

Madame Rosalinda's psychic predictions had sounded so exciting, but absolutely nothing significant had happened on the trip. There had been *no* perils to overcome. Definitely no love affairs. And no incidents that called for heroic action on her part.

Instead, she had spent a very peaceful weekend walking along the pristine California shoreline and exploring the expensive boutiques in the mall downtown. At least it had been a good rest and a nice getaway.

The sensible side of Taylor's personality was now convinced Madame Rosalinda's mysterious predictions were merely an exercise in the dramatic. But her desire and willingness to believe in inexplicable things kept at least some of her expectations a tiny bit alive.

As she began to feel drowsy from the soothing rhythm of the train, memories of the fair—and her father—filled her mind with dreamy images.

Taylor stirred from her nap as she felt the train slowing down. She cupped her hands on the cool glass and peered out the window into the inky darkness. The station sign wasn't quite readable, and she didn't recognize the stop. She knew the trip from Santa Barbara south to San Diego included numerous small-town stops for weekday commuters who rode the train rather than fight the freeway traffic.

She must have slept through most of them. All in all, it had been a quiet ride, with few passengers to disturb her sporadic napping.

Resettling in her seat as the train pulled away from the station, Taylor mentally replayed the events of the day at the fair. What was the message? Maybe she'd missed something, she thought.

As she carefully pictured the inside of Madame Rosalinda's tent, a chill shuddered down her spine. A second chill traveled over her skin and she rubbed her arms to stop the crawl of her flesh. Eyes closed, once again she tried to sleep.

. . . Waking with a start, Taylor realized that the train was again slowing; it should be coming into the downtown station, by her estimate. She yawned and stretched her arms, rocking her head from side to side to work out the kinks.

As the train came slowly to a stop, Taylor grabbed the bowler-style straw hat she had bought on impulse in Santa Barbara and placed it on her head. She was dressed casually in a collarless white shirt and beige linen vest, with summer-weight tailored trousers in a chocolate brown cotton. Flax-colored canvas wingtips completed her look.

As she glanced around, Taylor saw that she was the only person disembarking from her car. The other few passengers must have quietly gotten off at previous stops, she thought, while she'd napped.

Taylor clutched her small leather suitcase and walked down the dark aisle. Why aren't the lights coming on? she thought. Why did it seem so dark at the station? She checked her watch, activating its built-in indigo blue light. Eleven-thirty. The train was overdue. She sighed, hoping she wouldn't have too much trouble finding a cab at this late hour.

As Taylor carefully navigated the steps leading down from the car, she peered at her feet in the darkness. Cautiously, she stepped onto a wooden platform that was barely visible, and then onto hard-packed earth. A sudden gust of wind blew her hat to the ground and she ran a few quick steps to retrieve it.

"Hey, watch out! You there!"

Taylor swung around, then froze—gaping in astonishment at a horse and buggy speeding toward her. She sidestepped out of the way, tripped on the edge of a wooden boardwalk, and fell back violently against the clapboard wall of a building. The impact knocked the breath out of her and she struggled for air. As her eyes became more used to the darkness, Taylor began to examine her surroundings.

The dirt road before her was rutted and next to now *empty* railroad tracks. The sleek, shiny Amtrak train was no longer there, though she hadn't seen or heard it depart. Some distance down the block she saw what she assumed was an old-fashioned electric lamp on a tower at least a hundred feet high. The subdued light it cast bathed everything in an unearthly glow.

Taylor stared in disbelief. *This can't be happening to me,* she thought in confusion. Had she gotten off at the wrong stop?

Then, at her feet, she noticed a discarded magazine, its pages turning in the slight breeze. With great trepidation Taylor picked it up and examined the cover.

In the dim light, she read, "*The Golden Era,* An Illustrated Monthly Magazine Devoted to the Artistic and Industrial Progress of the West. The Golden Era Company, San Diego, California. July 1888."

Taylor stared at the date. It couldn't be true.

This can't be right, she thought. Panic spread from the pit of her stomach and she struggled to fight the very real feeling she was going to throw up. A few feet away she saw a large wooden barrel and ran to it, praying it was filled with water.

She dipped in with both hands and splashed her face several times. The water was cool and helped, at least temporarily, to pacify her rattled nerves. Her face still dripping, she took another look at her surroundings.

The wooden building behind her appeared to be a general store, darkened at the late hour. She stared at the window display, reading aloud, "Finally a Cure for Female Weaknesses. Try Mrs. Pinkham's Vegetable Compound. It's Been Curing Since 1873."

She continued, peering into the next window. "To Cure

a Cold in One Day, Take Laxative Bromo Quinine, 25 Cents—No Cure, No Pay."

Either downtown San Diego has developed a sudden interest in nostalgia or she was going crazy. Taylor walked back for her suitcase and tried to make sense of things.

This is insane. Okay. I'm going to walk around the corner and everything is going to be just fine.

Taylor grasped her suitcase tightly and walked briskly to the corner, silently wishing with all her heart that she would soon see the familiar sights of a modern downtown San Diego. As she reached the corner of the building, Taylor hesitated—just in time to avoid a collision with an extremely intoxicated man who was rather unsuccessfully trying to navigate the long, dark road.

"Whoa there, fella! You just about scared the pants offa me!" As the man stumbled in his dazed condition, he grabbed Taylor's arm for support.

"Are you all right?" Taylor turned her head, trying to avoid the unmistakable rank odor of alcohol on the man's breath.

"Is that you, Willie?" The man peered at her, his eyes squinting in concentration.

Without thinking, she answered, "No, it's Taylor."

"Oh, Taylor, Taylor, Taaaay-lor." The man swayed to an upright position and wrapped his arm tightly around her shoulder. "Come on, Taylor, let's go get us a drink. I'm buyin', too!" He cackled loudly and dragged Taylor along with him across the street.

As she struggled to stay upright, she could do nothing else but go along.

Taylor stumbled as they turned sharply into the doorway of a building; her suitcase banged painfully against her leg. She gasped in shock as she stared at what looked like a saloon right out of the old Wild West.

The room was crowded with a mix of rough-looking cowboys and dozens of finely dressed men in black string ties and fancy brocaded vests. Scantily clad women in satin and lace were scattered throughout the room, seductively draped over the men's shoulders or in their laps. Card games were being played at every table and an occasional triumphant cry burst from the crowd, followed by the conspicuous slap of cards from the losers.

Taylor's companion enthusiastically dragged her across the rough wooden floor through the noisy crowd and successfully maneuvered them both into a small space at the bar.

"Hey, Jackson, give us rakes a couple o' beers and a shot o' yer best whiskey—an' don't be pouring none o' that rotgut. My friend Taylor, here, is right thirsty."

The man leaned heavily against the curved polished edge of the bar and finally loosened his death grip on her shoulder.

As she bent to place the small suitcase against the bar at her feet, Taylor flexed her weary shoulders. Her back to the raucous crowd, she nervously stared straight ahead. Above the back of the bar was a long series of mirrors, each with a gilded filigree frame. A delicate floral border was etched into each one. It was an unexpected touch of elegance in the bawdy environment.

Taylor stared at her own reflection in the mirror as the bartender poured their drinks. In the dim light, she instantly understood why the drunk had assumed she was a man, especially in her bowler hat and tailored trousers. She appeared to be a fresh-scrubbed young man in his twenties, perhaps a traveler from a place where fashion was unconventional, to say the least. *Thank God I'm not in my pink silk suit,* she thought.

It quickly dawned on Taylor that she needed to continue to pretend to be a man until she figured out just how to escape from the saloon.

"This round's on me, Taylor!" The man slapped her sharply on the back, and sent her hat soaring over the bar, where it landed neatly at the feet of the bartender.

Taylor's hand flew to her head in alarm. In the shadowy

light, though, she could see her short hair lay close to her head in a somewhat masculine style. She looked into the questioning blue eyes of the bartender.

She cleared her throat and consciously thought about lowering her voice a little before she spoke. "Could I have my hat, please?"

The bartender reached for the bowler and gently placed it on the bar in front of Taylor. A moment later came two foaming mugs of beer and two large shot glasses filled with amber-colored whiskey. "Here you go, Henry."

"You're a good man, Jackson. Now, drink up, Taylor, it's gonna be a good night for us—I think yer gonna be bringin' me the luck I need at the faro tables. Let's drink to our luck tonight." Henry raised his shot glass to Taylor, sloshing a little on the floor in his haste.

Taylor raised her glass and drank the shot in one large gulp. It was strong enough to make her eyes water, and she was thankful for what she always called her inherited taste and tolerance for whiskey. *Thanks, Dad,* she thought as the liquid warmed her throat and stomach.

"It'll be okay."

Taylor looked up, but saw only her own anxious expression in the mirror. *Dad?* she asked silently.

"I'll be here when you need me."

She whirled around and searched for her father's face in the crowd. Was he there with her? She must be going crazy, she thought. When the feeling vanished, Taylor turned to face the bar and found Jackson staring at her.

"I thought I heard someone. I thought it was someone I knew. . . ." Taylor picked up the mug of beer and drank deeply, simultaneously wishing the man would stop looking at her.

As Jackson turned away to pour more drinks, Taylor watched him. Busy as he was, in the cramped space behind the bar, he moved with easy grace, as though he was most comfortable in constant motion. Like a cat, she thought.

He was neatly dressed in a clean white shirt and ornate

crimson and black brocaded vest. Wisps of curly hair peeked from above the loosely knotted silk string tie. His inky black hair was combed back, and seemed to be cut in longer layers than most of the other men's. A few untamed tendrils curled onto his forehead. He was clean shaven, with a generous mouth that, Taylor noticed, was quick to smile.

Taylor took another swallow of beer and tried to distract herself, self-conscious and embarrassed by her attraction to the man. She watched Jackson's reflection in the mirror as he worked. The muscular outline of his broad shoulders strained against the fabric of his shirt as he constantly reached for bottles and glasses. She looked downward to a waist that revealed an obviously flat stomach and narrow hips.

Taylor blinked, now more than a little shocked at her brazen staring. It must be the whiskey, she thought. Why else would she be on the verge of fantasizing about a man who—with any luck—believed *she* was a man?

And add to *that* the fact that at least it appeared she was actually sitting in a saloon in San Diego in 1888.

Taylor closed her eyes. What am I going to do? she thought. *Just what am I supposed to do?*

"Taaaay-lor! C'mon with me—we're gonna play some cards!" An even more inebriated Henry put an arm around Taylor and dragged her to a nearby card table.

Taylor stood stiffly next to Henry in front of the saloon's large faro table. It was covered in dark green felt, with the images of thirteen cards intricately painted along one side, running from the ace to the king of spades.

At least a dozen people were elbow-to-elbow around the edge, waiting for the betting action to begin. The dealer scanned the crowd for players and quickly welcomed Henry as a newcomer to the round.

"Relax, Taylor, and you'll be fine."

Taylor's ears pricked up at her father's soothing words. She'd never seen anything like the card game they were

playing and she searched for clues as to what she was supposed to do.

Henry threw the last of his gold pieces on the table and
demanded playing chips for the next round. The house
banker shuffled the deck of cards, cut it, and placed it
faceup in the dealing box. The top card showing was the
queen of hearts.

Henry turned to Taylor and asked, "Well, what'll it be,
pal? Choose me a card to win this turn and the first spoils
are yours."

A feeling of panic threatened to suffocate Taylor.

She watched as the game started. The dealer showed the
top card in the box—a queen. Other players dropped chips
onto the painted card images as they shouted their predictions as to what card would appear after the next shown.

"Bet ten dollars on the king."

"Ten on the king," she repeated aloud.

Henry slapped Taylor heartily on the back and said,
"That's the spirit! Here we go!" He placed two red chips
on the table's painted king of spades as the dealer reached
for the visible top card—the queen of hearts—to begin the
first round.

With a practiced hand, the dealer slid the top card out of
the slit at the side of the wooden box and discarded it to
his right, while he explained every move in a singsong
voice. "The next card is the 'loser' and the dealer shows
another queen—the queen of diamonds."

Taylor gasped as she realized the next card exposed
would have to be a king or an ace to beat it.

Dad, are you sure about this? Taylor demanded silently,
then felt her father's presence disappear. She forced her
attention to the faro box, crossed her fingers, and visualized
the next card to be a king.

Henry cheered thunderously as the dealer slid the queen
of diamonds out of the box and exposed the king of hearts
as the winner for that round. Taylor stared in disbelief as
Henry merrily placed four red chips in her hands.

"And here's twenty for your trouble, Taylor." Henry winked and turned back to the table for the next round, thrilled at his change in luck.

Taylor backed away from the table, clasping the chips tightly. She returned to her place at the bar, finished her lukewarm beer, and placed her bowler back on her head just as Jackson walked toward her.

"Another beer?"

"I don't think so, but where can I cash these in?" Taylor opened her hand to show him the chips.

"You had good luck at the tables, I see." There was a warmth in Jackson's smile that echoed in his voice as he reached out to take the chips from Taylor. "I can take care of that for you."

As he scooped up the chips from Taylor's outstretched hand, Jackson abruptly stepped back and turned away, transferring the chips to his other hand and shaking out his fingers.

Odd, Taylor thought as she followed his movements. She did note, though, that as Jackson's fingers had grazed her palm a pleasant tingle had traveled from her hand, up her arm, and ended in the pit of her stomach. Something in the man's easy manner soothed her and, though there was no reason for it, he seemed somehow familiar and safe.

As Jackson cashed in her chips, Taylor suppressed a yawn. It was well past midnight, and she held on to the thought that if she could just find a safe place to sleep, she would either wake from the crazy dream she was having or at least be rested enough to try to deal with the strangeness of a new reality.

At some level, Taylor struggled to try to accept her bizarre situation, but at that moment she simply wanted to close her eyes and sleep. Things might seem more clear in the light of day, she reassured herself.

"Here you go, Taylor. I'm Jackson, by the way, Jackson Hoyt." He extended his hand with a smile.

As she reached out to grasp Jackson's hand, Taylor returned his smile. His hand felt warm in hers and she felt a shiver of pleasure as he squeezed her fingers. "Thanks. Maybe you can do me another favor and tell me where I could get a room for tonight."

"At this hour, you'll probably want to try the hotel next door, though I think they're full tonight. There was a big land auction today that brought in a lot of people from up north."

Taylor bit her lower lip, trying to hide her immediate feeling of frustration.

"If they're full, just come on back and you can use the cot in the storeroom for tonight." Jackson's smile quickly faded, almost as though he regretted the words he'd spoken.

Taylor bent for her suitcase, then forced her mouth into a thin-lipped smile and turned to forge a path through the boisterous crowd. She tried to imagine herself in a soft, clean bed, her head snuggled into a big feather pillow.

As she reached the doorway, Taylor tripped over an uneven floorboard and felt herself falling. Strong arms reached out to catch her just before her knee could make contact with the floor.

"Hey, there! Watch yourself, now. I don't want nobody breakin' a leg in my gamblin' house tonight."

Taylor quickly recovered her footing and looked into her rescuer's face to thank him. Before her stood a tall, classically handsome man with deep-set blue eyes, dark blond hair, and a long handlebar mustache.

"You all right, little fella?"

Taylor struggled to her feet, adjusting her vest and pulling her hat low onto her forehead. She felt vulnerable and small next to the man. "Yes, I'm fine. I just tripped. Thank you, Mr. ——?"

"It's Earp. Wyatt Earp. Now, you're sure you're not hurt?"

Taylor's eyes widened in amazement as, sickeningly, the room whirled and she lost her tenuous hold on reality. Her body went limp in a dead faint, still in the arms of the famous frontier marshal.

Chapter 4

TAYLOR WOKE WITH a start, her heart thumping madly and her eyes snapping open. She had no idea where she was or what had happened.

Breathing in shallow, quick gasps, she searched for something familiar, something to help her clear the haze. Eyes closed now in desperation, she told herself to breathe slowly and calm down, to try to make sense of things. As her mind floundered, she frantically grasped for reality.

Think, think, she commanded herself. She remembered fainting in the arms of Wyatt Earp, but had no luck remembering anything after that.

Sounds of heavy, steady breathing came from the other side of the room. Eyes again open wide, Taylor listened. As her vision adjusted to the darkness, her gaze focused on a narrow cot across the room. Someone was asleep there—a body was hidden beneath a thin blanket. She envied the peaceful slumber, suddenly feeling like she was trapped in an unwanted, never-ending nightmare.

The body rolled over and faced her direction. She carefully pushed away her own blanket, relieved to find herself still fully clothed except for her shoes. Then she stepped over her suitcase and hat, and tiptoed silently across the room.

It was Jackson.

His sleep looked as peaceful as a child's, she thought, as she knelt on the floor beside him. A black tendril of hair had fallen onto his forehead and she gently brushed it back. Jackson's mouth curved into an unconscious smile, and, for some strange reason, it comforted her.

The room suddenly darkened and Taylor looked up, her heart pounding as a shadow passed in front of the window. She saw the silhouette of someone peering in, hands cupped around his eyes. Quickly she stepped back across the room and into her bed, her heart now in her throat. Through half-closed eyes, she watched and waited.

The man at the window began to tap quietly but persistently. Taylor pulled the blanket up to her nose, hoping to muffle her own anxious breathing.

She heard Jackson stirring, then turned toward him. She watched as he cocked his head toward the sound of the tapping. In one quick movement, he pulled a knife from under his pillow and leapt out of his bed. He appeared instantly alert and ready for anything. Then he walked noiselessly to the window and motioned to the man to go around the corner.

Then he turned toward her.

Taylor closed her eyes and forced herself to breathe evenly. Soon she felt Jackson's own breath on her cheek as he checked to see if she was asleep. She waited until she was sure he had left the room before she opened her eyes again. Carefully, she slipped out of her bed and walked toward the doorway. Muffled, low voices came from the hallway, and she moved closer, listening.

"We're countin' on you, Jackson."

"Stop worrying," Jackson hissed. "I've got everything under control. The marshal trusts me like a brother now, so all we have left to do is pick the right time. And I don't think you should come here anymore. It's getting too dangerous. Now go."

Taylor heard footsteps and dashed back to her bed. She had just pulled the blanket back into its original position when Jackson entered the room.

This time, Jackson didn't come near her. She heard the creak of the cot as he settled himself, then a soft moan.

Taylor listened for his breathing to become slow and steady, waiting until she was absolutely certain he was asleep, before she finally opened her eyes. She looked first at the shape of Jackson on the cot, and then toward the window. What in the world had just happened? she wondered.

Whatever it was, she didn't have a good feeling about it.

Taylor settled back on the cot and clasped her hands behind her head, staring at the ceiling. She spent the next few hours willing the sun to rise, certain it would help bring some kind of clarity to the situation she was in.

Okay, somehow I'm stuck here. In the past. In the back room of a saloon owned by Wyatt Earp. In San Diego. I guess that part's good, though I sure wish I remembered more local history.

Taylor reevaluated everything that had happened since she had stepped off the train earlier that night. After the fifth time through the scenario, she relaxed and fell into an exhausted sleep. This time she slept soundly.

"And who might this be, Wyatt?"

Taylor's eyes fluttered open to the sound of a woman's cheerful voice.

"Ah, you *are* awake. What's your name?"

Taylor focused on the face of the young woman who stood next to her bed. "Taylor. Taylor Martin."

"Well, hello, Taylor. I'm Mrs. Earp. You may call me Josie."

Taylor opened her eyes fully and took in the entire image

of the woman who stood next to Wyatt Earp. She guessed her to be in her early twenties, with a very youthful face surrounded by long dark hair that she wore loose and draped over her shoulders. The woman looked very exotic and Taylor liked her immediately.

Taylor cleared her throat before speaking again. "Good morning. I'll just get my things and be on my way. I'll be checking into the hotel next door."

"Wyatt, dear, aren't they full next door? Didn't you tell me they had no vacancies?" Josie asked.

Taylor straightened her clothes, then sat up and reached for her shoes.

"Oh, no rush, now. It's just that Wyatt thought you might be sick, collapsing and all last night. Are you sure you're well?"

Taylor stared back at Josie Earp, whose expression now seemed like a mix of puzzlement and concern. Then she moved her gaze toward Wyatt. "I'm fine, really. And thank you for letting me stay here last night." Looking into the deep blue eyes of the famous marshal, she offered her most sincere smile. What she really wanted was to be on her way before any more questions were asked.

Wyatt stared at Taylor. "Have we met somewhere before?"

Taylor flushed, but remained silent.

Wyatt continued to scrutinize Taylor. "Now you're sure you're feeling up to moving around? Are you stayin' a while in San Diego?"

Taylor placed her hat on her head, stood up with suitcase in hand, and tried her best to look organized and confident. "Well, I haven't really decided yet, but—"

"Wyatt, aren't you looking for some help around here?" Josie nudged her husband and gave him an encouraging glance. "San Diego's a wild city, and not a safe place for anyone to be alone."

"Well, Taylor," he said, "I sure could use some cleanin' help here during the afternoons. Why don't you think about comin' back here in a couple days, after you're good 'n' rested, and we can talk about it." Wyatt wrapped one arm around his wife's waist and gave her an affectionate squeeze. "Now, we should let Taylor, here, go find a proper room."

Josie smiled and allowed her husband to lead her out of the dingy back room.

Relieved to be away from their friendly inquisition, Taylor followed closely behind, hoping to make a quick exit.

In her peripheral vision, she saw Jackson was behind the bar busily cleaning the mirrors. She waved at him and hurried outside before he could speak to her. The strange events of the night made her cautious about the seemingly congenial bartender. It was obvious that he was involved in some kind of devious plot, and logic and instinct told her she should stay as far away from him as possible.

Taylor stepped through the door to the street outside and took a deep breath to steady her nerves. The day was alive with city noises that brought unfamiliar sounds to her ears. She stood for a moment to acclimate. Instead of the mechanical sounds of cars and trolleys, she heard buggies creaking and horses neighing. The wooden boardwalk was crowded with men and women involved in their daily routines, with most too busy to notice her curious stares.

She stepped into the street, motivated by her rumbling stomach. At least, having won money at the faro table, she could afford a good meal and a clean bed, Taylor thought. She crossed the busy street, walking toward a café nestled between a bank and a hardware store.

As she stood in the doorway, Taylor heard the clatter of plates and cheerful laughter coming from the back of the room.

A young voice called out, "Just sit anywhere you like and I'll be right with you."

Taylor chose a table in the far corner of the room. With her suitcase stowed and her hat hung on the back of the chair, she simultaneously caught the smell of strong coffee and the mouth-watering aroma of freshly baked bread. Suddenly she felt as though she hadn't eaten in a week.

As Taylor looked around the room, she noticed a piece of butcher paper tacked on the wall that gave the morning fare: BREAKFAST WITH EVERYTHING: 25 CENTS. BISCUITS AND GRAVY: 5 CENTS. At least her twenty dollars would go further than she thought.

"What can I get for you?"

Taylor looked up and smiled at the young girl standing beside her table. Probably all of fourteen or so, the girl had the look of a young woman just beginning to blossom. Her waitress attire consisted of a white blouse, well worn but clean, and an apron covering her plain blue, ankle-length skirt.

"The biggest breakfast you can bring me," Taylor answered, "and a regular coffee with half and half."

"Half and what?"

"Coffee with cream," she corrected herself.

"Right away, sir." The young girl hurried off to the kitchen, visibly pleased at her order for a full breakfast.

Her stomach rumbling in response to the appetizing smells in the café, Taylor distracted herself by examining the other diners in the room. She noticed a shabby-looking family of five sitting at a table near the door.

The mother was shushing two young boys who sat next to her while both wriggled in their chairs and teased each other. She was firm but loving in her approach, careful not to draw public attention to the scolding. The father seemed quite a bit older than his wife, and Taylor watched as he closed his eyes for a moment as if saying a silent prayer. His forehead wrinkled in a worried frown for just an instant. Then his eyes opened and he smiled at his family, reaching out to pat the primly folded hands of his daughter.

The family's clothes were covered with reddish-brown dust and they looked like they had been traveling a long time. Two suitcases and three tapestry satchels sat under their table. The family shared a single order of biscuits and gravy.

"They don't have much money."

Taylor gasped, then closed her eyes and listened anxiously for her father's voice to continue. She heard nothing more. Just as she opened her eyes, the young waitress appeared with a mug of coffee and a small pitcher of cream.

"It'll be just a little while for the meat to get hot," she said, her voiced warmed by a friendly grin. "Here's your coffee and cream."

"The family by the door," Taylor began, "would you bring each of them a full breakfast and add it to my bill?"

The young girl's eyes widened in surprise and disbelief that a stranger would be ordering for the vagabond group. "That's gonna be a dollar and fifty cents total," she whispered, then glanced warily at the family.

"I know, I know. I can pay in advance. Here's two dollars right now. And you can keep the change, okay?" Taylor watched in amusement as the girl's mouth dropped open at the request. "And don't say it's from me."

"But what will I say to them?"

"Well, I think they're so hungry they probably won't care. But if they make a fuss, why don't you just say that they won their breakfast. Tell them the tables are numbered and theirs was this week's winner. Try that."

The young waitress's eyes sparkled in delight, then she turned and almost ran back to the kitchen. Before long, the girl reappeared with a woman from the kitchen, both carrying bowls and platters of food to serve the family.

Taylor observed the father's meager protests, while the children ignored him and cheered. On the table before the group was a feast of huge, steaming biscuits, thick slices of ham, bowls of thick gravy, a gigantic platter of fried sliced potatoes, and a basket of fresh peaches. The waitress returned in a moment with silverware, plates, three glasses of milk, and two mugs of coffee for the mother and father.

Taylor covered her grin, trying not to give herself away by reacting to the heartwarming scene.

"That was perfect, Taylor."

Thanks, Dad. And you would have done exactly the same. Her own breakfast soon appeared before her and she ate with gusto, relishing every bite. She could feel her strength return as she replenished her body with the good, home-made food.

"More coffee, sir?"

"Definitely," Taylor replied. "Excuse me, but could you recommend a hotel nearby? I need a place to stay for a few days."

"Let me go ask my mother," the girl answered. "I'll be right back." The young waitress skipped back to the kitchen, obviously pleased that the morning had turned out to be so profitable.

As Taylor watched the family finish the meal, she saw renewed hope in their faces. The mother and father smiled deeply at each other and happily watched the children eat their fill. The leftover fruit was carefully packed away in one of their traveling bags, and the oldest girl neatly stacked the dishes to make the table easier to clear.

Taylor looked up to see someone observing the family from the doorway of the kitchen. The woman grinned, then smoothed her apron and made her way to the family's table.

"Why, aren't you sweet to make the table easier for us to clear. Thank you," she said. "My name is Martha. Martha Reed. And I own this place. What might your name be?" She directed her gaze at the girl at the table.

"Annabelle Johnson, ma'am, and this is my ma and pa and my brothers, Frank and John. We sure enjoyed your cookin'. Why, it's just about as good as my pa's!" When she realized what she said, Annabelle slapped her hand over her mouth in embarrassment.

Mrs. Reed stifled a laugh, bringing her hand to her mouth. When she seemed under control, she cleared her throat before she spoke. "Now, don't worry, dear. My feelings aren't hurt a bit. In fact, I was just thinking I needed someone to help me do some of the cooking around here. I haven't met too many cooks that were men, though. Do you bake, Mr. Johnson?"

Mr. Johnson's eyes lit up as he answered, "Yes, in fact I have several specialties."

"Oh, his cakes are exceptional and his dark, sweet bread was the talk of our town back home." Mrs. Johnson eagerly interrupted her husband, unmistakably proud of his abilities, smiling broadly.

"Well, that sounds wonderful to me," Martha continued. "Now, make this a perfect morning, Mrs. Johnson, and tell me you might be a woman talented in keeping numbers and such."

"That I am. In fact, I had my own business back in Kansas, and I handled the books for the general store *and* the restaurant where my husband worked. We moved out here for the climate, you see. John, our youngest, has the asthma, and the doctors heard about the healing California waters. So here we are." Mrs. Johnson tousled young John's hair playfully. "We're making a brand-new start today."

"Well," said Martha, "then I'm certainly glad we had this chance to meet. I propose that you both work for me—Mr. Johnson could be my baker and you, ma'am, could be my bookkeeper. Annabelle, you could help my Jane, if you want, with serving the café customers. I can't pay much just yet, but I can give you room and board and three dollars a week to start. What do you say?"

Amazed at the positive turn of events for the family, Taylor watched as Mr. Johnson leapt to his feet and pumped Martha's hand enthusiastically. Mrs. Johnson looked at her children in astonishment—then they too caught the excitement of the moment and broke into spontaneous applause.

"Now, gather your things and Jane will show you to your rooms upstairs. You all just have a good rest today, and then we'll talk more at supper." Martha watched the group as they followed her daughter, then she turned and approached Taylor's table. "And I have you to thank."

Taylor was silent, unsure of the woman's intention.

"Because you, sir, were kind enough to feed this family, they stayed long enough for me to see they were just what I needed. Thank you." She smiled warmly at Taylor. "And Jane tells me you're looking for a place to stay for a few days, is that right?"

"Can you recommend a hotel around here?"

"Most of them are full of land speculators, with the auctions being so popular and all. But do this: when you leave, go left on Fifth Avenue and go down about four blocks. Turn right, go one block to Island and you'll see the Gaslamp Quarter Hotel near the corner. It's a two-story brick with a balcony on the second floor. Go around back and knock at the kitchen door and ask for Maylee. Tell her Martha Reed sent you, and she'll find a room for you."

"Thanks, I really appreciate your help," Taylor said. "And I'm glad it worked out with that family. They seemed like they needed a chance."

Martha nodded. "Things sure do have a way of changing," she muttered, turning to return to her kitchen.

Finishing the last of her coffee, Taylor gathered her things. With suitcase in hand, she left the café, determined to find the hotel Martha Reed recommended.

Staggered by the hustle and bustle of the streets, Taylor dodged the constant flow of people streaming toward her. Catching her breath, she stopped in front of a store window filled with dresses, hats, and boots.

Having noticed more than a few curious looks from passersby on the street, she realized she needed to invest in some more normal-looking clothing. She dismissed the picture in her mind of the reception the jeans and T-shirt she had in her suitcase would surely get. Looking up at the shop's sign, she read aloud, "City of Paris."

Inside, the proprietor looked up and greeted her. His puzzled stare confirmed that her appearance was just different enough to get a reaction. Hoping to diffuse any growing suspicions he might have, she headed for a display of men's clothing.

Looking through a stack of clothing, she quickly chose a gray shirt and baggy black slacks.

"My sister asked me to pick something up for her," she said as she walked toward the ladies' side of the shop.

Before the man could protest, several customers entered the store and distracted his attention away from her.

After a glance around the area, she chose a pair of black lace-up boots, a long turquoise-blue skirt, and an ecru lace blouse that buttoned up the front to a high collar.

Against the back wall, petticoats and corsets were displayed. Taylor looked again toward the shopkeeper. After confirming he was still busy with other customers, she picked up one of the corsets. The material felt like strong, coarse cotton and had very stiff edges where the lacing ran. Extremely stiff wires were placed vertically along each panel. She imagined they would be pure torture to wear.

Next to the corsets were several strange-looking devices—polished wood rings, hard rubber rings on leashes attached to waistbands, and steel springs with rubber cups at their coiled ends. Mystified, she picked up a brochure that described the devices, called pessaries. She read:

If you are a corset wearer, you need uterine support. We recommend Dr. Morrell's Uterine and Abdominal Supporter. Physicians advise the consistent use of a pelvic pessary to reposition the sagging uterus. Choose from many styles available. Most will not interfere with the act of coition.

Taylor stared at the graphic drawings that explained how the devices were vaginally inserted to support a woman's uterus. They looked truly painful, she thought. *Why would any woman wear such disgusting things?*

Shifting her attention from pessaries to petticoats, Taylor

chose an unadorned, ruffled cotton slip, then gathered her merchandise and looked for the proprietor.

Just as she found him, a familiar, handsome face appeared in the doorway.

Jackson Hoyt had entered the shop.

Chapter 5

"Hello, Jackson, what can I help you with today?" The shopkeeper greeted him with a warm smile and a handshake.

"Mornin', Charlie, did my vest get here yet?"

"I think it did, but I'll have to take a look."

Jackson leaned against the counter as the shopkeeper went into the back room to check on his order.

Out of view behind a thick, rough-lumbered post, Taylor took advantage of the opportunity to examine Jackson. Leaning against the counter, his long legs extended, he looked like a runner stretching for a race. With a shudder, she remembered the ominous conversation she'd overheard during the night, and wished there was no reason for suspicion.

Charlie returned with the vest. "Here it is, Jackson."

That's strange, Taylor thought, it looks just like the one he had on last night at the bar. Why would he special-order a vest that was exactly the same?

Jackson inspected the vest carefully as Charlie stepped away to assist another customer. She watched as he quickly located an almost invisible pocket built into the heavy lining. "Perfect," he whispered, then called out, "Hey, thanks, Charlie. Put it on my credit?"

"Sure, Jackson. Glad it meets with your approval." Charlie waved and returned his attention to another customer.

Taylor watched as Jackson slipped the vest on and turned to leave. She shivered at his smile. This time it was more of a grimace. Her brow wrinkled into a frown and she shook her head. Something was wrong.

She made her way to the counter to pay for the clothing she'd chosen, keeping her head bowed, hoping to leave without any questions. With her purchases wrapped in brown paper and bundled up with string, she returned to the boardwalk to continue her journey to the Gaslamp Quarter Hotel.

Still deep in thought as she walked, Taylor looked up just in time to see the two-story red brick building on the corner. As Martha Reed had instructed, she went around to the back and knocked at the kitchen door. She stood for a moment, eyes closed, hoping a room would be available.

The door opened and her stare was met by the stern face of a large Asian woman. As round and wide as she was tall, the woman's small black eyes squinted at Taylor with distrust.

"Well, what do we have here? And what might *you* be lookin' for?"

"Martha Reed sent me. Are you Maylee?" Taylor did her best to sound confident and friendly, though fatigue had begun to get the best of her. She longed to rest and soak away her troubled thoughts in a hot bath.

"I am. And who are you?" Maylee stood motionless, arms folded on her chest, her ample bulk filling the doorway. She looked angry, and unafraid, but still a little cautious.

"My name is Taylor Martin, and Mrs. Reed thought you might be able to find a room for me—I need a place to stay for a few days."

Maylee's glare softened, and her face broke into a grin that instantly transformed her face into that of the Cheshire cat. "Ohhhhh. Well, if Martha thinks I can work a miracle today, I guess I just better try. You come in here and sit at the table. I'll be right back."

Taylor followed the woman into the kitchen and sat at the table.

Maylee returned in a moment, frowning. "I'm sorry, there just isn't a spot I can put you here. Even the tiny room under the stairs is occupied. In a couple of days, though, some of the land speculators are planning to leave—they've filled us up for the last week and a half."

Taylor looked away as her eyes filled with unexpected tears. Then she felt Maylee's large hand on her shoulder.

"Taylor, you don't happen to know anything about gardens and such, do you? Someone I know needs a caretaker for her flower garden—she just lost her regular man—and I know she let him stay in an extra room at the house."

Taylor stared at the woman. "Sounds like a perfect solution. I'm sure I could handle a flower garden. Is it close by?"

Maylee grabbed her hat from a hook by the door and said, "It's just next door, but I'll have to walk over with you and talk to my friend. Let's go."

Taylor took a deep breath and gathered her things once more. She followed Maylee out the back door, struggling to keep up with the unexpectedly fast pace of the heavyset woman.

The two women hurried along the side of the hotel, then followed a narrow alley that ended at a tall fence. Abruptly, Maylee stopped at the fence's gate.

"Wait here."

Taylor put her suitcase on the ground and hugged the bundled new clothes to her chest, wondering what she was getting herself into.

Maylee returned a few minutes later. A smile filled her face, and her eyes danced. "It's all set. She'll take you. The lady of the house will meet you in the garden and show you to your room. You just do as she asks and you'll be fine. Come see me in a couple of days if it doesn't work out."

Before Taylor could say much more than a quick thank-you, Maylee was already on her way back down the alley to her kitchen.

Picking up her suitcase, Taylor pushed the gate open with her left hip, and backed her way into the yard. Then she put her suitcase on the lawn so she could relatch the gate behind her.

Slowly she turned around, and her breath caught in her throat. Before her was more than just a garden. It was an exact replica of the Victorian garden she had seen at the fair.

This can't be real, she thought.

"It's beautiful, isn't it, Taylor?"

Her father's voice rang inside her head as she walked up to a brand-new version of the same table and chairs she had seen in the exhibit at the garden pavilion.

The same two wooden chairs were there on either side of the table, though this time they were polished and new. A green leather-bound book was open on one chair and clean garden shears were lying on the other. The same. A china tea set was on the table next to a plate of butter cookies. A vase held an enormous bouquet of flowers. Taylor picked up the shears, placed them on the table, and sat down. She felt a little faint from the impact of seeing the identical scene.

Taylor closed her eyes and willed her father to speak.

"You're supposed to be here," she heard him say.

A warm breeze blew and Taylor removed her hat. She ran her fingers through her hair and tilted her face to the late-morning summer sun. She had to admit, she did feel safe in the garden. What a peaceful place, she thought. And for no good reason, it *did* feel like she was supposed to be there.

A movement inside the house caught Taylor's attention and she stared at a woman peeking from behind a curtain. The face disappeared, reappearing at the door when the woman pushed it open and made her way outside. The back door slammed behind her with a loud crack.

Taylor stood and quickly put her hat back on her head, watching the woman's angry approach.

"What's this—you put your hat *on* when a lady approaches? What kind of manners do you have?" The woman snatched the hat from Taylor's head and tossed it to the ground.

Taylor's gaze locked on the woman, studying her carefully. She was utterly stunning—with brilliant, glowing auburn hair carefully coiffed in an elaborate style of waves and curls. The woman's face was beginning to show the graceful signs of age, though not dramatically. The gown she wore was a rich emerald-green satin, with yards of black lace circling the hem. Her waist was tiny, and her generous bosom nearly burst from the low neckline. The woman's complexion was pale and flawless.

"And you stare—lower your eyes, young man, and let me see your hands."

Taylor, still speechless, obediently held out her hands.

"These do not look like the hands of a gardener." She shook her head and waited for a response.

Pulling her hands away, Taylor tried to explain. "My father was an avid gardener and I grew up helping him— I know I can keep your garden looking good. And I really need a place to stay." Taylor glanced up to gauge the response to her explanation and her plea.

"Well, sit down then, and tell me about yourself," the woman snapped. "Maylee says your name is Taylor. So tell me, Taylor, exactly why a young woman like you is dressed in men's clothing."

Taylor gasped and stepped back, nearly falling over the chair behind her.

The woman quickly reached out to grasp her arm and helped ease Taylor into the chair.

"Relax. I'm ready for an interesting tale today. Have some tea and tell Ida all about it." She smiled broadly and poured two cups of tea, then picked up her book and sat down.

"So far you're the first to figure it out."

Ida laughed loudly. "Well, you might call me a specialist when it comes to men, and I'd have to say it's obvious to me that you *aren't* one. Are you running from the law, perhaps?" She smiled at Taylor over her cup of tea.

"No, no . . . nothing like that."

Ida's voice was tender when she spoke again. "Well, I truly need a gardener, Taylor, so I'll let you stay for now. All I need is for you to keep the garden neat, weeded, and watered. It's my greatest pleasure to be able to come out here and enjoy quiet moments when I need them. Do you understand?" Ida smiled at Taylor and reached out to touch her cheek. "Now, don't worry. You'll be safe here."

"Thanks—"

"Ida. I'm Ida Bailey, the proud madame of Sherman House. I have thirteen girls working here in this class establishment. Do you know what I mean, Taylor?"

"What you're saying is—"

"Yes, Taylor, my girls are working girls. But they're all good girls, and I allow no smoking or cussing in my house. And the men who come here are expected to be gentlemen, or I introduce them to the curb. We have an elite clientele; bankers, attorneys—why, even the famous marshal Earp visits now and then."

At the mention of Wyatt's name, Taylor blushed and smiled. "I really appreciate your taking me in, Ida. I'll work hard for you . . . in the garden, I mean."

Ida smiled back. "I have a feeling you will. Taylor, you look to me like you might want to freshen up a little, so finish your tea and gather your things. Follow me."

Taylor gulped the last of her tea, retrieved her suitcase,

hat, and parcel, and followed Ida into the house. They walked through the large kitchen to a narrow staircase.

"These are the servants' stairs. You can use them to come and go, and be out of view," Ida explained as they climbed to the second floor.

The top of the stairs opened into an elegant hallway. "And this is the main bathroom." Ida pushed open the large door on the right.

Inside, Taylor saw a large tin bathtub and a wood stove. There was a pump and a sink next to the stove, and shelves stacked with thick white towels.

"The water closet is in this other room," Ida said as she pointed to the narrow door across the hall. "And your room is here, next to the bathroom. It used to be a storage room, but I think you'll find it comfortable enough." Ida pushed back heavy drapes that hung in the narrow doorway, and Taylor followed her into the small room.

"My old gardener left some clothes in the wardrobe. They'll probably fit you—he was a small man." Ida went to the window, opened it, and a warm breeze filled the room. "You can see the shed from here. You'll find all the tools you'll need in there."

Taylor gazed at the garden. From here the flower beds looked immense, and she realized she had her work cut out for her.

"Oh my, the day's already getting pretty warm. Perhaps you should just acquaint yourself with the yard, and this afternoon you can enjoy a bath and a rest. How does that sound?"

Taylor put her suitcase under the small bed, then opened her bundle of new clothes. The cozy room would be just fine.

"I'll go through my extra closet and see if we can come up with some dresses and pretty things for you—that is, if you want to wear something other than men's clothing." Ida squinted at Taylor, as though evaluating her figure.

"I'd like that. I did buy this skirt and blouse on the way

over here, though," Taylor said as she hung both in the wardrobe. Next she neatly folded the man's shirt and slacks and placed them on a shelf.

"Well, you'll need something a bit dressier for dinner, at least. I'm sure I can find an outfit or two that I'm not using. We eat dinner rather early here—at five," Ida said, "and our evening of business usually begins at seven or so."

Ida and Taylor exchanged one last look. Taylor smiled her thanks, grateful Ida's questions, at least for the time being, were minimal.

Taylor pulled from the wardrobe a pair of thin cotton trousers and a lightweight tunic-styled shirt, work clothes left by the previous gardener. Perfect for yard work, she thought, and undressed. She rolled up the cuffs on the pants and tucked in the loose shirt. Well-worn boots were on the floor next to the bed, which fit fine when she put on two pairs of her own socks.

She made her way down the stairs and out to the garden. Inside the shed she found a pile of dirt-caked tools, a watering can, and an old, battered straw hat. She put the hat on and carried the tools outside to clean. Finding a stiff wire brush in a wooden box behind the shed, she scrubbed each tool until they all gleamed. After discovering a hammer and some rusty nails, she made a place for each tool on the walls of the shed so everything could be neatly hung. There, she thought, now she could at least find what she needed.

"My, that looks wonderful," Ida exclaimed.

Taylor jumped at the sound of her voice. "Sorry, I didn't know you were there."

"I've set the table with sandwiches and lemonade. Help yourself and enjoy the rest of the day, Taylor. You've earned it. Feel free to take a bath before dinner. Oh, and I've put some things in your room for you to try on." Ida seemed quite pleased at Taylor's efforts to put the toolshed in order. "I'll see you at dinner, dear."

Ida returned to the house and Taylor sat down to her

lunch, surprised at her appetite. Thoroughly satisfied, she carried her empty plate and glass to the kitchen, then quietly made her way up the stairs back to her room.

As she reached the top of the stairs, Ida's loud laughter rang through the hall.

"I declare, Jackson Hoyt, you're the only man I know who only comes here for the hot water—and not to get in some." Ida giggled at her own joke. "And you won't even take me up on my offer of a free girl your first time. You are a strange one, Jackson."

"Ida," Jackson groaned, "all I want today is a hot bath and some peace and quiet."

Taylor took two steps back down the stairs to stay out of view.

"Now, I know you are partial to brunettes, Jackson, so you just say the word when you get a hankering." Ida chuckled as she walked away.

Taylor heard a door open and close, then she noiselessly made her way to her room.

Why can't I get away from this guy? Taylor shook her head at how Jackson's path seemed continually to cross hers. At the washstand, she poured water from the large tin pitcher into the washbowl, removed her sweat-stained clothes, and rinsed the grime off her face and arms.

As she washed, she listened to the sounds coming from the bathroom—sounds of water being poured from the large buckets she'd seen on the hot stove. Finally she heard the sound of the hand pump as the buckets were refilled with water.

Finished with her sponge bath, Taylor wrapped herself in a large towel and ducked out into the hall to visit the water closet. When she returned to her room, she eyed the small bed. It seemed sensible to try to snooze through the heat of the day, she thought.

As she neared the bed, Taylor noticed a glint of sunlight coming through the wall her room shared with the bathroom. Kneeling on the bed, the small knothole was now at

eye level. And when she looked through it, she had a perfect view of the bathtub.

Jackson removed his shirt and new vest and hung them
neatly on the wooden hooks along the wall. At the wash-
basin, he prepared the shaving kit that Ida let him keep in
the drawer. After adding a dipperful of hot water, he lath-
ered the soap, applied it to his face, and carefully began to
shave.

Everything was going as planned.

The vest was perfect—its hidden pocket would carefully
conceal the tiny .32-caliber Harrington & Richardson's revolver. It had been an exasperating glitch that Jackson
hadn't even considered. He hadn't known Marshal Earp's
meticulous habit of checking everyone for firearms before
they entered the saloon, even employees. Absolutely no
guns were allowed during business hours.

All his plans had been delayed until the vest could be
made to his exact specifications. But it had given him time,
he realized, to get to know the Earps. They trusted him,
and he could use that to his own advantage.

Now, with everything in place, he only needed to meet
a few more times with the McLaurey boys to pick the night,
take delivery of the revolver, make sure everyone knew
their part, and time their getaway.

It had been a long time coming, but he knew the revenge
would be sweet. As a young man he had lain awake many
nights, planning the death of the famous Marshal Earp for
the murder of his father. The pain was still as sharp today
as it had felt ten years ago. It was almost time.

Jackson rinsed his face and dried it with the hand towel
that hung from the washstand. He finished getting undressed and walked to the tub.

Still wrapped in her towel and kneeling on the bed in her
room, Taylor peeked once again through the knothole in
the wall. With a hand over her own mouth to quiet her

gasp, she watched Jackson's now nude body come into
view. His shoulders were muscular, his body well propor-
tioned. Conscious of his athletic physique, she allowed her
gaze to continue down toward his slender waist and firm
buttocks. A warm tingling began in the pit of Taylor's
stomach that she couldn't resist. . . .

Steam gently rose from the water's surface, and Jackson
tested its warmth with one hand. Next to the tub, Ida kept
a shelf of glass bottles filled with scented oils. He reached
for one and uncorked it.

As he breathed in the sweet aroma of the rosewater, a
woman's face appeared behind his closed eyes. The face
was young, with pleading emerald eyes. Her lips were moving as though she were asking a question, and he guessed
that she was naked beneath her silky red robe. . . .

Jackson opened his eyes in surprise. He had the distinct
feeling that he knew the face. Smiling, he wondered if Ida
was putting more than rose petals in the bath oil. After he
poured some of the oil into the bathwater, he climbed into
the tub, standing for a few moments before luxuriously
sinking into the hot water.

Taylor continued to watch Jackson with uncensored scrutiny. Silky black hair covered Jackson's chest like a fine,
curly carpet, and her fingers unconsciously flexed, ready to
caress. Her gaze followed the pattern of hair as it tapered
to his flat, muscular stomach, only to begin again below.
Her stare boldly resumed, her body beginning to ache deliciously. Her gaze slid downward still. A delightful shiver
of wanting ran through her and her pulse quickened at the
speculation of touching him there. Mentally, she caressed
and stroked him, completely mesmerized. . . .

Jackson felt his muscles relax, one by one, soothed by the
hot water. He slid further into the tub, until the back of his
neck cradled its edge. With every breath he inhaled the

scent of roses, and recalled the vision of the mystery woman's face.

A blurred image reappeared in his mind and he began to examine it for any detail that might make sense. Her eyes were a deep emerald green and they had a sheen of purpose. Wisps of rich, mahogany brown hair framed her face, and she had the look of both delicacy and strength. Mentally, he commanded the image to drop her robe. She did as he asked with a dimpled smile that sent his pulse racing. His body responded instantly, throbbing and hard. The woman's body arched toward him. Her breasts were firm and high-perched, and her nipples hardened before his eyes. She was slender, almost willowy, with a narrow waist and slim hips.

Taylor watched Jackson in amazement and realized her own body was at the same point of arousal. She felt passion rising in her like the hottest fire, clouding her brain. Falling back onto the bed, she felt the vibration of liquid fire between her legs. Closing her eyes, she suddenly soared to an awesome, shuddering ecstasy, her pleasure pure and explosive. Feeling sweetly drained, she succumbed to a numbed sleep. . . .

Jackson's eyes snapped open in response to his body's physical reaction to the vision of the willowy beauty. *This is crazy,* he thought, and abruptly stood up in the tub. His body felt as if it were half ice and half flame. The contrasting cool air served to calm his throbbing arousal and he shook his head to clear it of the image of the dark-haired woman.

I don't have time for daydreams, he thought angrily, and sank back into the tub. His skin still tingling, he roughly scrubbed away any lingering feelings of desire. Maybe he needed to take Ida up on her offer after all. He wondered if such a girl existed in Ida's harem.

He finished his bath with a thorough soaping of his long black hair, then toweled off quickly and dressed. He had an appointment with the McLaureys.

It was time to finish things.

Chapter 6

TAYLOR STIRRED FROM her nap, and roused a dream-image of Jackson. In her dream she'd joined him in the tub for a delicious, erotic shared bath. As she rubbed her eyes, she brought herself back to reality. She felt almost drugged—in a half-asleep and half-awake state—and, for a moment, forgot where she was.

Late-afternoon sunlight filtered through the window and she sighed with the realization that she was still in the little room at Ida Bailey's. With her towel secured anew, she stepped out of her room to again use the privy across the hall. Then she knocked on the bathroom door to make sure it was not occupied.

She entered the room and immediately quivered from the memory of Jackson, both embarrassed and mystified by her own tremendous physical reaction to him—especially the unexpected orgasm.

She had never felt such desire before and was not quite sure how to handle it. Her boyfriends of the past all had a certain common thread of boring security, and each had—at least in the beginning—respected her wish to delay their lovemaking. To her it hadn't seemed right to make love without any of the passionate desire she expected to feel. Eventually, though, each had issued an ultimatum and she'd sent them on their way. At first she'd figured it was just a string of bad luck. But her fear was that she'd never find that special someone. She'd lost the desire to even look.

No one had ever made her feel as erotic as she'd felt watching Jackson, and she wasn't used to feeling the lack of control. It felt like the passion she'd imagined existed between two people that were meant to be together. This was the passion she'd imagined must have existed between her mother and father.

But why *him?* she wondered, shivering at the thought. Why should *he* be the one to evoke the long-suppressed feelings within her?

After hanging her towel on one of the hooks, Taylor lifted a steaming bucket of hot water and poured it into the tub. Then she added another bucket of hot water and then added cold until it felt perfect. Impulsively, she reached for the bottle that Jackson had poured from for own his bathwater. Uncorking the bottle, she breathed in the delicate smell of flowers. Rosewater, she decided, and added some to the bathwater.

Efficiently and quickly she washed, soaped, and rinsed her short hair. Minutes later she stepped out of the tub and toweled off. As the water drained, she felt restless and a little uneasy, as though she were waiting for something to happen.

Back in her room, Taylor opened the wardrobe to dress for dinner. Several dresses now hung next to her own newly purchased clothes. Her fingers touched the smooth, satiny material and she was amazed at the intricacy of some of the lacework. Finally she chose a rosy-pink dress with a full, ruffled skirt. Its bodice was fitted and the neckline didn't look too low, she thought. She put the dress on and added her own petticoat and the white cotton stockings Ida had provided. The short boots she'd bought fit well enough, and with a quick brush of her hair, she was ready.

Ida knocked on the wall outside Taylor's curtained doorway. "Are you ready for dinner, my dear? May I come in?"

"Of course, Ida. Thank you so much for the dresses—come see."

Ida drew back the curtain. "My goodness, you certainly look different in a dress. And that one was always one of my favorites." She smiled at Taylor.

"And I brought you something else. I don't know why you've cut your beautiful hair, but why don't we pin this on." Ida held out a fall of brunette hair, carefully curled into a flowing, feminine style. She secured it to the back of Taylor's head. It blended perfectly.

"There, now you look absolutely wonderful," she exclaimed. Retrieving a case from her pocket, she added, "With a touch of rouge to your cheeks and lips, you're complete. Now, come with me, and I'll introduce you to the girls."

Taylor took a quick peek into the mirror, amazed at the transformation. "It doesn't even look like me."

"Taylor, should I introduce you as that . . . or perhaps you need a different name for tonight? None of my girls use their given names, actually. Do you have a middle name, my dear?"

"Yes, it's Rose."

"Ah, much better. That's what I shall call you—at least when you're wearing a dress." Ida chuckled softly as she led Taylor down the hall to the front stairs.

As they made their way to the dining room, Taylor heard the sounds of laughter and conversation. The large dining table was surrounded by at least a dozen young women enjoying a meal of baked chicken and fresh summer vegetables. They quickly added a chair at the table for her and dished up a heaping plate of food.

"Everyone," Ida said, tapping her spoon on the edge of a glass, "this is Rose. She'll be staying with us for a while. And no need to raise those eyebrows, now—she'll be working in my garden, that's all. So all of you be nice to her."

Taylor stared at the women. They were all gorgeous, with beautiful gowns, coiffed hair, and lightly made-up faces. They were not what she expected. Each looked happy and well cared for, she thought, and it was obvious that Ida carefully maintained their environment. The place definitely felt more like a home than a brothel.

"So give Rose her privacy, and make her feel at home, girls. And pass down those biscuits," Ida added, patting Taylor's hand in a motherly way.

The lively conversation resumed and Taylor quietly ate her dinner, marveling at the volume at the table. As the girls finished, one by one they retired to the parlor to wait for their evening to begin. As she cleared the table, she was surprised to find Maylee in the kitchen preparing the sink for the dirty dishes.

"My, my. And who might you be? You're new here, aren't you?" Maylee squinted to get a better look at Taylor. "Why, you're that boy that Martha Reed sent to my back door, aren't you?" Maylee put her hands on her hips and roared with laughter. "Well, you are full of surprises, now, aren't you?"

Taylor stood in the doorway with her mouth agape.

"Now, don't you worry. It's certainly none of my business what you're up to. Besides, if my friend Martha thinks you're respectable enough to send to me, it's good enough for me. Now bring me those dishes before you get that pretty dress dirty." Maylee beckoned to Taylor.

"I . . . don't know what to say," Taylor began. "It's a little complicated. And Ida asked me to dress for dinner, but I'm still only working in the garden—"

"Well, you sure could pass for one of her gals, you know. With that pretty long hair and that lovely dress, you just better stay out of the parlor." Maylee chortled at the thought and waved Taylor back to the dining room for more dishes.

"Now, tell me again what your name is," Maylee asked

when Taylor returned to the kitchen. "It was some kind of man's name, wasn't it?"

"Well, my name really is Taylor," she answered, "but Ida introduced me by my middle name tonight—it's Rose."

"Ah, now that suits you just fine. Well, Rose, we're finished in here. Time for me to go back to the hotel. I just come over here sometimes to serve dinner and clean up a little. Thank you for helping. You know, I have a job tomorrow night that I sure could use some help with. Are you up to doing some extra evening work?" Maylee asked. "It's a nice place. The master of the house is a bit eccentric, but he pays well."

"I'd be happy to help you."

"Wonderful—we'll leave here after dinner tomorrow night. Wear your fanciest dress, too," she instructed. "You'll be serving some very important people, maybe even royalty. Mr. Shepard throws some impressive parties, and he knows everyone who's important in this city."

Maylee waved at Taylor as she walked out the back door and headed toward the garden gate.

"See you tomorrow, Maylee," Taylor called. She followed the cook out into the backyard, intending to enjoy the rest of the evening in the garden. Sounds drifted out from the parlor—piano music and lilting feminine laughter, both eventually muffled by the rowdy sounds of masculine voices.

Glad to offer her help to Maylee, she was even more pleased to have any kind of future plans at this point. It made her existence seem somehow more real. It had finally sunk in that she had to face the fact that she was here. Really here. In the past. And living at a brothel, no less. At least she had a roof over her head and a job of sorts, and she knew things could certainly be worse.

Taylor sighed. This is all too strange, she thought, and so hard to believe it was only yesterday she was on a train going home from Santa Barbara—and a few days before that, at the fair. As she sat in one of the chairs, she closed her eyes and thought about the chain of events that had catapulted her into the past.

"Remember what was predicted, Taylor."

Her father's voice rang clearly in her, sending a shock of realization through her.

What did he mean?

Taylor recalled details of the psychic reading she'd had with Madame Rosalinda and her father's voice reminding her that the predictions did indeed seem to be happening. But what was she doing there? What was she supposed to accomplish? And what about the danger?

Taylor shivered, remembering her suspicions about Jackson. Is he the danger? Could he be the false friend?

As she felt her father's presence pull away from her, her confidence drained away with it. Taylor's eyes filled with tears. *I wish you were here, Dad.*

"Well, Jackson, did you decide to finally take me up on my offer for a free gal?" Ida's eyes twinkled as she gave him a playful jab in the ribs.

Jackson had just walked in Ida's front door, breathless. "It's my night off from the bar. Actually, I have an appointment and just wanted to wait here for a while, that's all."

"Well, suit yourself. Just don't go distracting any of my girls, then. There's some of Maylee's peach pie in the kitchen if you're hungry. Now shoo!" Ida waved him toward the kitchen and returned her attention to the men gathered around the piano in the parlor. There, several of Ida's girls were chatting with them, looking quite innocent and virginal. Within the conversation, however, selections were being made and soon the parlor would be empty except for the piano player and Ida—another successful night of business was underway.

Slipping into Ida's on his way to find the McLaurey boys, Jackson was certain someone was following him. He knew he should take his own sweet time getting to their meeting place. Better safe than sorry, he thought. He probably had at least an hour before they'd be there.

Jackson made his way into the kitchen for some of the pie Ida had mentioned. As he stood by the back door, enjoying each sweet forkful, he gazed out at a dark-haired woman walking across the manicured backyard. He watched her hips sway as she made her way to the garden shed. There, she put on a pair of leather work gloves, grabbed a flat willow basket, and selected a pair of pruning shears. Why would one of Ida's girls be out working in the yard?

Walking over to one of the side flower beds, the woman bent over a bush of miniature yellow roses and quickly cut off the dead flower heads, letting them drop into the basket. Working her way toward the house, she continued to prune until all the bushes were neat and trimmed.

Jackson stood watching, openly staring at her as she bent over to prune the rosebushes, affording him a provocative peek at the top of each breast. Fearing she would see him as she came closer to the door, he backed away and turned to put his dish and fork in the sink. When he returned to the door, he watched her put her things away in the garden shed, then sit down at the table, primly waiting. It looked as though she were waiting for him.

Taylor looked up as Jackson walked across the lawn directly toward her.

"Evening. I thought I might join you . . . may I sit with you? I'm Jackson Hoyt." Jackson bowed slightly and graciously extended his hand to Taylor. "I'm sorry, I don't believe I know your name."

Taylor stared, baffled that Jackson had managed to find her again. Her breath escaped with relief. At least he hadn't recognized her. "I'm Ta . . . my name is Rose. Pleased to meet you, Mr. Hoyt." Taylor did her best to distract him with her warmest smile, hoping her awkward reply would go unnoticed. She held out her hand.

As Jackson leaned closer to her, she smelled the delicate aroma of roses. The bathwater, she remembered dizzily. In the dreamy light of dusk, his dark hair looked so touchable—soft and silky, with a few loose tendrils caressing his forehead. His eyes were a pale blue. Almost a sky blue, she thought. His newly shaven face was already showing the shadow of regrowth. And he had a perfect, full mouth. Gorgeous—dressed or naked, she thought. Her cheeks blazed with sudden heat.

As Jackson touched Taylor's slender fingers, he pulled his hand away quickly and stepped back. His eyes narrowed, then he motioned for Taylor's permission to sit down. After she nodded, he joined her at the table.

"Rose, you seem to know how to care for your namesake. How do you know about flowers?" Jackson leaned forward, placing both hands on his knees.

"Actually, my father was the avid gardener in my family, but I learned the basics by watching him." Taylor stared into Jackson's blue eyes. She had felt an unexplained warmth when their hands had touched, just as she had in the bar when they'd first met. She wondered if he'd felt it too. Concentrate on his eyes, she instructed herself, forcing a smile.

"And how long have you been here in San Diego, Rose, and why have I never seen you before?" Jackson's gaze held hers.

"Actually, I just got here. I'm visiting from . . . up the coast."

"Ah, and how do you like our wild and beautiful San Diego?"

Taylor's breathing was becoming labored as she grew more and more uncomfortable. Though it was obvious he was very interested in her, instinct told her to keep her distance. Against her better judgment, she allowed her curiosity to get the best of her. She couldn't help wondering if Jackson would be truthful with her.

"I love it here. And what type of work do you do here, Mr. Hoyt?"

Jackson paused, running his fingers through his hair. "I'm a . . . land speculator, looking to buy some property."

"Interesting." Why was he lying to her? There was nothing wrong with an honest job in a bar. "And have you purchased anything, Mr. Hoyt?" she continued, hoping to see if his fabrication might lead to an explanation of the ominous whisperings she'd heard between him and the man at Wyatt Earp's gambling house. She grasped for remembered phrases—something about having things under control, and something about picking a time? What she clearly remembered was how his voice had sounded quite harsh and cruel.

"Just looking, right now. And this evening, Miss Rose, the scenery is the most lovely I've seen in San Diego." Jackson checked his pocket watch, blinked seductively, and whispered, "I'd really like to spend some time with you but, unfortunately, I have an appointment."

"Oh, with whom?" Taylor held his gaze. *Probably with that man you met in the middle of the night.*

"Excuse me, ma'am, I'd better be on my way. Though, I'd like to come back to see you a little bit later, Rose, if I may."

He assumed she was one of Ida's girls. *And I've given him no reason to think otherwise. This kind of complication I don't need.*

"I'm sorry, but I don't think so." She dropped her gaze from his pleading eyes and focused on her folded hands.

Jackson stood and once again extended his hand to Taylor. "Well, perhaps another time, then. Good night, sweet Rose."

As he brought her fingers to his warm lips for a gentlemanly kiss, again Taylor reacted to his touch, though this time the energy surge was more of a feverish glow. The touch of his lips on her skin was heavenly, but the degree to which her body instantly responded stunned her.

Rose pulled her hand away from Jackson and returned it to her lap.

Jackson waited, and she wondered if he had changed his mind about leaving. He stared at her, burying his hands deep in his pockets. Did he sense her reaction to his touch? She blushed at the thought.

"Evenin', Rose."

Taylor watched Jackson return to the house, and then followed behind him a few moments later. Racing up the servants' stairs, she ducked into her room, unpinned her borrowed long hair, and quickly slipped out of her dress in one fluid motion. She hastily wiped the rouge from her cheeks and lips, and put on her own slacks, shirt, and vest. With her bowler hat on her head, she quietly made her way down the main stairs just as Jackson closed the front door behind him.

She would see for herself who he was meeting tonight and find out exactly what he was scheming.

Chapter 7

ON IDA'S PORCH, Jackson looked keenly at the parade of people passing by, searching for anyone that might be out of place. He still felt certain someone had been following him when he'd ducked into Ida's place, though now he saw no one that seemed suspicious. Somewhere a clock chimed nine times.

Time to go, he thought. Time to let things begin.

Jackson walked around the corner and a block east. If the McLaurey boys were on time for their meeting, he knew he'd find them at the infamous Acme Saloon. Visitors and locals alike were attracted to the Acme, and owner Till Burnes had created a piece of the real frontier in his establishment. The Acme was as rough and tough as any western saloon, and Till even offered gawkers an up-close look at the Wild West in the form of his caged pet bear. Jackson had laughed the first time he'd seen a mob of people ogling at the animal. It certainly drew the crowds in, he'd thought. Till was quite the businessman.

Taylor's gaze locked on the image of Jackson as he walked casually down the street. She followed, careful to stay in

the shadows close to the buildings. His slow pace didn't
give the appearance he was in a hurry to get anywhere, she
thought.

Then, abruptly, Jackson stepped out of sight into a doorway. Taylor paused, hoping that, inside, he would move
enough from the entrance so she would escape his notice
when she entered. Dressed in the same masculine attire
she'd been wearing when they'd met at Wyatt Earp's, Taylor didn't want Jackson even to notice her, let alone pos-
sibly see through her disguise.

She pulled her hat lower over her eyes, counted to ten,
and walked into the doorway of the Acme Saloon.

The air inside was murky, filled with smoke and the
noise of a very raucous party on the verge of becoming
almost dangerous. Most of the men at the bar were enjoying
cigars and drinking large mugs of beer that they gulped
down without pausing for air.

Taylor took a deep breath and tried to relax. She felt a
terrible tenseness in her body and, with a surge of panic,
she realized that she could very easily find herself in trouble.

She began scanning the room, trying to see if Jackson
was anywhere in sight. If not, she thought, she would be
out of there as fast as she could get back out the door.

Along the rear wall, she could see several curtained
rooms. It was obvious that men were being entertained
there by the colorfully dressed women that paraded across
the room. The women pranced from corner to corner, calling and gesturing to regulars and strangers alike, leading
them to the back area.

On her right, Taylor noticed an archway and a sign that
pointed the way to a reading room. Under the archway
looked like a much safer place to stand and would give her
the chance to really look around.

Making her way over to the archway, Taylor kept her
gaze downward. No one seemed to notice her or even be

interested in her presence. *Good,* she thought as she tucked herself just around the corner of the arch.

Almost immediately, Taylor heard the muffled voices of three men arguing. Making her way along the wall to gain a better vantage point, she recognized Jackson's voice.

"The vest is ready, Will. I picked it up today. When will you have the gun? It's time to finish this."

"Relax, Jackson, we're still waitin' on Pete Spence's gun connection. It should be any day now. Them little vest guns ain't that easy to get. Yer soundin' a little too anxious about this. Relax. Cool down a little."

"You have no idea how hard it's getting for me," Jackson said. "I don't know how much longer I can stand working for that murdering marshal—smiling and being his cheerful employee."

"Now, Jackson," Will replied, "don't go and get all nervous at this stage. We just have to wait a little longer. Pete Spence wants Earp dead just as bad as you do, but you gotta have a gun on you if this is going to work. Now, let's go over it one more time, since we're all here."

Taylor heard the scrape of chairs as the men sat down at one of the tables. She flattened herself against the wall and crept a little closer. Fear and anger knotted inside her, and she shivered as the fearful images of a shootout built in her mind. And now she knew Jackson was definitely involved.

"Now, Dean and I will be at the faro table that's at the back of the room. Jackson, you'll need to keep an eye out so you'll be ready to cover us. We've seen how fast Earp is with a gun—we saw how quick he killed your pa in Dodge City."

Taylor covered her mouth with a quivering hand, smothering her labored breathing. She was afraid to leave, but was also beginning to feel she just might not want to hear the rest.

"I don't know what we're waitin' for anyway." A new voice spoke. "I bet we could sneak in our own guns and just take him down whenever we please—that marshal can't see everything all the time, and—"

"Quiet, Dean, and listen. Your loud mouth'll get us in trouble yet—simmer down or I'll be sendin' ya back to Arizona with yer tail between yer legs. I don't know why I thought you could handle this job anyway—"

"Aw, Will—you know I'm a good shot and—"

"I don't care how good a shot you are, Dean, keep yer trap shut and listen!"

No one said a word for several minutes and Taylor only heard the sharp clink of a bottle against glass, then the slamming of glasses on the table.

"We'll keep bettin' at the faro game," Will continued, his voice not quite as harsh, "and we'll start fussin' about somethin'. Dean, you'll give me a shove off my chair. Jackson, you come over to help get us under control. Earp won't be far behind, you can bet on that. You can also bet that he'll have a gun with him—"

"I don't know, Will," Jackson interrupted. "In all the cleaning and stocking I've done since I started tending bar, I've never seen a gun in the place. Are you sure he'll have one?" Jackson's voice clearly sounded uneasy about Will's claim.

"Relax, Jackson. We *know* Earp. That's how he's always handled it before, and that's the way he'll do it here too. You relax, and quit thinkin' so much. You ain't changin' your mind, are ya?"

"No, no—"

"Jackson," Will interrupted, "you and us—we got a common bond that's real strong. That bastard took the life of our uncle at the OK Corral—just the *same* way he took your pa's. Murdered. In cold blood."

"I just want to make sure. It'll look a lot better if his own gun is drawn.",

"Like I said, don't worry." Will paused a moment. "Partners, right?"

"Partners," Jackson answered.

"All right—now, by this time I'm on the floor and, Dean, you put your hands 'round my throat like you're gonna choke me to death right then and there. Jackson, you'll be makin' your way over to help, right?"

"Right."

"Dean," Will continued, "you need to make it look like you're really gonna kill me and just wait. When Earp gets there, he'll most likely come up next to you with his gun pulled out. You just remember to keep still and look 'im in the eye. Jackson, you'll have plenty of time to pull your gun and finish him off. In all the commotion, we'll make a run for the back room and get out through the window. It'll be easy as pie, as long as everyone does his job."

"Got it," Dean replied. "It'll be easy. Jackson, you just make sure you do some straight shootin', that's all. That Earp deserves what he's got comin' and we're gonna give it to 'im!"

Taylor heard a heavy hand slap the table followed by ugly laughter.

"Hey, pretty boy, you ain't gettin' cold feet, are ya?"

Jackson's voice was even and calm. "You just get the gun and leave it with Charlie at the City of Paris store. One thing, though, I don't think we should be seen together anymore," Jackson added. "It's too dangerous. Just leave a note with the gun with the date we're going to do this. I'm ready."

"Fine with me," Will replied. "Your daddy would sure be proud of you, Jackson. It'll be a pleasure takin' care of business with you."

Taylor heard the grating sound of chairs being pushed away from the table as the men finished their discussion. She turned, then quickly walked toward the archway to leave before they appeared. Luckily, the bar was even more crowded now and she placed herself in the middle of a boisterous group as Dean and Will McLaurey walked out of the reading room. They stopped momentarily, appearing to decide whether to take their place at the bar or scout for

a table in the packed gambling area. Taylor stared at the
men, memorizing their faces. She watched them walk to
the bar, turn their backs to her, and order a drink.

Taylor waited for Jackson to appear next. After an un-
comfortably long five minutes she concluded he had used
a back door or perhaps was waiting long enough to be
certain there would be no connection made between him
and the two men. Her clenched stomach muscles confirmed
it was time for her to get out of there.

Jackson sat back down at the table in the reading room.
Things were progressing much more slowly than he'd
hoped, and it had already been a long and agonizing journey for him.

Since his mother had died of consumption nine years
ago, Jackson had pretty much been on his own. His life
had changed dramatically due to his mother's death, but
more so because she had tearfully divulged the truth about
his father. Jackson had grown up thinking his father had
died before his own birth. On her deathbed, Jackson's
mother revealed that his father had in fact died only the
year before.

That last conversation had been painful for both of them,
Jackson remembered. His mother told him that she had
fallen in love with his father, a man named George Hoyt,
who had promised to take her west for a life of adventure.
After a quick courtship, he'd left to secure their new home,
promising to send for her in a month. By the second month,
she knew he wasn't coming back to marry her and, worst
of all, she was with child—his child. To save face, Jackson's mother had told everyone that she and George had
secretly married before he'd left.

Jackson closed his eyes against sudden tears. He remembered how his mother had often looked to the west at sunset
with a dreamy, wistful expression. Now he understood what
she'd been dreaming about. Even after all those years, she
still waited for his father to return. As a young boy, Jackson

had fallen in love with the idea of traveling west, to seek out the adventures he'd read about, where lawless towns established their own ways to deal with right and wrong. Now he knew he had inherited his own mother's wish to explore and experience a wilder side of life.

Jackson had tirelessly cared for his mother, especially that last year. He prayed he'd never see anyone suffer as much as she did, struggling to breathe, sometimes without enough strength to eat. That last pain-racked day, she tenderly told Jackson she couldn't die without telling him the truth—how she and his father had never married, and that his father didn't even know he had a son. She'd also heard that he had been killed in Dodge City by the marshal there, though she wasn't sure how or why.

Jackson closed his eyes, picturing his sick mother—pale, weak, and gasping for air. He had reassured her that everything would be fine, that *he* would be fine. He held her hand while she took her last breath. He was sixteen, and alone.

After his mother's burial, he continued to wonder about his father. He finished his schooling and worked on a neighbor's ranch. And occasionally he would go into town and work Saturday nights at the saloon there. He'd decided he would save the extra money to make the trip someday to Dodge City, to find out once and for all what happened to his father, and then head west.

After almost ten years, Jackson had enough money saved to pay for the satisfaction of his own curiosity. He set out for Dodge City. The first night there, Jackson met Will and Dean McLaurey.

He'd asked them if they knew anything about the killing of a George Hoyt. They had been very interested, he remembered, especially when he told them he'd just learned that George Hoyt was his father. The three of them began to plan a journey to find Wyatt Earp. They intended to even the score for the killing of Jackson's father and their own uncle, Tom McLaurey. Will told Jackson he might as well

go back home and wait for word from them. They'd contact
him when they found the murderous marshal, and he could
join them then.

Brought back to reality by the overflow noise from the
saloon crowd, Jackson sighed. It had been a long ten years.
And now he needed to be patient for just a little longer.

Feeling fatigued and emotionally drained, Jackson
pushed his chair away from the table. Maybe there was time
for a little distraction, he mused. Perhaps the beautiful Rose
was just what he needed to keep from becoming too anxious. Jackson walked out of the Acme Saloon and made his
way back to Ida Bailey's.

Chapter 8

SHIVERING MORE FROM the overheard conversation than from the chilly night air, Taylor hurried away from the saloon. So Jackson was the predicted false friend, she thought.

"No."

Taylor stopped walking, startled to hear her father's voice. How could he say that when she'd just overheard him plotting with two men to kill Wyatt Earp?

Taylor strained to hear her father's voice, but she heard only the sounds of a buggy going by.

It seemed simple on the surface—they were all after some kind of macho revenge—an eye for an eye.

"Look for the truth."

Taylor's jaws tightened. Was she supposed to figure out who the conspirators were, and then stop them by finding out the truth? The truth about what?

"Jackson is no killer."

Dad, I heard what they said. I heard about the gun, the plot, everything.

"Taylor . . . look deeper. Trust your feelings."

His presence melted away and Taylor shivered, feeling even more confused. Look deeper—at what? she wondered.

The only benefit to her father's interference, she thought, was the growing possibility that Jackson might not be what he appeared to be. In her heart of hearts, Taylor hoped he wasn't the ruthless assassin that two overheard conversations suggested he could be. He just didn't have the look of an outlaw. The other two men were picture-perfect examples of bandits of the old West. They could have walked on any western movie set and fit in nicely. And they gave her the creeps.

Reaching Ida's front porch, Taylor looked around to confirm she was alone. She quietly opened the front door and closed it behind her, leaning against it with a sigh of relief. She quickly decided to go upstairs the back way so there would be less chance of being seen.

Moments later, Taylor was safe in her room changing out of her pants and vest. On her bed lay a red silk robe and a note from Ida.

Rose,

This never did fit me and I thought you might enjoy wearing it. Noticed you were gone and hope all is well. See you in the morning after ten or so for tea.

Ida

Taylor picked up the robe, holding it out to take a better look. *Sweet Ida. How nice she has been to me.* Her fingers lingered on the luxurious satiny fabric, enjoying the sensuous feel of the cloth. Impulsively, she removed her underwear and bra and slid the robe over her bare skin. It felt velvety and warm against her cool flesh. Looking in the mirror, she saw the robe almost shimmering in the moonlight.

Taylor reached for the big china pitcher and poured some water into the washbasin. She washed her face and hands in the cool water, immediately feeling revived from her long day. The damp edges of her hair curled toward her face, and she felt very feminine, the robe a dramatic contrast to the boyish clothing she had just removed.

Sounds of the night's carnal business drifted into Taylor's room—high-pitched squeals followed by heavy footsteps and laughter. Bed springs signaled a great deal of activity was underway just down the hall from her curtained doorway.

Knowing she would be unable to sleep, she felt suddenly restless and walked to the window overlooking the garden. The moonglow was bright, and she was drawn to go outside for the peace and quiet. Grabbing an extra blanket from a shelf, she tiptoed down the back stairs, through the kitchen, and out the back door.

The grass was as soft as carpet on her bare feet, and the air was warm and still in the protected garden. The scent of flowers was thick and almost intoxicating. She spread the blanket out next to the rosebushes and sat down. The stars overhead seemed larger than life, sparkling like diamond chips against a black satin sky. No smog to blur their light, Taylor thought. Stretching out onto her back now, she clasped her hands behind her head and felt her entire body relax.

Jackson walked into Ida's carrying the same feeling that someone was watching him. Just nervous, he thought. Though he had seen no one, he had walked four blocks out of the way and doubled back, just as a precaution. Walking into the parlor, he greeted Ida. Two of her girls were sitting on a plush sofa, and they instantly focused their attention on him with friendly smiles.

"Ah, my friend Jackson has returned," Ida exclaimed. "Are you here to accept my offer, then?" Jackson's immediate and obvious discomfort drew giggles from Ida and the girls on the sofa.

"Just here for a room, Ida. The large one on the end—

is it available?" He took a few steps backward, hoping Ida would leave well enough alone for the night.

"Oh, come on, Jackson. When are you going to relax and have some fun? You're too serious for your own good," Ida said. One of the girls rose from the sofa, smiling warmly at him. Her long honey-blond hair draped across her shoulders and onto firm, jutting breasts that were barely covered by a lacy pink camisole.

Jackson looked pleadingly at Ida. "Just a room tonight, Ida." He watched the lips of the blond beauty pucker into a provocative pout as she sank back down to the sofa.

"Come on then, I'll show you to your room." She motioned for Jackson to follow her up the stairs.

"Ida, who's Rose?"

Ida stopped on the stairs and glanced back at him, her eyes twinkling. "Oh, that one. She's just a temporary, you could say. Did you like her?"

"Just curious, that's all."

They continued down the hallway, neither breaking the silence.

Ida turned toward Jackson as she stood in front of the door with the key. "You look more than curious to me." She handed the key to him with a smile.

Jackson stretched his neck and looked up at the ceiling, sorry he had brought it up at all.

"She's very special, Jackson," Ida said softly. "Just remember that. And she makes her own decisions at my house. She's independent, if you know what I mean."

Jackson returned Ida's gaze, drawing his eyebrows together as he considered her explanation. "Independent?"

"Self-governing. Free to do as she pleases," Ida replied, then chuckled. "Sleep well, then, Jackson. And you're welcome to help yourself to breakfast before you go back to work in the morning. Good night." Ida retrieved her pocket watch to check the time, and firmly knocked on selected doors. "Time," she called out as she made her way down the hallway.

Jackson unlocked the door. He loved that particular room and spent a couple of nights each week there when tips ran high enough to indulge in the pleasure. The room was luxurious in contrast to his meager accommodations at the saloon, and sinfully lavish compared to any room he'd ever slept in. The shining brass bed was the ultimate in comfort, with crisp, clean sheets and a patchwork quilt. At the head of the bed, six pillows were heaped—each filled with the softest down.

The room had its own bathtub, which was its greatest extravagance. A small wood stove was ready to heat water, and every flat surface in the room held a vase filled with roses from Ida's garden. Even though the room was expensive, he had grown to think of it as a much-deserved indulgence.

At the window, Jackson pulled back the lacy curtains to allow the night breeze into the room. Closing his eyes, he breathed in the heavy aroma of summer flowers. Opening his eyes, he gazed out at the lawn and garden, soon spotting a lone figure in a crimson robe. Immediately he flashed back to the vision he'd had in his bath. The woman in the red robe. *Red As a Rose.*

He narrowed his eyes, focusing on the figure in the dreamy moonlight. *So, perhaps we shall meet again.*

Chapter 9

TAYLOR REACHED UP to shoo away what felt like an insect on her nose, then reluctantly opened her eyes to discover a blade of grass was gently tickling her, held by Jackson Hoyt.

Crouched on the grass next to her, he grinned. "Sorry, I couldn't resist. You just looked far too comfortable in your slumber on this beautiful moonlit night, sweet Rose." He stared into her sea green eyes, noticing a faint glint of humor.

Taylor sat up, holding her robe together at her neck. Her other hand soon found its way to the back of her head, where her long hair was no longer attached.

His gaze followed her movements, pausing deliciously at her creamy white neck. With surprise, he noticed her short-cropped hair. "What happened to your hair?"

"This is the way I normally I wear my hair," she explained. "I borrowed a fall from Ida earlier." Her fingers nervously fluffed her locks. "It's easier this way."

He reached out, gently rearranging an errant wave back behind her ear. "It's nice. It's just different than most women." Ida was right, he thought, she is independent. Most women would rather lose a limb than cut their hair. He cocked his head and looked at her disheveled dark hair, and how her wispy bangs fell across her forehead. Different, but nice, he decided.

Keenly aware of his scrutiny, Taylor dropped her eyes. She felt her nipples harden against the silkiness of her robe.

"I have some brandy from my room. Would you like some?" Jackson reached for the bottle on the grass and half filled the two small snifters he'd brought down. He handed one to her and gently touched his own glass to hers. "What shall we toast to?"

As she swirled her glass, she inhaled the mellow aroma of the brandy. Remembering her father's reference to finding the truth, she replied, "To fulfillment."

"To fulfillment, then," he echoed, taking a sip. "May I sit with you?"

"Certainly," she said, moving over to make room on the blanket. She took a generous swallow of brandy, hoping it would help her relax. Already she felt a tumble of confused thoughts and emotions, knowing she should take advantage of this opportunity—ask him some questions, look for the truth her father had alluded to. Her heart began to pound an erratic rhythm, and there was a tingle of excitement inside her. Taylor swallowed tightly as Jackson settled himself next to her on the blanket.

"It's a beautiful night." Jackson sighed, looking up at the stars.

She noticed his faint smile held a touch of sadness. "What are you thinking?"

For an instant a wistful look stole into his expression. "I think I'm missing home," he said. "I guess I just feel unsettled right now."

"Where's home?" Taylor repositioned herself to see Jackson more directly, kneeling next to him. His expressive face changed and became almost somber.

"I grew up in Kansas. It seems like a long time ago . . .

are you sure you want to hear my life story after only one brandy?" His mouth quirked with amusement.

"Never," she began, "never reveal your life story until the second brandy." She tipped her glass at her lips, drinking the last swallow. There was an immediate rush of warmth from her throat to the pit of her stomach.

He stared at her and then burst out laughing. "Agreed." He finished his brandy with a quick jerk of his wrist, and poured two fresh glasses.

"All right," she said, "now you may begin." She watched the play of emotions on his face. *Talk to me. Tell me about what's really happening here. Help me find the truth.*

Jackson stretched out on his side, elbow bent to support his head to continue looking at her. "Well, let's see. I had a regular childhood, I guess."

"Brothers and sisters?"

"Just me. My mother and I lived a ways outside of town. She took in wash and mending and, when I could, I worked on a neighbor's farm. She died of consumption when I was sixteen."

Taylor knew tuberculosis was not an easy way to go. "Were you there when she died?"

His eyes glistened with tears. "I cared for her until the end. Consumption is an ugly, painful way to die."

"Tell me about her. What was she like?"

After taking a swallow of brandy, he continued. "She was beautiful and—kind, mostly. And she always wanted to come out west. I think she would have liked it here. I get my restlessness from her, I think." He paused for a moment. "She was fair and strict with me. Made me promise to finish school. We had a good life until she got sick."

"How did you cope?"

"What?"

"How did you deal with her death? You were young to have to go through that," she said softly.

"I don't know," he replied, closing his eyes for a moment. "The end was the worst. She just couldn't breathe.

And she was too weak to eat, so she just got weaker and weaker until she couldn't go on. I stayed with her as much as I could."

"Why were you alone? Where was your father?" Taylor saw anger light his eyes and wondered if he would tell her the truth.

"He courted her and left, promising to send for her later. He never knew about me."

His gaze held hers for a long moment and she wondered if he was searching her eyes for signs of shock or, perhaps, rejection. "Did you ever wonder where he was?"

"The day my mother died, she told me the truth—how she and my father had never married. She also heard that my father was living in Dodge City, but he'd been killed the year before."

"Killed?"

"Well, murdered actually. Why am I telling you all this?" He turned away from her and gazed into the sky. "Perhaps I'll blame the brandy—or have you cast a spell on me, beautiful Rose?" He looked at her again, then cupped her chin gently in his free hand, stroking her jawline slowly with his thumb. "I feel bewitched when I look into your eyes."

Taylor leaned back, away from his reach. "Was the murderer ever found?" Silently, she urged him to be truthful.

"*I* found him, and he'll pay for his crime." Jackson drained his glass. "Tell me about you, now."

Taylor sipped her brandy, stalling. "Not much to tell, really."

What was she supposed to say? That she lived a hundred years in the future and was supposed to be here for some important reason that she hadn't quite figured out yet? *And, oh, yes, my dead father shows up every once in a while and tells me what to do. Great. Oh, and by the way, sometimes I dress up like a man and use another name and I've seen you in the buff already and . . .*

"What are you thinking? You look like you're miles away."

Taylor forced herself to meet his stare, feeling the hot redness spread on her cheeks. "Well, like I said before, I'm just visiting here from up the coast."

"So you don't plan to stay in San Diego, then? I was hoping we'd have time to . . . get to know each other better."

"I honestly don't know." At least her answer was accurate. "And you? How long will you be looking at property here?" Another chance for him to tell her the truth.

Jackson looked into his glass and shook his head. "I'm not a land speculator, actually—though there've been plenty of times I've thought I'd like to live here. I just don't think that's what's going to happen."

Stretching out on the blanket, Jackson gazed to the heavens, then closed his eyes. After a few moments, the frown on his face disappeared and he looked completely at ease.

Taylor examined his face carefully. It was impossible to imagine him in the role of an assassin. What she had seen in him was a determined man filled with the pain of his mother's betrayal, his unknown father's death, and an overwhelming sense of obligation to right a wrong. The lines in his face had betrayed his outward calm and she had seen clear signs he was weary with the heavy burden of revenge. His face now relaxed, she could see the beginning of a smile tip the corners of his mouth.

"And now what are you thinking?" she asked softly.

"I just feel good right now—thinking how beautiful you are. How peaceful it feels here with you. It's been a while . . ."

Once again, Taylor felt the uncontrollable pull of attraction building, and her fingers ached to touch him. A black tendril curled against his forehead and, just as she had done the night she'd spent in the back room of the saloon, she gently brushed it back.

Jackson reached for Taylor's hand and brought it to his lips.

Taylor gasped at the pleasure that radiated inward. Then he tenderly kissed the palm of her hand. His touch was suddenly almost unbearable to her in its tenderness.

Gently pulling her closer, Jackson opened his eyes. Pausing, he looked at her speculatively, and for a long moment she looked back at him. He waited.

Taylor's heart jolted and her pulse pounded. Jackson's gaze was as soft as a caress and she slowly leaned forward, her own gaze now frozen on his mouth. Her lips slowly descended to meet his, and she quivered at the tenderness of their first kiss.

Soon she felt his hand at the base of her neck, pulling her more firmly to him; and her own hands moved to his muscular chest. The touch of his lips was a delicious sensation, and she felt a dreamy intimacy in the kiss. She returned his kiss with abandon and hunger, and she felt her calm shatter. Finally raising herself up and taking her mouth from his, she gazed into his eyes.

A delightful shiver of wanting ran through her as Jackson seemed to search her eyes. She wondered if his body ached for hers too. Then his gaze dropped. Her robe had slipped open and she knew his gaze fell to the tops of her breasts, plainly in view. He reached out and softly outlined the circle of her breast with his finger.

Taylor breathed lightly between parted lips, her senses reeling as if they had short-circuited. His gentle touch sent currents of desire through her. He fondled each breast, teasing each taut nipple until she moaned softly. Their peaks grew hard as he aroused her passion.

"Jackson, stop," she managed to whisper.

"Why?" He pulled her to his lips again and buried any response she may have given. He moved his mouth over hers, devouring its softness.

The kiss sent the pit of her stomach into a wild swirl and eagerly she drank in its sweetness. Pulling away slightly, her tongue traced the softness of his lower lip, then she pressed her open lips to his, the tips of their tongues meeting with a tentative flick.

Jackson reached out with his tongue and she tasted the honey sweetness of his mouth as he explored her teeth, searching for her tongue. Blood pounded in her brain as the hot tide of passion raged on.

He pulled her to him, so that her breasts were against his chest, her body half covering his.

Breathlessly, she pulled her lips from his. Passion radiated from the soft core of her body and she yearned to yield to his seduction. She felt his hands move gently down the length of her back, massaging his way down her spine. She saw a clear invitation in the smoldering depths of his eyes.

"Rose, you decide where we go from here." He studied her face, as though reaching for her thoughts.

He couldn't disguise his body's reaction to her—she'd felt his hardness, how strongly he'd responded to her.

Taylor breathed deeply. "I have to go." She self-consciously pulled her robe together and scooted away from him.

Jackson ran his hands through his hair. She made him feel absolutely crazy with desire. He continued to stare into her eyes, then watched her expression change from passionate desire to one of controlled detachment.

Perhaps she was able to remove herself more easily from physical attraction, he thought. All he knew was how confused he felt. Some long-buried part of him wanted to explore her potential friendship, and another wanted to savagely explore her soft flesh, feel her writhing beneath him. He watched her stand and take a step off the blanket.

"I'll stay here a while, then, sweet Rose." He stood and folded the blanket, then handed it to her. In one forward motion, his arms encircled her, one hand in the small of her back.

With the folded blanket now between them, at least he was spared the guaranteed tingle of full body contact. Her breath softly fanned his face and he gazed into her clear, bright green eyes.

"You're sure you have to go?" he asked again.

"Yes."

As Taylor lightly kissed his chin and smiled, he smiled back and planted a kiss in the hollow of her neck.

"Good night, then." He watched as she made her way back to the house. Then he bent to retrieve the bottle of brandy and glasses and walked slowly to the table in the middle of the lawn. He could use another drink to calm his nerves, distract him from the overwhelming urge to follow her to her room.

Sitting at the table, Jackson sipped his brandy and considered what had happened. Who *was* she? Was she a highly paid harlot just toying with him? She had seemed genuinely friendly during their conversation, and why had he felt so compelled to answer her questions honestly? A voice whispered in his head. *Why had she asked so many questions in the first place?*

A cold knot formed in his stomach. Did she suspect why he was there? Had *she* been the one following him? He'd have to be careful, he decided, finishing his drink.

This mysterious Rose could be his biggest danger, for all he knew. Somehow, he determined, he would have to find out more about her.

Chapter 10

TAYLOR WOKE ON her own small bed, still wrapped in the red silk robe. The night had been filled with dreams of Jackson, though now they were only vague images, just out of reach. Rubbing her eyes, she realized the laziness she was feeling was probably the leftover effect of the brandy they'd shared in the garden.

The view from the window offered signs of another warm, beautiful day. Birds were making merry music, perched on the fence. Hummingbirds were drinking from the lush flowers, flitting like miniature helicopters from bloom to bloom.

She was already getting used to being there. Strange, she thought, she knew she should be trying to figure out how to get back to the real world, but she had to admit all she seemed to be feeling was how *nice* it all seemed.

Pulling her suitcase from under her bed, she retrieved her watch, toothbrush, toothpaste, and disposable razor, certain she'd feel better after she cleaned up, even if the water wasn't hot.

So far she really hadn't missed much as far as modern

conveniences. She was becoming accustomed to wearing no makeup, other than the cheek rouge that Ida had left for her. And she certainly was enjoying the quiet—no telephones ringing, no televisions blaring, no sirens disturbing the serenity. She glanced at her watch. Seven. Too early for much activity at Sherman House. As she returned everything to her suitcase, Taylor said a silent prayer that Ida wouldn't snoop and discover her modern things. It would be difficult to try to explain, she mused.

After getting into her gardening clothes, she quietly made her way down the back stairs to the kitchen. There she buttered two thick slices of Maylee's homemade bread and spooned on some strawberry preserves. She ate quickly, looking forward to having morning tea when Ida surfaced later. There were weeds that needed her attention, and she worked ceaselessly in the garden for the next three hours.

Upstairs in his room, Jackson woke with a start, a dream image of Taylor still crystal clear in his mind. He groaned in frustration, and closed his eyes to recapture the picture of her reclining on his bed, beckoning to him. Her image faded instantly, and he opened his eyes.

Sunshine poured into the room and a warm breeze fluttered the lace curtains at the open window. He stretched, then swung his legs to the floor and walked to the window. Jackson could see Taylor busily pulling weeds at the far fence, kneeling in the grass. It didn't make sense, he thought. What was she doing working in Ida's garden anyway?

With only an hour to get back to the saloon, Jackson cleaned up, dressed, and gathered his things. He relished his Sunday nights off from the bar, and silently vowed to return to Ida's as soon as he could, hoping to find out more about the mysterious Rose. He also vowed to gain more control over his own feelings about her. There were other things to be concentrating on right now, and the morning light reminded him to keep his mind on his mission. Distractions he didn't need.

Back in the saloon, he busied himself sweeping the floor and polishing the bar. Glasses needed to be washed and stock levels needed to be checked. He had a full day ahead of him just to get ready for the evening crowd. He'd learned a lot about running a saloon from his job. The hours were long, but wages were good.

"I brought you some lunch, Jackson."

Startled in his reverie, Jackson jerked around at the sound of the voice of Josie Earp.

"Are you ready for a break? I thought I'd join you. Wyatt's gone to look at some property and I hate to dine alone." Josie put a large, draped tray on a nearby table.

He stared at her, frowning slightly. "I was just thinking of stopping, actually."

"Good. There's a new cook at Martha Reed's place, and you tell me if this doesn't look absolutely delicious." Josie removed the checked cloth, uncovering two steaming plates of beef stew, with thick slices of dark bread on the side. "And even fresh peach cobbler for dessert," she added. "Now, why don't you sit with me here, Jackson." She smiled flirtatiously and sat in one of the chairs.

"Looks great, Mrs. Earp."

"Call me Josie. Please."

Jackson came out from behind the bar and sat opposite her at the table. "Thanks. I guess I was more hungry than I thought."

Josie took a bite of stew. "Wyatt's rather pleased with your work here, you know."

He looked at her questioningly. "Excuse me?"

Josie stared at him. "I just thought I'd let you know that Wyatt thinks you're a good employee. Do you enjoy your work, Jackson?"

"Sure," he answered between mouthfuls of stew.

They sat silently for a while, Jackson concentrating on his meal and Josie stealing glances at him.

Josie dabbed at her mouth with a napkin. "Did you have a good night off last night?" Josie carefully searched his eyes for the slightest sign of guilt or suspicion. She'd been terrified he'd seen her following him to the Acme Saloon the night before, but now saw nothing in his expression to indicate he had. Tremendously relieved, she smiled. "What do you do, Jackson, besides work?"

Jackson's expression was neutral. "Nothing much, I guess. Usually I just relax and rest."

. . . and meet with hooligans and outlaws. Josie finished his thought with her own. From behind one of the curtained rooms at the Acme Saloon, she had seen the McLaurey boys join him in the reading room. She had also seen Taylor crouched along the wall listening. "That doesn't sound too exciting to me. Have you had a chance to explore San Diego since you've been here?"

"Not too much, actually." Jackson threw her a sidelong glance as he finished his cobbler and leaned back in his chair.

She smiled. "Hope you enjoyed the lunch. We'll have to do this again sometime." She placed the empty dishes back on the tray. "I'll just get these back to Martha. I won't keep you any longer."

Jackson watched as Josie carried the tray out the door, and shook his head.

In Martha Reed's café, Josie made her way to the kitchen to return the tray of dirty dishes. Mr. Johnson was checking a batch of biscuits in the oven, while Martha busily washed dishes.

"How was lunch, Josie?"

"Just fine, Martha, just fine. And Mr. Johnson, the peach cobbler was just divine." She smiled warmly at Martha's new cook, surprised and rather pleased to see a man in the kitchen. "Martha, may I ask you a question?"

"Well, certainly, Josie. What is it?"

"Yesterday, a stranger had breakfast here. A small, thin

young man wearing a light-colored vest and a bowler hat.
Do you remember him, by any chance?"

"As a matter of fact, I do," Martha replied. "He was quite
nice. I remember he asked about lodging, and I sent him
to see Maylee at the Gaslamp Quarter Hotel. He might have
gotten a room there."

"Do you remember anything else?"

"Nothing, really. He just seemed like a nice young fel-
low."

"Thanks, Martha, lunch was wonderful as usual." Josie
walked back through the café and headed for the Gaslamp
Quarter Hotel. Perhaps Maylee would add to the story.

A few minutes later, Maylee told her the stranger had
ended up as Ida Bailey's new gardener. Josie was beginning
to feel like she was on a wild-goose chase. Peeking through
the fence slats into Ida's garden, Josie could see Taylor
pulling weeds along the back wall. Carefully, she opened
the gate and closed it silently behind her. Eyes fixed on
Taylor's back, she walked up to her.

"Hello, Taylor."

With a gasp, Taylor stood up and turned toward the
voice. "Jeez, you scared me half to death!" She brought her
hand above her eyes to shade them from the sun. "Oh,
hello, Mrs. Earp. What brings you here?"

"Well, you, actually," she answered. "Could we sit down
and talk for a while?" Josie walked stiffly to the table and
chairs and sat down. "I need some information, Taylor. I
hope you can help me."

Josie watched Taylor sit down in the empty chair and
remove her leather work gloves and hat, placing them on
the ground at her feet. Again she had the feeling there was
something not quite right about the stranger, but was unable
to put her finger on it.

Taylor sat silently, eyes downcast, waiting.

Josie continued to stare, examining her for a clue, some
sort of sign that would explain why she felt so cautious.
She gazed at Taylor's short hair, damp and wavy from

working in the day's heat. She looked at her small ears and clear skin. The loose shirt she wore did well to disguise body type or muscular development. Her examination ended at Taylor's small feet, wearing old boots two sizes too big. Leaning forward, closer to her, Josie took a deep breath and sat back in surprise. Well, for one thing, she thought, this creature was not a man. No man could hide the masculine odors created by the sweat of working in the summer sun. Taylor simply *smelled* too good.

"Tell me who you really are, Taylor. And your real name, too."

"Taylor really is my name."

"You had me fooled yesterday, but not now. I can see that you are masquerading as a man, so enlighten me as to your reasons." Josie leaned back in her chair, arms folded and chin raised. She was right. And she was sure the stranger was hiding something. And what was the connection between her, Jackson, and the McLaurey boys?

"I'm waiting. . . ." Josie spoke with cool authority.

"Things are a little . . . complicated for me right now, and all I really needed was a place to stay. Maylee brought me over to meet Ida and I'm filling in as her gardener."

"Do Maylee and Ida know of your charade?"

"Actually, yes. I know it sounds strange, but—"

Josie smiled. The stranger's story might prove to be interesting after all. "Are you running from someone? The law, maybe?"

"No, nothing like that. It just seemed easier to get around dressed like a man—at least when I first got here."

"So, I'm just to believe there is no danger from you being here? Then why were you following Wyatt's bartender to the Acme Saloon last night?"

Taylor stared, her jaw dropped in surprise. "You were there?"

"I was. I saw you listening to a conversation between Jackson and two men. Tell me what interested you, Miss Taylor."

"Well, actually I was trying to learn more about something I'd overheard Jackson say, and I ended up following him to the saloon. I couldn't hear much of what they said, though. I couldn't get close enough."

Josie peered at her, searching her eyes for the truth. "Did it have something to do with my husband?"

"I'm just not quite sure. I promise you, though, that if I learn anything more, I'll tell you."

"Very well, then." Josie paused, returning her gaze. *I guess I'll have to be patient a little while longer with this stranger.* "Taylor—is that what Ida calls you?"

"Maylee and Ida call me by my middle name . . . Rose."

"Do you prefer Taylor to Rose?" Josie couldn't help but find it amusing that this young woman had successfully fooled at least some of the people in San Diego. And she seemed to be a very spirited young woman. She found she was unable to fight a feeling of fondness for the young woman's—what was it?—quirkiness?

"My father was the only one who ever called me Rose."

"If you will call me Josie from now on, then I shall call you Rose. Are you sure there's no trouble that you need help with?" Josie felt a tug at her heart now that she sensed the uncertainty within the young woman's position. There was undoubtedly more to her story, but she knew she'd have to earn the young woman's trust before she might learn more from her. Besides, she had more investigating to do. Primarily, she needed to find out why the McLaurey boys were in town. She strongly suspected that it had something to do with Wyatt, and probably something to do with Pete Spence.

"May I ask you something?"

Josie nodded.

"What is it like being married to Wyatt Earp?"

A thoughtful smile curved Josie's mouth. "Well, we certainly do have our ups and downs, but we are *madly* in love. I can't imagine my life without him. And you . . . do you have a man in your life, Rose?" She watched a smile appear tentatively on Taylor's face. "Ah, I can see that you do. Tell me about him," she encouraged.

"There's no one, actually."

Josie considered her words, suspicious at the hesitant reply. "Is that why you were following Jackson? Is it something to do with him?" Josie reached out to touch Taylor's fidgeting hands. "Rose, please be careful. As far as I could tell, Jackson may have met two men at the Acme that certainly are not what you or I would call gentlemen. Promise me you'll be careful."

Taylor exchanged a smile with her. "I promise. And I promise I'll let you know if I find out anything serious— anything you should know."

"All right, then. I'll rely on you for that." Josie patted Taylor's hand. "I have to go. You send word to me anytime, and if you need anything, let me know. I don't mind telling you that I wasn't at all sure about you when I came to talk with you today, and I'm still not. But I can wait for details, for the time when you feel you can share more with me. I hope we can be friends, Rose. Good day for now." Josie made her way back out the gate, leaving Taylor alone, once again, in the garden.

Relieved that Josie hadn't thought she seemed out of place, Taylor sat back in her chair. But why had Josie been following Jackson? Did she have her own suspicions? Obviously she would do anything to protect her husband, Taylor thought.

"Be careful, Taylor."

Taylor tilted her head, listening carefully. Of Josie? She thought a moment. She supposed Josie could be the false friend mentioned in the Tarot card reading.

Taylor shook her head and waited for anything else her father might share. Only silence. She dismissed the thought of Josie being a danger—in fact, she liked her, and doubted she was doing more than being a dutiful, protective wife. Even so, caution seemed to be the safest path until she could sort things out more.

"Find the truth."

What was her father talking about anyway—the truth about Jackson? About Wyatt Earp? About what?

"Jackson is no killer."

Taylor had a distinct feeling he would be unless she could figure out how she might convince him to change his mind. She got up from her chair and began pacing. She wished her father's brief messages were more clear. If he knew something, she thought, why didn't he just come out and tell her?

"I can't."

Can't, she thought, or won't? She believed her father was there to help, but instinctively knew she was the one who would be ultimately responsible to find the truth he kept alluding to. She struggled to hold on to logic, but her emotions were winning.

Dad, I wish you were here. Taylor abruptly stopped her pacing, feeling suddenly very much out of place and realizing just how awkward she felt.

Then Taylor sensed her father's spirit fade away. *Dad?*

"Rose, are you ready for some tea?" Ida called to Taylor from the back door. "You look like you're ready for some company. Are you all right?"

"I'm fine, Ida. Tea sounds good." She waved to Ida.

"Maylee's on her way over with some fresh date nut bread. Wash up and we'll meet you in the kitchen." Ida shut the door. She had been standing for several minutes watching Taylor pace back and forth next to the rose bed and occasionally cock her head as though she were listening.

Taylor finished washing her hands and face at the pump as Maylee came through the back gate.

"Hello, Rose. Come on inside and have a piece of my fresh bread." Maylee continued toward the back door, with Taylor close behind.

"Hello, Maylee."

"How are you on this fine day, Rose? You look a little

tired to me." Maylee glanced at her as they all sat at the large wooden kitchen table.

"A little tired from working outside, I suppose," she replied. "The bread smells wonderful, and a cup of tea sounds perfect." She smiled at the two women sitting across from her. Ida was already dressed and coiffed. Taylor had never seen her unkempt or casual. Maylee was perspiring a bit from her walk from the hotel, and was frowning at her with motherly concern. "And you two should both stop worrying about me," Taylor suggested.

Ida poured three cups of tea and passed the honey and cream to Taylor. "The garden is looking better already, Rose. Your skills are obvious and I am very pleased at your progress. I must say, you work harder than my previous gardener." Ida smiled at Taylor. "I think you are trying to spoil me."

Taylor returned her smile with a heartfelt grin. "I'm enjoying myself—I just hope you'll let me stay a while."

"Rose, please stay as long as you like. Now, Maylee, pass some of your bread this way. I've already told Rose it's delicious."

Maylee beamed and passed the plate of sliced bread to Ida. "Hush, now. It's not even my best," she said. "Rose, are you still planning to come with me tonight to Mr. Shepard's?"

Taylor nodded.

"Good. I thought I'd better let you know that sometimes Mr. Shepard's parties are quite long. We might not be back until rather late. We'll leave from here after dinner tonight."

"Sound's fine."

"And wear something fancy if you've got it."

Ida clapped her hands together. "I know just the gown you can wear. My old blue satin one—it will be perfect. I'll help you with your hair and let you borrow my silver and pearl necklace. You'll be stunning."

Taylor warmed in the glow of the attention from Maylee and Ida. More and more, they felt like aunts to her. Family.

Ida drained her cup and spun it clockwise, three times. Then she turned it upside down, allowing the last few droplets to fall onto the table. Finally she handed the empty cup to Maylee.

"Maylee, what do you see?" she asked. "Tell us."

Maylee bit her lip in concentration, tilting the cup for a better look. "Well, I see what looks like a kettle. At the base of a tree. This says illness or injury, but with recovery." Maylee looked up at Ida. "How have you been feeling?"

"Fit as a fiddle, in fact."

"Perhaps it's not you. Maybe one of the girls, do you think?"

Ida frowned. "Perhaps, perhaps. Rose, your turn. Drink your tea and swirl the empty cup to the right three times."

Taylor obeyed, mimicking Ida. She handed her cup to Maylee and watched her peer into the cup—fighting an instant, unexpected feeling of regret.

"I see two things," she murmured, "a boat and a chair. This doesn't make much sense to me."

"What doesn't make sense?"

"Well, a boat usually means a visit from a close friend with bad news and a chair means there will be an unexpected visitor. I'm not sure which one of the images dominates. Do you have friends here, Rose?"

Taylor shook her head. "No one." She wondered if it could be Jackson, or maybe Josie.

Maylee shrugged. "I just do this for fun, right, Ida? It's a good excuse to stop by for a cup of tea, anyway." She smiled and drained her own cup, reaching for the last slice of bread. "I'll be going now. See you at eight, Rose. You might have a rest this afternoon. I expect the evening won't end until well past midnight." She pushed away from the table and quickly retreated out the back door.

Taylor stared into the bottom of her teacup, squinting. All she saw were specks of tea leaves. No boat. No chair.

"Never you mind, Rose. Sometimes Maylee's teacup

readings are right, and sometimes she's miles off target."
Ida patted her shoulder.

Taylor smiled at her concern about Maylee's rather ominous interpretations of the tea leaves.

Ida continued, "There's chicken soup warming on the
stove when you're hungry. I have to run some errands in
town, so I'll see you at about five. I'll need your help with
dinner tonight, and when we're finished, I'll help you dress
for your evening. I'll get out the blue gown and the necklace for you."

"I'm not worried about the tea leaves," Taylor called
after Ida as the older woman left the kitchen.

She admitted how much she liked the woman and, somehow, her profession as a madame didn't seem that shock-
ing. It was obvious that Ida cared for her girls, and had
made certain Sherman House was safe and comfortable for
them. And she had certainly opened up her heart and home
to *her*. Taylor shuddered at the thought of trying to deal
with life in 1888 alone and hiding behind a fairly weak
disguise as a man.

And she felt safe there. Just like she'd felt when she'd
seen the Victorian garden scene at the fair. Was there a
connection she was missing? It was obvious that the scenes
were identical, but was there more?

Over her bowl of soup, she went over in her mind everything that had happened to her so far, trying to identify
clues to her purpose there but came up with nothing.

Relaxed and full, Taylor wiped off the kitchen table and
finished rinsing out the dishes. A high-pitched scream shattered the afternoon stillness and she dropped one of Ida's
teacups to the floor.

Chapter 11

TAYLOR WAS SURE the scream had come from the second floor. She raced up the back stairs, taking two at a time. At the landing, she stopped to listen. From behind the bathroom door, she heard the muffled sounds of crying.

She checked the knob and found the door unlocked. "Are you hurt? What's wrong?" No reply answered her questions, so she turned the knob and opened the door just wide enough to see into the room.

"It's me . . . Rose. What happened?" She could see one of Ida's girls dressed in a camisole and petticoat, standing with her back toward the door, her body quivering. Suddenly the girl's knees buckled, sending her to the floor in a heap. Taylor bounded into the room just in time to keep the girl's head from landing on the hardwood floor.

The girl had fainted. But why? And what had made her scream? As she grabbed for towels to elevate the girl's legs, she almost slipped on the puddle of water on the floor. Steaming, hot water. Then she looked at the girl's face— her left cheek and arm were both bright red with what looked like a first- or second-degree burn from the tipped hot water bucket.

"What happened to Audrey? Oh, look at her face!"

Soon the small room filled with the other girls who had run down the hall to see what had happened.

"Someone go down to the icebox and chip some ice into a clean dishcloth," Taylor shouted.

"But you should put butter on a burn right away and—"

"Just go and get the ice. Do it! We have to work quickly before the blisters come. Now go!" Taylor glared at the young woman who stood paralyzed in the doorway, wringing her hands. "What's your name?" Taylor asked, forcing her voice to sound calm and firm.

"Lizabeth."

"Please, Lizabeth, go get some chips of ice. It'll be okay, but you have to do what I say." She smiled at the young woman, keeping her voice quiet. "Please?"

Lizabeth finally turned and ran down the stairs.

Taylor returned her attention to the injured girl, who was beginning to stir from her faint. "Fill the bowl with cold water and put it on the floor . . . here. And bring me some more towels." She pointed to the sink. "Now!"

This time, the rest of the girls obeyed without hesitation. She placed more towels under Audrey's arm, hoping to reduce the swelling that had already begun. She soon had cold, wet towels placed on her arm and cheek.

Suddenly Audrey's eyes fluttered open in painful surprise. "My face! Oh, my face!" Her hand flew up to touch her injured cheek, and Taylor deftly caught it in midair.

"Listen to me. You're fine. The water burned you, but it's not a bad burn."

Audrey began to whimper, tears rolling slowly down her face.

"It's going to be fine. Don't worry. Look how everyone is helping." The other girls had surrounded Audrey, each on her knees. "And here's Lizabeth with our ice chips. Good job. They're perfect," she said as she repacked half the chips into a soft, clean cloth.

Audrey looked questioningly, but allowed her to place the cold pack on her cheek.

"Lizabeth, put the rest of the chips in the other towel for Audrey's arm."

Lizabeth quickly complied, carefully placing the second ice pack on the reddest part of Audrey's upper arm.

"The pain should be getting less. Is it starting to feel better?" Taylor brushed a stray honey-blond curl from Audrey's forehead. She could see the fear in her eyes, and knew how devastating the thought of a scarred face would be to her.

"It's better," Audrey whispered.

Taylor lifted the ice pack long enough to take another look at the burned cheek. "It shouldn't even blister," she said. "I think we got the ice on it quick enough—thanks to Lizabeth."

Audrey smiled, obviously relieved. "I never heard of putting ice on a burn before. Won't my skin freeze?"

Taylor recognized that her twentieth-century first aid methods were clearly not the current treatment for burns. She didn't care. If she hadn't used the ice, there would have been at least some blistering on Audrey's face, and her delicate skin would probably have scarred.

"Doesn't the cold make it feel better, Audrey?" Taylor hoped she would just accept the fact that the pain had decreased and not question her method any further.

"Does it really feel better, Audrey?" Lizabeth asked.

"Yes," she answered, smiling. "It hardly hurts at all now. How long does the ice stay on?"

"Just a few minutes longer," Taylor reassured her, "just until the fire is out of the burn. You try to relax for a few minutes. You're going to be fine."

The group of worried young women breathed a collective sigh of relief. They busied themselves mopping up the spilled water, refilling the bucket for the stove, and taking the wet cloths out to the laundry. One by one they left the bathroom, finally convinced that everything was under control and their friend was going to be all right.

Taylor looked up to see Lizabeth hesitating in the door-way. "You want to stay and help?" She could see that the girl was curious and still concerned about Audrey.

Lizabeth nodded. "What can I do?"

"Let's take a peek first," Taylor said, lifting away the ice packs and wet cloths. "What do you think?"

"It looks red still, but different."

"We'll leave the cold off for a little while now, and see if the pain returns. If it does, then the ice goes back on."

Lizabeth knelt down beside Audrey and held her hand. "How does it feel, Audrey? Better?"

"It hardly hurts at all now. I was so scared. . . ."

"I know," Taylor said, "a burn on the face is bound to scare anyone. You did just fine, though. Do you want to try sitting up?"

Audrey carefully sat up and gave Lizabeth a quick hug. "Thanks, Lizzie, I'm glad you were here."

"I'm just so glad everything turned out all right. Thanks to Rose, that is. And you be more careful with these buckets, too," Lizabeth scolded.

"Audrey, promise me you'll just rest today and tomorrow, and I'm sure you'll be just fine. A burn is a shock to the system. I'll check on you tomorrow." Taylor could see that the redness was already diminishing, and Audrey's burns would probably not even need a dressing. *Thank goodness for the icebox.*

"Rose, are you a healer?" Lizabeth stared at Taylor with a serious expression. "Can you teach me?"

Taylor stared back at the girl. She'd already influenced how this group of women would think about treating burns for the rest of their lives. She needed to be careful. "Actually, I'm really just a gardener. Plain and simple. I just read somewhere you should try to take the fire out of a burn to prevent blisters . . . and I thought ice would do a good job. It sure worked, huh?"

Audrey and Lizabeth nodded.

"You make sure she rests, Lizabeth. I'm counting on you. Now, off to bed with you, Audrey, and I'll look in on you tomorrow. I'll finish cleaning up in here."

Taylor watched the two girls walk down the hall and out of sight. Having deposited the rest of the wet towels into the laundry baskets, she returned to the kitchen to sweep up the shattered teacup, wondering if she might find a replacement at a store in town.

The thought of returning to the streets of San Diego was appealing. She returned to her room and chose a simple skirt and blouse to wear. Looking in the mirror, she was again surprised at how accustomed she was becoming to her appearance. As a final touch, she added the long hair to the back of her head. Satisfied, she slipped some money into her pocket and walked down the front stairs.

"How can we help you today, miss?"

After several inquiries of passersby as to where she might go for a teacup, Taylor found her way back to the same store where Jackson had picked up his vest. This time, though, the shopkeeper was much more attentive.

"Were you interested in a new gown or perhaps a new bonnet?" Charlie asked.

"Actually," she said, holding out a piece of Ida's broken teacup, "I need to replace this cup. You wouldn't happen to have this pattern in stock, would you?"

Charlie took the piece of delicate china from her. "Let me check for you. I'll be a few minutes, though, because my china storage is way in the back. Please feel free to browse." The shopkeeper smiled and soon disappeared through a curtained doorway.

Just as she turned to examine some books on a shelf nearby, she heard the bell on the door jingle as a customer entered the shop. She recognized the man as Mr. Johnson, the father of the vagabond family from Mrs. Reed's café. He looked well scrubbed and quite happy. What a contrast, she thought.

"Afternoon, miss."

"Good afternoon. I'm afraid the shopkeeper is in the back looking for a teacup for me."

"Not to worry. I'm in no hurry today. My name's Johnson, by the way. My family and I just moved here from Kansas. Have you been in San Diego a while?" Mr. Johnson extended his hand to Taylor.

"Mr. Johnson," said Taylor as she extended her own hand. "I'm Ta . . . Rose Martin," Taylor stammered, "and I've just been here a short while myself. It certainly is an exciting city, though."

"I'll agree with you there, Miss Martin. My family and I have had nothing but good luck since we arrived here. We have jobs and a place to stay and my children are as happy as can be. In fact, I'm here to buy some supplies for Mrs. Reed. Do you know her?"

Taylor hesitated. "Well, I've eaten at her café—"

"Well, I'm her new baker," he interrupted, "so I hope you'll drop in to try some of my sweet breads and pastries. And my wife is her new bookkeeper."

Mr. Johnson's eyes filled with pride when he mentioned his wife, and Taylor could see the sparkle of true love there. "I will," she promised. "Would Mrs. Reed sell me a loaf today?"

"Don't know for sure, but I'll bet she'll start. I used to sell my bread every Friday back home. People liked someone else doin' all the work, that's for sure. I ended up taking orders to keep up with the demand."

Taylor smiled. She couldn't help feeling pleased at the impact she'd had on him and his family at the café. She mentally made a note to stop by the café soon to check on the rest of his family.

"You're in luck, miss," Charlie said, suddenly appearing at the counter with teacup in hand. "We had your pattern tucked away in the last box I checked."

Relieved, she paid him for her purchase and wished both men a good afternoon. On the busy street, she heard a clock chiming four. She'd have just enough time to slip the cup into the china cabinet and freshen up before Ida returned at five. She was looking forward to her evening with May-lee. A chance to "dress up" and meet the high society of San Diego.

Chapter 12

IDA CAREFULLY PINNED a short fall of perfect, mahogany-colored sausage curls onto the back of Taylor's head, giving it a little tug to confirm its secure attachment. "Now, let me fasten the necklace and you're all set."

Taylor stood patiently, marveling at Ida's effortless ability to transform her into a refined Victorian lady. She gazed into the mirror in disbelief. Before her was a stranger—a very feminine woman draped in yards of shiny, pale blue satin that cascaded behind her in a shimmering waterfall of cloth. Her hair was brushed back from her face so it mixed in with the brown hairpiece that hung in flawless curls to the nape of her neck. Ida's elegant silver and pearl necklace lay delicately around her neck, drawing attention to the heart-shaped neckline that was accented with delicate white lace. The bodice of the dress fastened in back with twenty-six small glass buttons and fit as though it were molded to her body.

For the first time in her life, she felt elegant and very ladylike. She had always been more of a tomboy growing up. She wasn't uncomfortable with her femininity, but she had definitely lacked the benefits of a female role model during her teenage years. Her father had always provided a listening ear, but she had mostly resorted to searching the downtown library for books that would answer her questions about men, relationships, sex, and love. When she looked in the mirror, she was surprised at the reflection of pure femininity.

"Rose, you look wonderful. I knew this dress would be perfect on you. It's a couple of years old, but the style is still acceptable, I'd say, and certainly sophisticated enough to serve the guests of Mr. Shepard tonight." Ida walked in a circle around Taylor, pausing to smooth a pleat and readjust the skirt.

"Well, I sure won't be able to eat anything—I'll burst my buttons. Are you positive it doesn't look too tight?"

"It's supposed to fit snug," Ida said, "and it fits you like a glove, my dear, like it was made for you." She sighed and a dreamy look glazed her eyes for an instant. "I envy your youth, Rose. You have your whole life ahead of you. Before you know it, the wrinkles come and no one thinks you're beautiful anymore."

Taylor noticed the change in her voice. "Are you happy, Ida? I mean, you have your own . . . business and . . ." Taylor paused. "At least you have your independence, right?"

Ida laughed, sincerely amused. "Yes, Rose, I do have my independence—as long as Madame Ida stays three steps ahead of the law, that is." She looked at herself in the mirror, stroking her neck, searching for the beginnings of a double chin. "And I was smart enough to know when to stop *doing* and start managing. My girls are happy here with me, I think. I pay them a good salary. I keep them safe. Sherman House has been good for all of us, I guess. I just hope this town keeps growing, then I'll be set for life."

Taylor gave her a quick hug. "You're still beautiful, Ida. And look what magic you make for your homely gardener."

Ida stared at her and then burst out laughing. "You are

a strange one, Rose. And there's absolutely nothing wrong with the way you normally look. But I'll admit it's been a pleasure for me to help you look more like a, well, perhaps like a San Diego socialite—like dressing up a doll, I suppose. You have plenty of good features, you know, and you just need to learn to look at yourself a little differently. Femininity is not defined by your gown or your hair. It comes from within, from liking yourself. From learning more about yourself. Now you scoot downstairs and wait for Maylee. It's almost time for you to go."

Taylor followed Ida down the front stairs to wait. Within moments she was seated next to Maylee inside a fancy black carriage on her way to Mr. Shepard's home.

Maylee's nonstop chattering made the trip go quickly, and her excitement grew as they neared their destination.

"Now, Rose, all you need to do is smile and serve the refreshments to the guests as they assemble in the music room. Mr. Shepard is a bit odd sometimes, but his parties are the talk of the town. I'll be downstairs in the kitchen most of the evening."

Taylor gazed out the window of the carriage and gasped, startled to see a familiar building come into view. "Maylee, is that where we're going?"

"Why, yes. They call it the Villa Montezuma. Isn't it grand?"

Taylor recognized the bizarre two-story Victorian mansion, with its Arabesque dome and many stained-glass windows. She stared at the outlandish roofline that was filled with gables, spires, and turrets and then, finally, at the odd, onion-shaped dome that was topped by a winged dragon.

Growing up in San Diego, she had visited the restored house many times, and found its eclectic look and exotic ornamentation fascinating. In modern-day San Diego it was a museum. Now she would have the opportunity to see the house in its original condition.

"Now, be careful you don't soil your dress," Maylee

said, "the road is so dusty. Follow me. We'll go around to the other side."

Taylor carefully gathered her skirt and stepped onto the walkway.

Maylee led her to the west side of the mansion to use the servants' entrance. "Watch your step here, we'll be going down to the kitchen."

Taylor followed. Gone was the "old" smell that she remembered vividly from school field trips. Instead she breathed in the scents of a house filled with life. Fresh flowers. Newly waxed floors. The refreshing aroma of clean linens.

Maylee reached for an apron from a hook on the wall next to the small cookstove. "I've got quite a bit of work to do to get things ready. This kitchen's too small for the both of us, so why don't you explore a bit so you'll know your way around by the time the guests arrive. I'll get my shortcake mixed and in the oven, and the brandied peaches will just need to be warmed up. You go have a look." Maylee was quickly absorbed in pulling out bowls and checking the cupboards and icebox for supplies.

"Are you sure it's all right for me to wander through the house? Where's Mr. Shepard?"

"I didn't notice any sign of him when we arrived, and no carriage was parked in the drive. I'll come get you if I see any sign of him. Now, out you go—you'll be busy enough when the guests begin arriving in an hour or so." Maylee turned away and busied herself with flour and mixing bowls.

Taylor made her way up the stairs to the main floor, running her hand along the polished surfaces. Wood gleamed everywhere and was obviously well cared for. Turning around, she knew she would see a stained-glass window at the top of the stairwell. Recalling a long-ago tour, she remembered being told that Mr. Shepard liked to hang a lantern there to illuminate the glass, making it visible to visitors who came up the hill. The glass depicted

Saint Cecelia playing an organ to signify this was the home of a musician.

Continuing her exploration, she walked next through the formal dining room, with its dramatic, blue-tiled fireplace, as beautiful as she remembered. More stained-glass windows—these representing Summer and Autumn as young girls gathering flowers. She paused to touch the fragments of glass, bright in their pristine condition.

She made her way to the front door, where Jesse Shepard's guests would arrive for the evening. She noticed a heavy curtain was drawn to close off the drawing room from view. Gazing up the intricate staircase, she shuddered unexpectedly.

It was a temptation to climb all the way up to the tower. There, she knew, Jesse Shepard had an unobstructed view of the city. She recalled tour guides' descriptions of his revolving desk and chair kept there, enabling him to enjoy the view from any side he wished while he wrote. Now she experienced a definite feeling of déjà vu—the same feeling of dread, a negative energy that had enveloped her whenever she'd visited the tower in her own time.

She turned away, her attention drawn to the reception room, which was decorated primarily in shades of pink. The upper walls had pink fleur-de-lis designs, the fabric of the chairs and drapes were in many shades of light cherry. Dusky rose pink candles stood ready for lighting on rich, dark wood tables. A maroon and pink Persian rug lay in the middle of the floor, with just an edge of the polished fir floor showing.

Beyond the pink room was the music room, the largest room of the house. It occupied the entire east side and was filled with exotic surprises. Taylor examined the conservatory alcove, a round room with a tiled floor. There she discovered strange-looking plants, huge ferns, and unusual orchids blooming. More stained glass enhanced the beauty of the alcove, flowers depicting the four seasons. Eyes closed, she breathed in the humid, fragrant air before continuing her exploration.

"Oh!" Taylor's voice shattered the deadly quiet of the room. She had tripped over the head of the polar bear skin rug that lay in front of the fireplace, landing painfully on one knee. The bear's open-mouthed snarl seemed much too real in the quiet room. Almost ready to rise and come to life. Taylor shivered. "Stay," she whispered dramatically.

Gathering her skirts so she could return to her feet, her attention was drawn to the piano at the far end of the room. Maylee had mentioned in her chatter that there would be a concert tonight, and she was looking forward to the chance to experience the music that was part of Jesse Shepard's fame.

"Go ahead. Play my favorite."

Dad? Taylor's hand flew to her chest to calm her suddenly fluttering heart. She was tempted to play, but fearful someone would come into the room. She listened for sounds of life, but heard only her own heart beating. She waited another moment, then sat down at the piano.

Taylor gently placed her fingers on the polished white keys, finding a chord. The piano had a bright tone, and was perfectly in tune. Slowly, she began to play her father's favorite ragtime tune, Scott Joplin's "The Entertainer." In her mind, she could hear his familiar whistle. It had been a long time since they'd been together at a piano.

She was surprised that, after many years since her lessons, she was able to find her way through the piece.

One more, she thought. This time *her* favorite, "Dear Heart." A smile spread her lips, remembering her father's teasing her by singing at the top of his lungs.

"I promise I won't sing. . . . Go on."

Taylor heard the faint sound of her father's chuckle as she began to play the old standard. As she finished, she felt her father's spirit disappear. She was glad he had insisted on her taking piano lessons, though she never felt she had much talent. Music was a pleasure to her, and she had grown to appreciate others' talents through the years.

"Quite remarkable—what music are you playing?"

Taylor gasped and stood up at the sound of the enthusiastic voice so close to her. How had she missed the approach of the man who now stood gazing at her? She recognized him immediately as Jesse Shepard, the host for the evening. His eyes were liquid brown with long lashes, gentle and contemplative. Dark, earth brown eyebrows raised inquiringly, causing the soft, brown curls on his forehead to shift. A full, curved mustache framed a kindly mouth. His features were so perfect, so symmetrical, that any more delicacy would have made him too beautiful for a man.

"I'm so sorry—"

"Tell me," he interrupted, "what is the name of that piece? And what of the first piece—the one with the ragged rhythm? I've never heard such rhythm, such uneven timing. Fascinating!"

Taylor nervously made her way out from behind the piano.

"Did you channel this music from the spirit world, or is it of earthly composition? Ah, I've frightened you, haven't I? Don't worry, then. I'll consider it a private performance, and my ears will treasure its memory forever."

She knew it was rumored that Shepard believed in mysticism and spiritualism. Some even said he held séances at the Villa Montezuma.

"Tell me your name." He extended his hand to her.

"It's Rose. Mr. Shepard." Her hand was dwarfed by his long fingers. "I came here with Maylee to help serve your guests this evening. I'll just wait down in the kitchen until the guests arrive."

"Nonsense," he replied, still grasping her hand. "The kitchen's quite small, and Maylee prefers to have it to herself anyway, correct? So please stay here, enjoy the music room—feel free to play the piano or perhaps read for a bit.

I'll be upstairs until the time draws nearer for the performance to begin."

His hand gently squeezed hers in reassurance, then he brought it up to his lips for a feather-soft kiss. "Until later, then, Rose."

She watched him return to the entryway and climb the stairs to his second-floor sanctuary—a room she knew was filled with artwork and sculpture from every corner of the world, including memorabilia from his own European musical tours.

He was both handsome and sweet, she thought. It was easy to see why so many people had fallen in love with him. He was definitely charming.

Against Mr. Shepard's invitation to stay, Taylor decided the safest place for her until the guests arrived was with Maylee, and she made her way back to the kitchen.

As instructed, Taylor smiled and greeted guests as they arrived at eight, explaining that Mr. Shepard would join them later for the concert. Most of the ladies pouted briefly, while their escorts rolled their eyes in overstated disgust. Some commented on the eccentricities of their host, or remarked how the gifted always took time for reflection before performing.

Displayed on the dining room table was Maylee's creation of fresh shortcake and brandied peaches, filling the room and entryway with a mouth-watering aroma. Lamps and candles flickered everywhere, creating pools of shimmering light where small groups of people stood discussing the arts over their delectable dessert. Conversations hummed with tension and anticipation of the evening before them. To be invited to Jesse Shepard's home for one of his musical events was a sure sign of society and celebrity. All were thrilled to be there, happily costumed in their finest formal attire.

Mingling through the crowd, gathering discarded dessert bowls, Taylor eavesdropped to her heart's content. It soon became evident, from overheard bits and pieces of dialogue, that the room was filled with poets, authors, artists, ministers, judges, politicians, and personal friends.

Her cheeks grew weary with the strain of smiling, and she turned her head away from the crowd for a moment to stretch her jaws in an exaggerated yawn. She saw Maylee beckoning to her from the hallway.

"Maylee, they love your shortcake, and several of the ladies said they thought Mr. Shepard must have imported the peaches."

Maylee blushed appreciatively. "Oh, such a simple dessert. It was nothing, really."

Suddenly, the sound of harp strings drew everyone's attention to the music room. Plates and forks were quickly laid on the dining table and the crowd very orderly filed into the next room, where chairs had been placed next to the piano.

"Our cue to start cleaning up," Taylor whispered.

"Now, I'll be doing the cleaning, Miss Hostess Rose. You have to keep Ida's gown clean." Maylee good-naturedly gathered plates and silver onto a large oval tray, ready to return to the kitchen.

"But—"

"You go enjoy the concert. I'll be taking a carriage home when I'm finished in the kitchen. You stay—the carriage will be back to fetch you home at the end of the evening. Do you mind?"

"Are you sure you don't need help?"

"I have to be up to make breakfast for the hotel tomorrow, and Mr. Shepard always wants someone to stay to see the guests out the door. You'll be doing me a favor by staying until the end, you see. He'll give you a purse at the close of the night and we can settle our pay tomorrow at teatime."

Taylor glanced toward the music room, where she heard the murmur of quiet whisperings among the guests.

"Shoo, now. You have a nice evening with the concert.

We'll chat over tea tomorrow." Maylee departed down the hallway, just as the sounds of soft chiming drifted out from the music room.

Taylor turned away, hoping to find a spot at the back of the room. One chair remained, as if it had been saved for her. On the seat had been placed a printed program of the evening's concert selections; as she opened the folded paper, several fresh rose petals fell into her lap. After tucking the scarlet petals away in her pocket, she quickly skimmed the selections listed in fine handwritten script on the interior of the program:

> *1st and 2nd movements of the 9th Symphony*
> *Grand Cavatina from the opera Sappho*
> *Echo Song (original)*
> *Grand Egyptian March,*
> *with imitations of Storm and Battle (original)*

Just as she finished reading, the lights began to dim. Candles were extinguished without a sound. The room was plunged into darkness and eerie stillness. She listened to the sound of hushed breathing, waiting with the crowd for the performance to begin.

Chapter 13

ONE BY ONE, candle flames came back to life, though Taylor had seen no one in the adjoining rooms relighting them. In the hushed silence she strained to listen to a whisper of a sound, a breeze upon which rode a hint of music—though it was unclear exactly where the sound was coming from or exactly what it was. Many audience members sat with eyes closed and heads tilted back, as though they were beginning a session in meditation.

Taylor closed her eyes and listened. It sounded like singing, though from very far away. Humming, perhaps, like someone in a valley, out of sight, with the sound rising to the clouds. A high voice. A woman's? Soft lullaby sounds, riding along on a summer breeze.

A very real breeze against her cheek startled her and the heavy lashes that shadowed her cheeks flew up. Jesse Shepard was now standing at the piano, smiling over the tops of everyone's heads, smiling directly at her.

"Welcome, my friends, and thank you for joining me this evening. I hope you will enjoy tonight's concert of carefully selected pieces, designed for your intimate pleasure."

With a quick nod of his head and a formal bow, Jesse sat at the Knabe piano to begin.

Taylor had never heard such lyrical melodies played with such ease and open emotion. Impossible combinations of sounds sang from the piano, achieved effortlessly and magically by their host. She glanced at the guests and saw many faces that looked almost delirious with the beauty of the music that surrounded them. Each piece was warmly received with much applause and spontaneous shouts of praise. She shared their elation, thrilled to experience the extraordinary performance. Jesse Shepard was undeniably a master entertainer, more than she could have imagined.

"This will be the final selection this evening. I thank you for your kind attention," Shepard said, smiling warmly at his captivated audience.

Taylor allowed her eyes to close, savoring the final piece for the evening, the "Grand Egyptian March." Miraculously from the piano came the sounds of approaching armies, complete with bugle call and the order, "Charge!" The music grew dramatically louder as the melodies built one upon the other until somehow, there were sounds of cannons and rifles. Then the clash of sabers and the anguished cries of the wounded and dying. The piece ended abruptly and the guests sat in stunned silence. Taylor wiped a tear from her cheek and began to applaud. The others jumped to their feet and joined in a standing ovation for their astonishing host.

Feeling drained from the emotional ending to the concert, Taylor forced her trembling legs to carry her to the entryway to take her position for the remainder of the evening, listening to the guests' comments as they filed past her to their carriages outside.

"It must be trickery. It's impossible to create the sounds of battle from a piano! We've been tricked, that's all."

"What a gift he has. And I've heard that he never had a lesson in his life. Can you imagine? It's a gift."

"Did you keep your program? I want to save it. We can

put it in the back of the Bible to keep it from getting wrinkled. No one will believe we were here tonight. Now we'll be able to show the program to prove it."

"What do you see in that man, really? With his curled hair and doe eyes, he doesn't look much of a man to me. I think he has all the ladies mesmerized, that's all. And the High brothers building this monstrosity of a mansion and just giving it to him. And for what, I ask you? Because he can play the piano?"

"Splendid performance tonight, don't you think? He's a genius, simply a genius. We are so fortunate to have him here with us in San Diego. He provides the culture that this wild city needs."

Taylor swallowed a yawn that threatened to escape, just as the last few guests made their way out the door into the night. Soon only the sounds of carriages were heard and she walked softly back to the music room to see if all the guests had indeed departed. To her surprise, she saw that most of the chairs were gone. Nine remained, and they had been evenly placed around an oval table that now stood in the center of the room.

"Ah, Rose. You were a perfect hostess this evening and I thank you for your services tonight." Shepard spoke enthusiastically as he entered the music room from the drawing room at the far end. "And here are your wages," he said as he handed a small velvet pouch to her.

Quickly tucking it away in the pocket of her dress, she asked, "Do you need anything else?"

"Actually, I was about to ask if you would care to stay a while longer. I thought you might be interested in joining me and some friends of mine, who will be arriving shortly, for a spiritual session. May I speak candidly with you, Rose?"

"Certainly."

"When I perform, I sometimes receive messages from the spirit world, and . . . sometimes my performance is enhanced, shall we say, by the influences of creative artists

that are no longer on this plane of existence. Do you understand what I am saying?"

"Actually, I do."

Shepard smiled at her, visibly pleased that she was reacting positively. "Let us say that I was given the message
that you should be invited to stay this evening, and share
in our spiritual circle."

"If you think it would be all right with the others . . ."

"It will be fine, I assure you. Please take a seat wherever
you like at the table. We will begin promptly at midnight.
My friends will let themselves in and join you shortly. I'll
be in my room resting and shall return when all have arrived. Please, make yourself comfortable."

She watched her host gracefully pivot, then walk toward
the drawing room. She knew his bedroom, the so-called
Red Room of the modern-day museum, was just beyond it.

Spiritual circle? Her fatigue vanished with her growing
excitement, and she chose a seat at the table.

Within minutes, the spiritual circle members had arrived
and let themselves into the house, joining her at the table.
All were silent, nodding and smiling at each other as they
took their places, sitting male-female-male-female. Two
seats remained empty, one next to Taylor and one directly
across the table. Each of the three women who had come
in were dressed in lily white gowns, their shoulders draped
with delicately fringed lace shawls or impossibly thin silk
scarves. In contrast, the three men wore plain dark suits
that matched their somber expressions. Some closed their
eyes, breathing deeply and evenly. One woman covered her
eyes with her left hand, resting her elbow on the table. She
looked as though she were trying to induce a trance.

Taylor found herself clenching and unclenching her
hands, anxious for Shepard's return. Though the others really looked perfectly normal and harmless, she questioned
her own eager willingness to participate in the eerie ritual.
She glanced toward the door as the last guest arrived.

When the young woman entered the music room, everyone instantly became alert; all eyes opened and were directed to her. Taylor followed their gaze. Unlike the other women, this last guest was not dressed in white. Instead, she wore an obsidian black gown that shimmered with every movement. The candles flickered ominously as she entered the room, sending a sudden chill up Taylor's spine.

"Hello, everyone. Ah, a newcomer, I see. Let me introduce myself. I am Madame Lana, your medium for the evening. And you are . . . ?"

"Rose Martin. Mr. Shepard asked me to stay tonight, I—"

"Indeed, I did. Hello, Lana." Shepard briskly walked into the room, greeting the others at the table with a brief smile and nod. "Please consider Rose our special guest tonight," he said, "and Lana, won't you take the seat next to her? I shall sit opposite you this evening."

Taylor noticed that he looked well rested and even more alert than his guests. She watched as he took his place across the table while the others adjusted their chairs, scooting in closer to the table. One by one, each placed both hands, palms down, on the table. Again she noticed that most began to breathe deeply and evenly. She placed her own trembling hands on the table and waited.

"Rose, our spiritual circle," Madame Lana began, "is designed to allow us to attempt communication with other planes of existence. Sometimes I am the vessel for that communication. Sometimes the spirits come to us more directly. I believe that our souls are not imprisoned in time, and that we have access to past and future souls. I truly believe that time is an illusion, you see, and you must remember that nothing is more important than belief."

Taylor nodded. Her throat felt suddenly dry, her mouth slightly sour with the taste of apprehension.

"Please don't be frightened, my dear."

Madame Lana reached for Taylor's hand in a gesture of reassurance, then pulled it abruptly away the moment her fingertips touched her hand. At the same instant, Taylor felt a charged tingle—an invisible jolt of electricity that caused her to gasp sharply.

"Is there someone you wish to contact, Rose?"

Taylor glanced at Shepard, then returned her gaze to Madame Lana. "I'm really not quite sure why I'm here," she began. *Or why I've made this leap in time,* she thought.

"Lana," Shepard began, "during my performance this evening, I received a message that indicated Rose should join us. There is someone waiting to contact *her,* actually. That's all I received."

"Ah, then we shall look forward to an interesting session tonight. Let's begin. Rose, please, just relax. Hopefully, the spirits will be with us in a few moments." Madame Lana closed her eyes and folded her hands primly in her lap.

Everyone at the table stared at the medium. Shepard gazed at Madame Lana, his eyes sharp and assessing, and brimmed with a visible conflict between curiosity and passion.

Taylor forced her own hands to remain on the table, waiting for something to happen. In her mind she called to her father.

"I'm here, Taylor."

She checked the others at the table to see if they had heard her father's voice. There was no indication they had. Each sat patiently staring at the medium.

Dad, will they be able to hear you? Is that what this is about? Taylor closed her eyes, concentrating on keeping her own breathing normal. She desperately wanted to know why she was there.

"Taylor, did you believe what the medium said of contacting past and future souls?"

Her father's voice sounded strangely serious, but calm. Well, her father had contacted her. And she was his future, he her past. A shared present was a little confusing, though. Was time an illusion?

"Everyone needs to find their own way of thinking about

*time, Taylor, and their own existence. Just believe, okay?
Believe. . . ."*

Her father's voice faded softly and, once again, she felt
the separation.

Madame Lana opened her eyes and began to speak.
"There are many spirits with us tonight in our circle. Please
send your welcoming thoughts to them," she instructed.
"Some souls are new to the other side, and some have been
there since ancient times. They are very excited . . . it's difficult to isolate the voices I hear. . . ." Madame Lana turned
her head from side to side as though trying to track the
spirits' voices.

"Ah, Mr. Miller," Madame Lana continued, "your father
extends his greetings and congratulations on your good
business fortune. He says to continue with the speculating
and all will come to you that you wish. And that he is
happy to see your mother is well."

Taylor watched as a man at the table nodded acknowledgment, smiling at the message.

"Sally, your sister sends her love. She says that your
suitor will bring you the item that you desire on Tuesday
next. Does this have meaning to you, Sally?"

Taylor watched as the woman at the far end of the table
nodded. So far, nothing too mysterious and profound, she
thought.

"I keep getting a queer message—something about
weaving or mending cloth. No, it's more like altering a
garment, a garment of the finest red cloth. Rose, are you a
seamstress?"

She shook her head no.

Unexpected laughter burst from Madame Lana, a private
joke she was experiencing. Curious glances and smiles
passed between the guests.

"The voice is clearer now," she explained, "and the picture I am given is someone tailoring a rosy pink–colored
gown. Rose, this message is being passed to you. Does it
have meaning to you?"

She nodded, smiling at the pun. *Tailored Rose.* Taylor Rose. She wondered if somehow Madame Lana had spoken with Maylee. Or perhaps she knew Ida. There must be a logical connection, she thought.

Madame Lana frowned. "The spirit says to tell you to believe in the voices—that she has a voice too."

The shock of discovery hit Taylor full force. More surprised than frightened, she asked, "It's a woman talking to you?"

"Yes. And she keeps giving me the message of a rose. She keeps insisting that she's not referring to you. That she is the Rose here. Do you know what she means?"

"My mother died after I was born. Her name was Rose."

"Yes, yes—she says that's it. Ah, well, that's what she was trying to say. You are both Rose. She's relieved now. She's asking if you believe. She's very concerned. She says to ask you."

Taylor hesitated, torn by conflicting emotions. It would be so easy to believe, she thought, that she would have the miracle of communicating with the mother she'd never known. It seemed too good to be true, though, and her father had taught her to be wary of anything that seemed too good to be true. But, he had also taught her to believe in miracles.

"Rose, she wants to come closer, to enter my body for just a few moments. She says she needs to tell you something . . . something very important—private and personal. She says to ask you if this is all right." Madame Lana gazed at Taylor, waiting for her reply.

She nodded, then felt an uncontrollable shudder along her spine as gooseflesh rose on every inch of skin. Even her scalp tingled.

Eyes closed, Madame Lana's head dropped suddenly. Her chin was now resting on her chest, her shoulders drooped. With a sudden gasp of air, her spine straightened and she lifted her head and stared wide-eyed at the group surrounding the table. Finally her gaze rested on Taylor and her eyes filled with tears.

Taylor stared as Madame Lana's hand rose slowly and came to rest on top of her own. She felt a comfortable warmth, almost as though their skin became liquid where they touched. It was strangely a feeling of tranquillity and safety.

Madame Lana cleared her throat, swallowing awkwardly. She brought her free hand to her throat as though speaking had become cumbersome. Finally, her lips parted.

Taylor leaned closer to her, fearful she might not hear the words that she was struggling to say.

"Yes," she whispered, "Taylor, it's me." The words were only audible to Taylor, though everyone at the table was leaning toward her, straining to hear.

Taylor shook her head in disbelief. "This isn't possible," she murmured.

"Your father's here with me. He's safe and happy. We're happy."

"How do I know—"

"Taylor Rose," she whispered. "Close your eyes and let me put my arms around you as I've dreamed of doing. I know you too have imagined this moment. . . . Believe. . . . Please."

Taylor's eyes brimmed with sudden tears at the chance to hug her mother. It was true that she'd imagined it countless times through the years. Her father had taught her to envision her mother's arms around her when she was frightened or sick. It had been a game for them, each imagining her there with them during bedtime stories and special times.

"Taylor, please. . . ."

Allowing her eyes to close, Taylor waited. Hot tears escaped from beneath her lashes as she felt soft arms wrap around her shoulders. A hand at the back of her head encouraged her to lean closer and find that soft part of every mother's neck. So many times she had imagined her mother's scent—a blended bouquet of new spring flowers and a warm ocean breeze. She breathed the aroma deeply, hoping to never lose the essence.

"Taylor Rose, my little girl. I've missed you in your lifetime, but I have seen much of it," she whispered. "I can't stay long. . . . Listen to your father, Taylor. Your purpose is real and you must keep searching for the truth. With truth, there is forgiveness. With forgiveness, the path for love is revealed."

Taylor felt her mother's arms relax as she pulled away, her hands now resting lightly on her shoulders. Taylor gazed into her mother's eyes, a million questions frozen in her own mind.

"And it's perfectly all right to wait for the magic, Taylor. Reach for the special love that your father and I found. You'll know when it's real."

"Don't go," Taylor whispered, her voice catching painfully in her throat.

"This is the first and last time for us. But talk to me, Taylor, anytime. I'll hear you. I'll be listening. . . ."

Madame Lana's body slumped in the chair. She groaned softly, as though stirring from a disturbing dream. Rubbing her eyes, she rolled her shoulders back, moving as though she were stiff and sore.

Taylor stared at her own hands, now limp in her lap.

"Did she come, Rose? It feels like she's been here. . . ." Madame Lana continued to stretch her neck from side to side.

She met her gaze and smiled. "Yes, she did. Thank you—it was amazing."

Visibly pleased, Madame Lana sighed. "It's amazing to me, too, Rose. I'm glad it was a good experience. Let's continue, then. Does anyone have any questions for the spirits? Mr. Shepard, is there a question tonight?" Madame Lana focused her attention on her host.

"Lana, ask the spirits if they see my writing career continuing," Shepard asked.

"I'm getting a positive response . . . yes, definitely continue on a literary path, I'm told. I'm also getting a picture . . . over water and beyond. Does this mean anything to you?"

"Yes, it does." Shepard leaned forward, resting his elbows on the table, concentrating on Madame Lana's face.

"Now I'm getting a picture of leaves, autumn leaves . . . somewhere far from here. Overseas. Europe, perhaps?"

"Yes, yes," Shepard murmured. "Shall I assume that I should travel to this place to pursue a project?"

"I'm getting a positive response. Oh! This place is France—is that where you intend to travel?"

Shepard nodded, rubbing his chin thoughtfully. "And will my project be successful?"

"I'm being told that this will most definitely happen . . . yes." Madame Lana cocked her head to one side. "Specifically, you are to remain overseas for one year. When you return, all your affairs will be quickly set in order. All will be well."

"Thank the spirits for the information. It is most interesting," Shepard replied, leaning back in his chair.

"Questions, anyone?" Madame Lana glanced from face to face, pausing to offer a sentence to each from the spirit world. When she had spoken to every guest, Madame Lana once again gazed at Taylor. Her eyelids grew unexpectedly heavy, and she allowed them to drop.

Each person appeared to have been given fairly specific advice or news that had distinct meaning. Once again, Taylor felt a sudden shudder along her spine and a tingle along her scalp.

Madame Lana opened her eyes. "Rose, there is another message for you. She says . . . she says to remember the cards, remember what was told to you. Does this have meaning for you?"

Instantly paralyzed from the impact of the question, Taylor stared wordlessly back into Madame Lana's eyes. How could she know?

"Now I'm getting a picture of a gun. Oh, my. . . . I see blood and darkness. . . . She says that it doesn't have to happen. . . . Someone is in danger! She says you have the power to change things . . . to stop someone? something? She says you know what the pictures mean. . . . Do you?"

Taylor forced her lungs to inflate. She felt light-headed from the momentary lack of oxygen. Nodding, she asked, "Who is speaking to you?"

"Strange . . . another Rose? No, I'm getting the name of . . . Rosa? Ah, Rosalinda . . . she says to tell you that you must continue to find . . . to find something. Do you know what this means, Rose?"

"Yes, I think so. Can you ask her what I'm supposed to do? How to find out what I need to find out?"

"She says it is your doing."

"Please . . . ask her about my future," Taylor whispered, not really wanting to know, but too afraid not to ask. "Am I going to stay here?"

"She's fading, Rose. I'm having trouble hearing her. . . . She says it is not certain—that you must grasp the moment, not the past or the future. The moment, she says." Madame Lana sighed, her head tipping back slightly. "She's gone."

Confused and weary from the emotions evoked during the séance, Taylor leaned back into her chair. She felt numb.

The séance continued for a few more minutes, as each of the other guests posed final questions to the spirits through Madame Lana. Taylor listened half-heartedly, longing for the peaceful escape of sleep. Slipping into her own thoughts, she focused on the messages she'd received from her mother and the spirit of the eerie clairvoyant of her own time, Rosalinda.

"Rose, are you feeling well enough?"

Taylor looked up into the sympathetic eyes of her host, surprised to realize that she was seated alone at the table.

"You've had quite an evening. I have a carriage outside to escort you home. Will you be all right?"

Taylor smiled weakly at her host. "It was a wonderful experience." The words caught in her throat and she swallowed painfully.

"I'm glad," he answered. "Please thank Maylee for sharing you with us tonight. I hope our paths will cross again. All I ask is that your experience only be shared with those very close to you. Many people in this city—in this world, for that matter—don't understand the mysteries of spiritualism. I myself sometimes struggle with its concepts." Shepard offered his hand, helping her to her feet.

Taylor allowed her host to walk her to the carriage outside. The ride back to Ida's went quickly and her mind, thankfully, was quiet.

Noiselessly, Taylor climbed the stairs to her room and undressed, carefully hanging the beautiful gown in the wardrobe and placing Ida's necklace on the bureau. Tomorrow, she decided, she'd begin to gain Jackson's confidence. Lives were at stake.

Chapter 14

TORRID SUMMER SUNSHINE made Taylor's room glow much too brightly as she struggled to open her eyes. She squinted against the glare, guessing at the time, suspecting she had overslept. During the night she had kicked off her light blanket and sheet, and the morning temperature was already climbing. The day felt decidedly slow and lazy, and she wasn't looking forward to the feel of the hot sun on her back in the garden.

"Hello, up there! Rose! Get out of bed for morning tea!"

She pushed back the curtain to wave at Maylee, who stood in the center of the backyard, sounding chipper and cheerful and looking very well rested. Maylee returned her wave.

"I'll join you in a minute—after I wash up a little," she answered. "Oh, and I have our money from last night. I'll bring it down." She looked forward to morning tea with Maylee and Ida. It had become a habit in the short time she'd been at Sherman House.

Maylee pulled open the back door, stepping into Ida's meticulous kitchen. She was at home enough to poke through the cupboards for teacups, and then for plates for the buttermilk biscuits she'd made. Water was already boiling on the stove, so Ida must be up and about. The table was set by the time Taylor arrived.

"My, you do look like you've had a rough night. I certainly hope it was to your benefit, child." Maylee chuckled as she pulled out a chair for Taylor. "Sit, now, and tell me how the rest of your evening went with Mr. Shepard."

Taylor smiled and handed the money purse to Maylee. She hungrily bit into a biscuit, suddenly famished, then added honey to her tea and stirred it thoughtfully. She wondered how much she should share with her.

"Come now, you've got me thinking that things became quite serious—what happened?" As she waited, Maylee carefully counted out the money they'd earned at the party, dividing it in half. She quickly put hers away in a pocket, deep in the folds of her beige cotton skirt, and left the rest on the table. She sat patiently waiting as Taylor grappled with her thoughts.

"Well, the concert was magnificent—unbelievably beautiful. Mr. Shepard really is a genius, like they say. You should have heard the sounds that came from that piano."

"So you knew of his talents, then?"

"Well, sort of. . . . I mean, I guess I'd heard that he was a fantastic musician, though I never thought I'd have a chance to hear him." *Or see him,* she thought. What a wondrous night she'd had.

"Go on," Maylee urged.

"After the concert, I—"

"I see you both saw fit to start without me this morning," Ida growled good-naturedly as she entered the room, looking groomed and gorgeous, as usual. Then she softened and turned to Taylor. "Are you all right this morning?"

"Fine, Ida, a little sleepy—why?"

"Last night, I heard sounds from your room and when I peeked in, you were sound asleep, crying. I was afraid to wake you."

Taylor frowned. She had no recollection of any disturbances in her sleep. She felt a little groggy, but that was all.

"Well, I'm happy it was nothing," Ida said, though her eyes betrayed her uncertainty.

"Oh, sit, sit. Rose was just beginning to tell about her evening." Maylee poured tea for Ida and passed her the plate of biscuits.

"Tell me you were the prettiest one there, Rose. That dress looked so lovely on you. What was everyone wearing?" Ida asked.

Taylor grinned at the two ladies' inquisition, delighted to recount the evening for their obvious pleasure. The sparkle in their eyes was reward alone.

"Ida, let her talk," Maylee chided.

Taylor described every detail she could remember—from the colors and styles of the gowns to the elaborate coiffures worn by the elite ladies of San Diego. As best she could, she recounted the way the music made her feel, and how impossible the melodies and sounds seemed. Maylee and Ida hung on her every word, especially demanding particulars of who said what and about whom.

"All right, now tell us what happened after the guests left," Maylee urged. She poured second cups of tea and settled in for Taylor's narrative.

"Maylee, did you know that Mr. Shepard has séances after his concerts? You should have at least warned me."

"I've honestly never stayed any time after the guests," she answered, "though I've heard that strange things have happened there. Ida, what do you know about this? You must have heard something."

"Actually," Ida said, "I have heard that Mr. Shepard is involved in the First Spiritualist Society, though I've also heard that he flat out denies this."

"He called the group a spiritual circle," Taylor began, "and said that during his performance, he'd been given a message to invite me to stay. The medium—she was the one who channeled the spirits—was a woman named Madame Lana, and she listened to messages and passed them on to everyone at the—"

"What do you mean, channeled?" Maylee interrupted.

"Someone who is supposed to be able to receive and transmit thoughts or actual messages from beyond the grave is said to channel a spirit, and sometimes even many different spirits will come."

"When I was a child," Maylee began, "I remember my grandmother acting strangely, going into a sleep but not quite asleep, you know? Then she would whisper and nod her head—is that what this woman did?"

"I guess it's possible," Taylor replied.

"Rose, how do you know these things?" Maylee asked.

"My father raised me to be curious about all religions, and we visited many different ceremonies and services. He also taught me to keep an open mind: not to insist on limits, to believe in the unexplainable—to believe in miracles." Taylor sent her silent thanks to her father, glad she had grown up in such an eclectic atmosphere.

"And what messages did Madame Lana have for you?" Ida asked quietly. "Perhaps that was what gave you bad dreams last night."

Taylor hesitated a moment, then began to relate the emotional experience of her mother entering the medium's body, finally revealing the intimate moment when she felt her mother's arms encircling her for the first time.

Maylee dabbed her eyes at the conclusion of her story, noisily blowing her nose into her handkerchief. "That's the most beautiful story I've ever heard. I don't care what people say or think, a child knows her own mother, and if you say it was your mother . . . then, it was."

Telling the story to Ida and Maylee brought Taylor's emotions to the surface, a little surprised how vividly she could still feel the touch of her mother's hand on her own. It had truly been a miracle, and one worth every moment of confusion and discomfort she'd felt over the past few

days. It felt like a gift, one she had wished for her entire
life.

"Rose, what do you think of leaving your garden today
and accompanying my girls and me to the beach? It's much
too warm to work outside, and we've decided we need a
day away. Interested?"

"I was hoping for a good excuse to leave the weeds alone
today, and now you've read my mind. What a fine idea.
Maylee, will you come too?"

"Not this time. Lots to do at the hotel today. In fact, I'd
better get myself back there and start some lunch for the
guests. You have a good time without me—just bring me
back a pretty shell if you find one." Maylee put her dishes
in the sink with a clatter and headed for the door.

"Maylee, are you sure you can't come with us today?
You need to take some time for yourself once in a while.
You work much too hard."

"Go. Go, and have fun enough for me, I have work to
do." Careful not to let the back door slam, Maylee hurried
back to the hotel.

"So, Miss Rose," Ida began, "find something cool to
wear and meet us out front in half an hour. I've rented one
of the transfer buses to take all of us to Ocean Beach today."

"A bus?"

"Well, my girls are not exactly welcome to join the rest
of society in traveling among the people of our fair city, so
I thought one of the pretty horse-drawn buses would be the
perfect thing. Now, go on upstairs and change. I'll pack our
lunch and we'll be on our way." Ida's pleasure showed in
the warm smile that lit her entire face.

As Taylor scampered up the back stairs, Ida reached for
a basket from the top of the cupboard and quickly organized a picnic. She gathered loaves of bread, jars of jam,
two large hunks of cheese, a dozen apples, and a bag of
fresh ginger cookies she had purchased at Mrs. Reed's café.
Martha's new cook was a master with sweets, and she had

already purchased several loaves of his dark bread. Having bundled several folded blankets and secured them to the top of the basket, her preparations were complete. She picked up an old brass school bell and let it ring, calling, "Girls! Let's go! Everyone out front in five minutes."

It had been some time since the occupants of Sherman House had participated in a day of rest and relaxation. To-day seemed the perfect day to laze in the summer sun, and a perfect day to probe for more information from the mysterious Taylor Rose. Ida loved a good challenge, and her own specialty had always been in the conversation department. Her mood seemed suddenly buoyant, and she knew the day would be filled with surprises.

Chapter 15

PARKED ON THE street outside Sherman House was a gaily painted San Diego and Coronado Transfer Company bus. The horse-drawn bus was actually an enclosed carriage designed to hold twelve people inside and as many on the upper open deck—as long as they were willing to hold on to a railing that only reached as high as the passengers' knees.

The bus was a bright daffodil yellow, with huge, snow-white spoked wheels. Decorating the sides were elaborate paintings of various landscapes, with intricate border designs. Four well-behaved horses waited patiently, ready to escort the bus and its contents to their destination.

Soon the air was filled with squeals of joy as Ida's girls discovered the day's mode of transportation. Clambering onto the bus, all jockeyed for window seats, settling in for the ride to the beach.

Ida watched from the front bay window, waiting for Taylor. She was surprised the horses didn't bolt and run with all the commotion the girls were causing. The front door opened and Ida smiled.

The first surprise of the day.

"Well, hello, Jackson," she said. "I see that you were able to fill in for the driver after all. It's difficult to secure someone to escort us sometimes—you know how this town is about ladies like us." Ida chuckled at Jackson's quick blush.

She turned to see Taylor standing in the doorway. "Rose, you've met Jackson. He'll be driving us to the beach today."

Taylor stared, complete surprise on her face. "Hello, Jackson."

"Hello, Rose, I'm happy to be escorting all of you today. And a pretty day it is." Jackson's voice was neutral but pleasant.

"Jackson, will you get the picnic basket?" Ida asked.

Jackson lifted the basket with a groan. "Shall we go? Ladies, after you." Jackson followed Ida and Taylor outside, nudging the door closed with his hip.

"Rose, I'm afraid you'll have to share the driver's bench with Jackson. The bus looks awfully full." Ida gave Taylor a brisk nod of encouragement and turned quickly away before Taylor could argue the point.

Jackson climbed into the front of the bus, secured the basket, and offered a helping hand to Taylor. Ida hummed a happy tune as she joined her boisterous girls inside the bus. They were all anxious to begin the day and were soon hanging out the windows shouting for Jackson to hurry along and get the horses moving. He obliged as soon as Taylor was secure next to him.

The sights of a wild and long-ago San Diego soon distracted Taylor from her initial thoughts of hesitation, and she soon had Jackson chattering away about the buildings and sights along their route to the beach.

Taylor began to feel the elation of liberation. She was on her way to the shore for a day with friends, she realized. Not so different from what she'd have chosen to do on a pretty summer day in her own time. She told herself to do as Ida suggested: relax and enjoy the break.

"Do you like the beach?" Jackson asked, breaking Taylor's momentary silence. He found her easy to talk to, though her fervent questions about the surroundings seemed just a bit curious. She appeared to have never seen the sights along the main road they traveled. Surely she had seen them when she arrived from up the coast, he thought. She seemed filled with wonder and surprise. Perhaps she'd arrived at night, or by ship, he reasoned.

"My father taught me to love the water. I've been swimming since I was three."

"Does he live up the coast?"

"He died about five years ago," Taylor answered, avoiding any specific reference to where he was from.

"I'm sorry, Rose. . . . And your mother?" Jackson continued.

"She died when I was a baby," Taylor answered softly.

"So you're alone, then?"

"Well, I suppose so, though I don't really feel alone. I have friends, of course, and plenty to keep me busy."

Jackson stole a quick glance at Taylor to see if her expression matched her optimistic words. He was surprised to see that it did. He gazed at Taylor, her profile sharp and confident, her chin tilted slightly upward. She wore her mahogany brown hair brushed back away from her face, without the false long curls she sometimes added.

Beneath her straw hat, Jackson noticed a few unruly curls that fringed the tops of Taylor's ears and caressed the sides of her slender neck. Her skin was like peach-tinted cream, beginning to glow from her daily exposure to the summer sun. Jackson felt an unwelcome surge of desire.

He tore his gaze away from her and returned his attention to the road. He was determined to maintain control over his attraction to her. What he really needed to do was find out more about her and make sure she didn't hinder his plans—and exactly what she was hiding.

"We're here!" squealed one of Ida's girls.

The bus stopped in front of the Ocean Beach Hotel, a splendid white wooden building, two stories high. The hotel's wide, roofed porch extended along the entire side, and ended with an elegant gazebo that was filled with guests sipping beverages and enjoying the soft ocean breeze.

Jackson tossed the reins to an awaiting stable attendant, who stood patiently next to the front wheel of the bus.

Ida's girls noisily exited the bus, waving cheerfully at the men on the porch. Wives tugged at their husbands' arms in aggravation, trying to distract them from ogling the busload of ladies of ill repute.

One man called out, "Halloo, Ida! Out for a day of play today?"

Recognizing him as one of her girls' regulars, Ida replied, "Why, yes, kind sir. Everyone needs a change of scenery now and then, wouldn't you agree?" She laughed at the women's prompt displays of disgust and the reddening cheeks of the men's faces.

A shrill voice from the porch called out, "You should be ashamed to bring those harlots to a respectable hotel!"

Though her life had been filled with jeers of unacceptance, Ida was satisfied with the sense of accomplishment she felt. She had seen a need and filled it well—Sherman House was a class establishment and a safe haven for her girls. She passed no judgment on them or the men they served. Having learned long ago that being judgmental was the greatest hindrance to happiness, Ida instead concentrated on living life to the fullest.

Jackson hoisted the picnic basket down from the floor of the driver's seat, then offered a hand to Taylor.

Their eyes locked for a long moment as she eyed him for signs of embarrassment or discomfort over the reaction of the hotel's guests to Ida's girls. She found only an expression of complete unconcern. He obviously was not bothered by the rude remarks. Keeping her own expression composed, she boldly stared into Jackson's eyes. A mischievous look came into his eyes, and she smiled in approval.

He answered her unuttered words. "No, it doesn't bother me to be here, surrounded by Ida's pretty girls . . . and you. Now, let's move this bevy of beauties to the beach where we won't distract these fine folk."

Both joined Ida and the girls, who were already making their way past the hotel and down to the waterfront. Jackson patiently followed as the women searched for the perfect site. Laughing and giggling, the group sounded more like young schoolgirls playing hooky.

Finally they reached an isolated area of beach with a long stretch of sandy shore. The spot was declared ideal and shoes were swiftly removed. Skirts were raised to keep them dry while small groups paired up to wade or search for shells along the wet sand. Ida asked Taylor to spread the blankets and secure the basket, nudging her gently toward the approaching Jackson. Before she could protest, Ida had left her alone and joined the others on the sand.

Taylor turned to wait for Jackson, taking the blanket bundle from him.

"I guess this is the spot." She spread each of the blankets out while he placed the picnic basket at his feet.

"Would you like to go for a walk?" he asked as he promptly sat down, quickly removing his shirt and shoes, and rolling up his pant legs. He looked up at Taylor, squinting from the bright glare. The sun behind her created an angelic halo-glow around her head, and he brought his hand up to shade his eyes from the brightness.

Taylor swiftly undid her skirt to reveal cotton trousers underneath that had already been rolled up in preparation. Her hat tossed aside, her blouse came off next, revealing a cotton tank top that would have produced more than a few gasps from the Victorian ladies at the hotel. Though she knew her black bikini would have been out of the question, Taylor had decided that the beach might be isolated enough at least to wear a sleeveless top.

Jackson's eyes widened slightly at her unconventional dress, but before he could utter a word, she had raced down to the shore.

"Let's go!" she called over her shoulder.

Jackson grabbed a small flannel blanket and wrapped it around his neck. Then he sprang to his feet to follow Taylor, who had already reached the waves that were gently lapping the sandy edge. He vowed to continue in his quest to discover more about her, but also decided that part of this day could be rest and relaxation. He had been so serious about gaining the trust of Wyatt Earp at the saloon that he'd taken few days off to enjoy the beautiful areas of San Diego. He was afraid of distraction, afraid to lose his focus on why he was there. Somewhere inside, he felt the tension ease—at least for the moment, at least for one day.

Taylor was ankle-deep in the water when he joined her. Bent over at the waist, she looked up at him with her fingers at her lips.

"Move slowly, and come here. There's a small stingray resting about three feet from me. Look," she whispered, pointing toward the beach.

Jackson followed her lead, but not before he noticed that the gap in her top revealed the crest of her bosom. He was surprised that she wore no undergarments. The immediate hardness in his loins shocked him, and his gaze lingered deliciously at the sight of the sunlight rippling on her ivory breasts. He imagined how it would feel to again bring their pink tips to crested peaks, as he had in the garden when he and the mysterious Rose had last spent time together.

"Do you see it?" she asked, glancing up at Jackson. Instantly, she realized where he had been gazing, and her cheeks burned in remembrance of his touch on her breasts. She felt her heartbeat throb in her ears and the unmistakable tingle of excitement between her thighs. She cleared her throat, pretending not to be affected.

Jackson severed his gaze from Taylor to the resting sting-

ray. He moved slowly closer to her and squatted in the
water to gain a better view of the animal.

Her attention drawn back to the water, Taylor moved
toward the ray, squatted, and reached out her hand. She
knew its skin was like velvet, having fed the tame rays at
Sea World in her own time. Now moving painstakingly
slowly, she stroked her forefinger along the back of the ray
before it flapped its wings and swam away with a splash.

Both stood, and Taylor grinned in delight. "They're so
soft, and such an odd creature, don't you think?"

"How do you know of such things?" he asked. "It's
called a stingray, you say? Have you studied sea creatures,
then?"

"Oh, not really, I've just seen them before. Let's walk
along the shore, shall we?" She turned and walked toward
the sandy beach, hoping to distract him from asking more
questions. Looking over her shoulder, she noticed some of
the girls were lounging on the blankets while others had
shed their outer clothes and were swimming in bloomers
and camisoles. She was tempted to join them. The water
was exceptionally warm and the sun was beginning to bake
her skin. She reached down for a handful of water and
splashed her arms and neck, letting some of the coolness
trickle down her front.

"The water feels great. Do you swim, Jackson?" She
turned to check his response. Nodding, he followed her
example and splashed his chest with the warm ocean water.
She briefly wondered if his broad shoulders ever tired of
the burden he carried, but soon she was distracted by his
inky black chest hair glistening with moisture. She stared
at him in simple adoration—his chest muscles were perfectly developed, and his stomach was flat and toned. Modern weight lifters would be envious of his athletic physique,
she knew, his defined muscles a product of hard work and
not from a daily regimen at the local health club.

Silently they walked side by side along the shore, and

both began to relax, enjoying the sunshine and the moist sea air.

"I do love it here," Jackson said pensively, his mood becoming slightly somber. He knew he would never again see the shores of San Diego once he'd completed his mission. He had accepted the fact that he might die in the process of avenging his father's murder, or be forced to live the rest of his life as a fugitive, or worse, in prison. Whatever happened, he knew he would soon leave this western paradise behind.

"It is the perfect climate, a beautiful shoreline . . ."

A heap of enormous boulders forced them to clamber over the rocks in order to continue their way down the shore. Instinctively he took her hand as they carefully made their way over the slippery surface of the boulders. Again, he felt a charge of electricity jolt up to his elbow. This time, he tightened his grasp on her hand until the tingle subsided into a warm glow.

Taylor didn't remove her hand from his until they had cleared the rocks and were once again on a small strip of sandy shore.

The small cove was beyond the view of the others, and the uneven shoreline had created a perfect bathing lagoon. A perfect spot to be alone with the beautiful Rose, he thought.

Chapter 16

TAYLOR STEPPED INTO the calm water of the protected cove and found it was as warm as bathwater. The still air intensified the heat of the late-morning sun.

"The water is perfect. I don't think I can resist getting in—the water's really warm here."

"Well, I think we've resisted long enough," Jackson said. "Avert your eyes, wench, I'm about to go skinny-dipping." Impulsively shedding his trousers and tossing them and the blanket up onto a dry rock, he entered the water. He playfully splashed Taylor's back to signal when he'd immersed himself.

She turned to retaliate, and splashed back. She was just as eager to be in the water. "Gaze to the horizon, kind sir, and I shall join you." She waited until he had obediently turned away before she removed her cotton trousers, panties, and top. Then she raced to the shore and shallow-dived into the water on the other side of the cove. Rising to the surface, she wiped the saltwater from her face, immediately refreshed and invigorated.

Jackson gazed at her. Her brown hair was the color of

polished rosewood, and slicked back from her dive into the water. Even from several feet away he could see her long eyelashes glistening with delicate drops of moisture. The color of her sea green eyes nearly matched the color of the still water of the pool—she looked like a mermaid. He imagined the taste of salt on her skin, of his tongue finding its way from the base of her slender neck to the vee above where her breasts lay hidden beneath the water's surface.

Taylor saw the unmistakable heat of desire in Jackson's stare, but didn't retreat as he made his way slowly through the water toward her. Though the water that lapped at the crown of her bosom was delightfully warm, she shivered and felt her nipples at once grow hard.

In the protected cove, it was as though she and Jackson were isolated from the rest of the world. Nothing else existed. Maybe time *was* an illusion. She lived only in the present, no future, no past. Jackson was no longer considering the self-destructive path of murder, she thought. There were no mysteries to solve, no truth to discover. All that was left to discover was each other. Succumbing to the delicious awareness of awakening passion, she took a step forward in the water and into the arms of Jackson Hoyt.

Gathering her into his arms, he held her weightless body snugly. He gasped at the shock of pleasure he felt as her soft curves molded to the contours of his own lean body. Skin to skin in the warm water, they were one.

Burying her face against his throat, Taylor felt her defenses weakening. She was acutely aware of his growing hardness pressing into the soft flesh of her belly, and she felt the tide of passion rise within her as a tremor heated her thighs and groin. Timeless moments passed as her doubts and fears sweetly drained away.

Gently she pulled away from him, just far enough to enable her to look up into his eyes. Her fingers were happily lost in the wet curls of his long black hair as she studied his expression carefully. The gaze he returned was as soft as a caress.

"Sweet Rose," he whispered, his mouth brushing against hers as he spoke, to taste the salt left there with the tip of his tongue.

Parting her lips, she returned his kiss with a hunger that contradicted her outward calm, shocked by her own eager response to the touch of his lips. Shivers of delight flamed within. Blood pounded in her brain, leapt from her heart, and made her knees tremble as she gave herself freely to the passion of the kiss.

Jackson's hands seared a downward path to explore the soft lines of her back, her waist, her hips. His hands lowered farther to gently cup her bottom, caressing the soft flesh like a cat kneading a pillow. Lifting her off the sandy floor, he encouraged her slender legs to encircle his waist as he locked his arms around her.

Again, she pulled away from him, this time to reassure him that she was willing to follow this perilous leap of her heart. She knew her eyes would reveal the ache for the fulfillment of his lovemaking—right there, right then.

"Jackson," she whispered hoarsely, "make love to me."

His hardness now perfectly repositioned between her open legs, she knew her folds were slick with readiness. She inhaled sharply at the contact, then trembled with pleasure. His hands massaged the small of her back, then encircled her waist, and pulled her down until she felt him buried deeply inside her.

She panted between parted lips, lost in the fiery imprisonment of his body now deep within hers. Intuitively she began to move, her knees now pressed against his hips, struggling to find a way to slide up and down against him. Soon his hands helped her move in a natural, primal rhythm that caused them both to soar simultaneously to an awesome, shuddering ecstasy. Electricity seemed to arc through them as they were consumed by the flames of passion.

A moan of rapture slipped through his lips as he moved his mouth over hers, devouring its softness. Their kisses became softer, more tender as both savored the sweet feeling of satisfaction.

A third time, she pulled away from him to gaze into his eyes.

Jackson returned her gaze, soon becoming lost in the swirling, moist green eyes of his mysterious Rose. Searching for words, he found none. Instead of speaking, he brushed a gentle kiss across her forehead, then touched his lips to each cheek.

Taylor sighed deeply and drank in the tenderness of each kiss. A deep feeling of peace entered her being. This was the passion she'd searched for, longed for. This was the magic she'd imagined must have existed between her mother and father. It felt wonderful. Just as she'd envisioned. Her eyes closed now, she cherished the afterglow of passion, relishing the amazing sense of completeness within her. Snuggling into Jackson's strong arms, she nuzzled his neck and nibbled at his earlobe.

"Jackson?"

"Yes, sweet Rose . . ."

"How do you feel?"

He responded wordlessly by holding her closer to him. He never wanted to release her, determined to capture the timeless moment forever. She had been well worth waiting for, he decided. His body ached from satisfaction, and he was surprised at the flood of emotions he felt. Uncontrollable joy. Shuddering ecstasy. The burn of passion's still-smoldering embers. Possession. But, did he possess her . . . or did she command him? Doubts threatened to diminish his elation, and he knew the solution to his questions was knowledge. He had to find out more about her. Bewitching as she was, he couldn't afford to blindly trust her. That, she would have to earn.

Loosening his embrace, he held her away from him and scrutinized her face. Slowly and seductively, his gaze slid downward to her still-hard nipples. She shivered as he gave her upper body a raking stare.

"I feel wonderful . . . and you look beautiful—like a sea fairy that has just enchanted an unsuspecting sailor."

She met his smile and boldly returned his stare. Jackson's black hair, now damp, seemed even longer. It gleamed in the sunlight and flowed from his face like a crest. Soft, unruly tendrils caressed his forehead and the sides of his neck. She touched his lips, following its edges with her fingertips as his mouth transformed into an irresistibly devastating grin. His sky blue eyes sparkled, mimicking the sunlight that danced on the water's surface.

"Unsuspecting? Not a chance." She splashed him playfully and, as he wiped the water from his face, she seized the moment to slip from his grasp. She dove underwater and swam away, beginning a frisky game of tag.

Having worked off their nervous energy in the water, both made their way to the sandy shore. Leaving Taylor knee-deep in the water, Jackson stepped ahead to retrieve the blanket from the rock next to their clothes. Then he spread it on the warm sand, careful to avert his eyes from Taylor's alluring, glistening, naked body, as she joined him. Out of the water, each felt unexpectedly awkward, shy. After the magical aqueous intimacy, stepping onto solid ground somehow brought an unwelcome feeling of reality.

"Why don't you dry in the sun for a bit. I'll be right back." Jackson grabbed his trousers and made his way around the bend to relieve himself.

Grateful, Taylor walked to the blanket and stretched out. She shared his feelings of confusion, surprised by their sudden shyness with each other out of the water. After such intimate contact, why would they flinch from seeing each other naked? The noonday sun quickly evaporated the clinging moisture, and she brushed the salty remains from her skin. Then she dressed and sat cross-legged on the blanket, waiting for Jackson's return.

"Ah, the mermaid has legs, I see." Jackson joined her on the blanket, matching her seaward gaze. Scooting closer to her, he put his arm around her waist and pulled her toward him.

Dropping her head on his firm shoulder, she sighed. She could get used to his touch. Pushing away any notions of resistance, she allowed herself the indulgence of the seemingly endless, timeless moment. No future, no past. Only the present reality, clear and tangible.

"What are you thinking, Rose? I'm not used to this silence," he teased. "Talk to me."

"Just enjoying the moment, I guess. It feels as though time has stopped. At least I want it to."

"I'm glad we made love," he interrupted, sensing that her wistfulness correlated to his own growing feelings of uncertainty. Their attraction was powerful, but his soul craved the satisfaction of information even more than his body had desired to be joined with hers.

"I'm glad too," she reassured him.

"Rose, why won't you ever answer me directly? You bent my ear with your questions on the ride here, but I never feel like you reveal anything about yourself, about where you're from, what your future holds. It feels like you're hiding something. . . . Are you?"

Taylor stiffened in response as her heart swelled with emotion. She wanted to answer truthfully, but she couldn't. Not yet. But she couldn't lie. Not now. It would simply be too painful to concoct an elaborate tale to the man she was falling in love with. Taking a deep breath, she searched for a compromise.

"It's not what you think," she began. "I just can't tell you everything about me, or my past. I know it's not fair, that it seems like I'm concealing circumstances that normally would be unimportant. . . . It's just . . ."

"It's all right. I don't need to know everything." He gave her waist a squeeze. "I just want to know you, Rose. Are you really just visiting San Diego? Ida told me you were different from her other girls."

She suppressed her surprise. He still thought she was a

prostitute. Great, she thought. Perhaps she had mistaken his passion for the typical male libido seizing an opportunity. She blinked back hot tears. How could she know what had really brought them together? Had it been just carnal attraction after all?

"Rose . . ." he persisted.

As casually as she could manage, she responded to his inquiries. "Well," she began, "I'm sort of on vacation, though I didn't really mean to even be here. I decided to stay when Ida offered a room to me. She's been very generous. And," she emphasized, "I work only in her garden."

"Then you're friends?" Her voice sounded sincere, he thought, but nagging doubts about her were still there.

"Well, we just met here, actually, though we've become friends. She's been like a mother to me."

"You said before that your mother died when you were a baby. Your father never married again?"

"No," she said pensively. "I always wished he had, even though he never seemed lonely to me. He used to tell me how special my mother was to him, and how he knew that she would be his only love—at least in that lifetime."

They sat silently for a few moments, each in deep thought.

Then Taylor continued, her voice hesitant. "He believed that people sort of 'find' each other—if they're lucky. And he always said that he and mom were soul mates that would find each other again . . . in another place, another lifetime."

"And you believe this too?" Jackson had read of such absurd sounding spiritual beliefs, but had never discussed them with anyone who really believed such nonsense. His Midwestern upbringing left little room for thoughts of the world being made up of ethereal beings—people that lived again and again. He shook his head in bewilderment, determined to change the subject.

"So, you grew up with only a father. Was this . . . close by?"

"Jackson, I can't tell you where. In a different place,

though. That's why I find this place so interesting. And why I ask so many questions."

"Yes, you do." He chuckled. "Well, tell me about you, then. What does your future hold? Do you plan to stay here or go back home—wherever that might be?"

She hesitated before answering him. "I'm honestly not sure. My stay here depends on lots of things." Her voice grew softer. "Right now, all I care about is today. Here and now. And getting to know more about you . . . and about us," she continued. There, she thought, at least she'd declared her intentions.

It was Jackson's turn to stiffen in response to Taylor's affirmation. Ida was right, he thought, she certainly is different. Fast moving. Unpredictable. But was she trustworthy? Honest? Time would tell, he decided.

In the silence, Taylor's stomach rumbled loudly. Jackson laughed in response.

"I'm famished. Are you ready to go back and see if there's anything left of the picnic?" she asked. Suddenly, she was inclined to be in the company of other people. Less chance for questions asked that she couldn't answer.

"Sure, let's go." Jackson helped her to her feet and stepped forward, clasping her body close to his.

She relaxed happily into the cushion of his arms, conscious of where his warm flesh touched her own tingling skin. Soon she felt the heady sensation of his lips against her neck. They kissed a path to her cheek, and finally to her mouth. As he caressed her lips, she returned his kiss, lingering, savoring every moment.

Breathless, Jackson pulled away, his heart thundering madly. Explosive currents raced through his body, ending where his groin throbbed painfully. The degree of desire she created in him was intimidating. A warning voice whispered in his head and aroused old fears and uncertainties. He had to remember who—and what—she was. After all, making a man crazy with desire was her expertise, he reminded himself. Enjoy what you want, he commanded himself, and keep her at arm's length.

He cleared his throat, hoping to gain control of his voice. "We'd better go, or they'll wonder where we are." He was hungry for her all over again. His body told him that. His brain told him to convert his appetite to one for information instead. He knew he needed to concentrate on discovering more about her. Perhaps it was Ida's turn to answer his questions.

Chapter 17

"WELL, HERE THEY are after all. The girls and I were just about ready to come searching for you." Ida inspected both Jackson and Taylor carefully, noting her rosy pink cheeks and his pleasantly tousled hair.

Taylor sank down on the blanket next to the picnic basket, reaching inside for a napkin. The food had been placed on the blanket next to it—thick slices of bread, canned preserves, chunks of cheese, crisp apples. Quickly, she made a cheese sandwich and sunk her teeth into the dark, sweet bread.

Ida turned to Jackson, a flash of humor crossing her face. "Been doing some exploring, Jackson?" The laugh that followed was low and throaty. When Ida laughed, she seemed ten years younger, her eyes bright with merriment.

Jackson colored fiercely and he sighed with exasperation.

"Perhaps you had better tell me about it . . . come over here and sit with me. I've made an extra sandwich." Ida wrapped her arm around his elbow, firmly directing him to a blanket a few yards away. "No arguments, now. . . ."

Jackson passively allowed Ida to lead him away. Looking

over his shoulder, he glanced at Taylor, who was gaily chatting with two of Ida's girls. She instantly met his gaze, her eyes sending him a private message. The look seemed to be both seductive and fearful. She was hiding something. He knew it.

"So tell me, Jackson. Have you and Rose finally become friends?" Ida watched Jackson carefully for reactions. She observed his hesitation, but also how his mouth curved into an unconscious smile. She knew his answer before he spoke the words.

"I suppose so. But I don't really know much about her. Ida, how well do you know her?" Jackson involuntarily clenched his jaw and narrowed his eyes.

Ida smiled to herself as he spoke. Their recent lovemaking hovered around him like a cloud of expensive perfume. She'd been right. They were meant to be with each other. Alone together, their attraction had been impossible to resist. She envied the potency of the sensual energy these two shared. Still, she sensed Jackson's reluctance to believe in his emotional response to Rose. She also sensed an underlying anger. His expressive face had changed and become almost melancholy. Something was wrong.

"Ida," Jackson pleaded, "tell me about Rose. What do you know about her? Where did she come from?"

Ida forced a demure smile. "And just why do you want to know?"

Jackson answered indulgently, "I need to know. I need to know who she is, that's all. Nothing sinister. It's just that I feel she's hiding something, something important. I don't want to get mixed up in anything right now that . . ."

"Ah, but you already are, aren't you?" Ida responded matter-of-factly.

When he spoke again, his voice was tender, almost a murmur. "I just need to know what I'm getting into. She's different, like you told me before. I don't need this kind of . . . distraction right now."

"Perhaps you do, Jackson. I've never seen you this con-

tent before. You come to Sherman House a couple times a
week, and I've never seen you smile like you do when you
look at Rose. Think about it. What are you afraid of? happiness? having a little fun? falling in love?"

Scowling, Jackson studied Ida intently.

Ida stared back in waiting silence. She'd finally struck a
nerve in the secretive Jackson. "Jackson, tell me what's
wrong. You know me. You can trust me."

"I know, I know. Nothing's wrong. It just seems awfully
peculiar that she just showed up, you know? She told me
that she didn't know you until you offered her a room. Then
she said something about not planning to be here at all, that
being here was some kind of mistake."

"What else did she say?"

"She told me her mother died when she was a baby. Her
father died about five years ago. She learned gardening
from him. That's about it." Jackson paused, taking a huge
bite of the sandwich Ida had given him. Put into words, he
really felt as though he knew next to nothing. His body, in
comparison, knew her intimately. The imbalance bothered
him.

"That's about all I know as well. You see the two girls
she's talking to?" Ida nodded toward Taylor. "Audrey told
me that Rose healed her burn with ice chips instead of
butter. Lizabeth was there and confirmed it all. She thinks
that Rose is some kind of healer, though when she asked
Rose, she wouldn't admit to it. Maybe she's afraid to let
on what she is, who she is. I don't know. I do know that
I like her, and I agree with you. I think she's hiding a great
deal, but it doesn't seem like it's dangerous."

Jackson's face began to relax. He listened intently, staring out to the sparkling water that was softly lapping at the
sandy shore.

Ida continued. "I went to her room the other night because I heard her sobbing in her sleep. I stayed with her
for a long time, until her breathing deepened and her crying
ended. Perhaps she's run away from someone who's abused

her, mistreated her in some way. Maybe there's some kind
of sadness she feels. I can't quite put my finger on it, but
I think you should just follow your heart, Jackson. You
don't get many chances for happiness."

Jackson concentrated as he listened. It still didn't ring
true. "She asks a lot of questions. Like she's investigating,
almost. And she doesn't know things that she should."

"I know what you mean," Ida agreed. "I still say there's
nothing to worry about. Enjoy yourself. Enjoy each other."

Jackson stood up abruptly, brushing the bread crumbs
from his legs. "I've got to think." He walked away from
Ida without a backward glance.

Ida sighed; a heaviness settled in her chest. Her instincts
warned her that Jackson's struggle to admit he cared for
Rose was his worst adversary. She hoped Rose would per-
sist and draw out the secrets that Jackson, too, concealed.

"Audrey, your face looks fine, just a little pink. You should
keep a hat on today, though, to keep the sun from the area."
Taylor inspected Audrey's face. The ice had been successful in keeping her fair skin from blistering.

"I'm extra careful now with the hot water," Audrey reassured her, "and I'm so grateful for what you did for me."
Lizabeth nodded in agreement.

Taylor smiled at the two girls. They couldn't be more
than eighteen, she decided. Audrey, the depiction of femininity, had long blond hair that flowed from a center part
and tumbled carelessly down her back. Lizabeth, in contrast, had a wealth of dark, coffee-hued hair that hung in
long, graceful curves over her shoulders. They were beauties. Very young beauties.

Taylor leaned forward and asked in a hushed voice,
"Will you tell me something?"

Both nodded.

"Why do you do what you do?"

"You mean . . . with men?" Audrey giggled in reply. "It's
not so bad, really. And what else could we do, anyway?

Lizzie and I came here to be in the theater. When it didn't work out, Ida rescued us right off the street. She's good to us, too. We make a good salary and she doesn't let any of the men take advantage of us."

"It's not so hard," Lizabeth added. "Ida's taught us what to do and what to say. She has rules and she makes the men follow them—not like in the Stingaree district. Gambling house whores aren't classy like us."

"But, what else do you want to do with your life? You know you can't do this forever, right?" Though Taylor empathized with the girls' plight, her stomach still soured at their apparently easy acceptance of their circumstances. It seemed as though they honestly didn't know what else to do.

Audrey shrugged dismissively. Lizabeth, though, squared her shoulders and said, "This is only temporary. And we're saving our money, all right."

"To do . . . ?" Taylor leaned forward, trying to make the girls feel comfortable, hoping they would feel that her questions were less an invasion of their privacy and more an illustration of her concern.

This time Audrey replied. "The truth is, we're really not good at anything else."

"I can't believe that's true. Tell me about what you enjoy. What do you like to do when you're not working? We'll start there."

"Well, Audrey sings like a bird," Lizabeth volunteered. "That's why we thought we could be in the theater here. The day we tried, though, there were a hundred other girls who sang just as well. And most of them didn't last anyway. Most of them are working just like us."

"Audrey, what were you good at when you were younger?"

"When I was in school, I used to help my mother keep the books for my father's laundry business. I guess I'm good at . . . numbers?"

"Good. And you, Lizabeth. What are your dreams?" Taylor watched as her face began to glow, and a secretive smile softened her lips. Instinctively, she felt that with a little encouragement, long-ignored aspirations might surface again for the two girls.

For an instant, a wistfulness stole into her expression and with a deep breath, Lizabeth began speaking in a hushed voice. "Back home in San Francisco, I used to help my uncle in his photography studio. I learned everything from him—using the camera, posing the people, developing the film. It's the only thing that I really miss."

"So . . . one of your dreams is to be a photographer?" Taylor observed the shock of realization sparkle in Lizabeth's eyes.

"But I'm a woman. I can't—"

"Nonsense. You're a perfect pair—two beautiful and talented businesswomen. You could open a photography studio, maybe specializing in women's photos. Audrey, you could handle the accounting and the appointments. Lizabeth, you could make *anyone* look beautiful. I'm telling you, people would be happy to pay for a flattering photograph. What do you think?"

Audrey and Elizabeth exchanged looks of interested amazement, then looked at Taylor in surprise.

"Rose, do you really think we could do it? Have our own business? Be our own bosses?" Lizabeth said the words tentatively as if testing the idea.

"But how would we get started? It still sounds impossible to me—I just figured if we could save enough to go back to San Francisco, that's all we had to look forward to."

Taylor knew it was difficult for the girls to see further than that simple plan. Just trying to get back home must have seemed hard enough. "First of all, tell Ida what you have in mind," Taylor began.

"But she'll laugh at us," Lizabeth interrupted.

"I guarantee you she won't. She'll be sorry to see you go, but I'll bet she'll help you. She knows people. She'll probably know of an empty storefront you could use."

Both girls stared at Taylor as they clenched and un-
clenched their hands nervously.

"Next," Taylor continued, "why don't you go into town
and talk with Mrs. Reed at the café? She runs the restaurant
with no man around, and I'll bet she would be willing to
give you some good start-up advice. My father taught me
to reach out to successful people and ignore those that dis-
courage you. You'll be surprised at what you can accomplish when you just make up your mind to try."

"Rose, you're wonderful!" Lizabeth declared. "I never
would have reached so high. It just never crossed my mind
to think we could own a business."

Audrey lifted her chin and tossed her hair back in a gesture of assurance. "Let's go for a walk, Lizabeth, and talk
about our future."

Taylor watched as the girls ran to the water, bursting
with upward spiraling confidence.

"Pretty pleased with yourself, aren't you?"

Startled to hear her father's voice, Taylor almost choked
on the last bite of her sandwich.

*"Those two young ladies are going to go far. You've
kindled quite a flame."*

Taylor felt, rather than heard, her father's voice fade into
the distance—just as though he had walked ahead of her
to the shoreline.

Grabbing the last apple, Taylor walked to the sand, hoping she could reconnect with her father. *Dad?*

She needed to talk and she desperately wanted to tell her
father, even though she knew it had to be a mistake, that
she was falling in love.

How could she let herself fall in love? She didn't even
know Jackson. All she really knew was that he had chosen
a path of murder that she was compelled to stop.

"Love is never a mistake, Taylor. Believe."

She wished with all her heart she could believe . . . believe with all the conviction Jackson had in his own plans.

But it was getting so complicated. And she had a growing, nagging feeling that time was running out.

Did her father know how much time she had? *Dad?*

The silence was deafening as Taylor waited for her father's reply. She whispered into the wind, "Dad, can you tell me how much time I have?"

"Time is running out, Taylor. Ask for the help of others; choose those you can trust, confide in them. Much as you think you can, you can't always fix things by yourself."

As her father's presence disappeared into the breeze, Taylor winced in recognition of her most painful trait. She invariably hesitated to ask for help, and it was her hardest lesson in life to learn. Who should she trust, though? Where should she place her confidence? with Ida? with Jackson?

Lost in thought, Taylor didn't react to Jackson's approach. He stared at the scowl on her face, a look of seriousness that he'd never seen before. His determination to elicit the truth had grown into an overwhelming desire and, this time, he would demand answers.

"Rose."

Taylor jumped at the angry sound of Jackson's voice.

"You startled me—"

"Rose, I want you to tell me why you're here. Did you run away from someone? something? It can't be that bad." Jackson's voice brimmed with resolve.

Taylor hesitated, torn by conflicting emotions. A flicker of apprehension coursed through her as she chose her words carefully. "Jackson, I have been sent here to prevent you from killing Wyatt Earp."

Chapter 18

THE SHOCK OF Taylor's statement siphoned the blood from Jackson's face. His luminous blue eyes widened in astonishment, then blazed azure fire. Jackson faced Taylor and glared at her with burning, reproachful eyes.

Biting her lip, Taylor turned away. Every fiber in her body warned her, heightening the awareness of her mistake as icy fear twisted around her heart.

"Who sent you?" Jackson spat out the words contemptuously.

"It's not what you think." Taylor choked on the words. She felt suddenly weak and vulnerable in the face of his instant rage.

"You are despicable! You used me."

The force of his seething reply took Taylor off guard. "Jackson, I—"

"Answer me. Who sent you?"

Taylor's eyes filled with tears of frustration. How could she make him understand? Trying to swallow the lump that lingered in her throat, she unsuccessfully searched for words.

"Who else knows?" he demanded.

"No one. Only me. Jackson, you have to believe me. . . . I . . ."

"So it *was* you who followed me the other night, wasn't it? Wasn't it?" His voice was quieter now, yet it held an undertone of cold contempt.

"Yes. I overheard your conversation with those two dreadful men at the bar. Jackson, you can't do this."

"It's none of your business!" Anger lit up Jackson's eyes as he grasped Taylor's arm roughly to force her to look at him.

The misery she felt was like a steel weight. How could she have thought he would believe her?

"I should have known. Did you enjoy taunting me with your body? Did you think I would confide in you? Is that it?"

"Jackson, no . . . that was real. How could you think that?"

He loosened his grip on her arm, fighting for control as he looked past Taylor to the horizon. She was vile, he thought, and, worst of all, she threatened his plans. This knowledge twisted and turned painfully inside. He had been reckless and irresponsible, allowing his attraction to her to place him in a perilous position. A renewed sense of urgency overwhelmed him. It was time, he decided, whether the McLaurey brothers were ready to carry out their part or not. His own path was clear.

"Jackson. Look at me," Taylor whispered.

Jackson turned and his angry gaze swung over her.

"I know things . . . I have been told things," she began awkwardly. "This isn't going to make much sense to you— it barely makes sense to me. But hear me out. I am here to find out something—something that will stop you from do- ing this . . . from killing—"

"Stop it! No more of your mysterious babble!"

"Jackson, please, please let me say what I have to say. I promise you, no one knows about this. Or why I'm here. I scarcely understand it myself. No one would believe me if I said you were conspiring to kill Wyatt Earp, anyway. Can't you see that? Can't you see that I'm no real danger to you?"

Jackson's voice was cold when he answered. "You . . . you stay away from me. My life and my plans don't concern you. I won't let anything or anyone interfere with what has to be done." He paused for a moment. "Am I making myself clear?"

Taylor shriveled at his expression. Its effect on her was shattering. He was deadly serious, and she realized that the time available to solve this puzzle had diminished dramatically.

"Yes," she whispered. "And you must believe me when I tell you that no one else knows."

Even in the storm of his anger, Jackson believed her.

"Halloo . . . Jackson! Rose! It's time to go!" Ida called out to Jackson and Taylor. She didn't like what she saw, especially how roughly Jackson had grabbed Taylor's arm. Out of earshot, she could only guess at their conversation, but whatever they were discussing, she had seen the immediate rage in Jackson. And she recognized the danger in his anger.

Jackson released Taylor and briskly walked toward the picnic area, quickly putting distance between them. Silently, he walked past Ida, heading back toward the hotel.

Taylor remained where she stood, rubbing her bruised arm. Terrible regrets filled her. Fighting tears, she bit her lip until it throbbed like her pulse. Her sense of loss nearly matched her tremendous ache of defeat.

Sighing heavily, Taylor forced herself to settle down. She couldn't afford to wallow in her emotions now. She drew a deep breath and forbade herself from losing her composure. Turning from the peaceful horizon, she walked purposefully away from the water.

• • •

"Rose," Ida said when Taylor was within earshot, "what happened? What were you and Jackson talking about? What's wrong?" Her stomach lurched with worry, and Ida sensed that the exchange between the two lovers was far more serious than she'd first guessed.

"Please, Ida, don't ask me . . . not right now." Taylor's lips were a tight line, a forced smile.

Ida leaned forward and lowered her voice. "Did he hurt you?"

"No . . . no . . . it's nothing like that. Please, Ida, let's just go . . . home. I'm fine. Don't worry."

Scrutinizing Taylor's face, Ida was even more certain that her alarm was justified. Something serious had happened between them. Unhappily, she vowed to keep silent, at least for now. Convinced that Rose would eventually confide in her, she shook her head in frustration.

Taylor dressed, found her hat, and then busied herself helping fold blankets and gathering the picnic remains.

Ida's girls chattered light-heartedly as they began the trek back to the Ocean Beach Hotel. Taylor placed herself in the middle of the throng of beauties, avoiding Ida. She was not looking forward to the ride back into town, knowing that sitting next to Jackson would be torture.

When they reached the hotel, Taylor saw that their horse-drawn bus was ready to board, but Jackson was not sitting in the driver's seat. Instead, a handsome young man stood next to the rear horse, reins in hand. His eyes searched the group of women until at last they locked on Taylor.

"The gentleman, Mr. Hoyt, asked me to take you back to the city. He said he had some . . . business to attend to . . . an appointment . . . that you'd know what he meant." The words were delivered blandly, well-rehearsed but without interpretation.

Taylor nodded wordlessly. The sense of time running out threatened to engulf her. A part of her wished that she could just close her eyes and will herself to return to her own time, to forget the seemingly impossible task that faced her.

"Rose?" Audrey tugged at Taylor's arm.

"I'm sorry, what?"

"Rose, would you mind if I sat up front . . . with him?" Audrey blushed as she nodded toward the substitute driver, obviously smitten with him.

"I wouldn't mind at all, Audrey. You go for it."

"What?"

"I mean, get on up there and talk to him." Taylor smiled at Audrey's crush, sending her thoughts of encouragement, watching the young man help Audrey up into the seat. His grin convinced her that his feelings matched Audrey's, and she was glad to see Audrey act on her impulse to get to know him. It was healthy. Normal. Her instincts told her that her father's prediction about Audrey and Lizabeth was probably right, that they would indeed do great things.

Taking a seat near the back, Taylor yawned and closed her eyes. She pretended to nap during the blissfully quiet journey back to Sherman House, hoping to avoid any more conversation. She considered her options, frightened that she would not choose the right path. Gathering her thoughts, she searched for clues until her mind felt numb and she drifted off to sleep.

Chapter 19

IDA GENTLY SHOOK Taylor's shoulder to wake her. "Rose, honey, we're home."

Home. That's exactly where I'd rather be right now. When Taylor's eyes fluttered open, she painfully realized that she still remained in the past—though at that moment the past no longer seemed quite as charming. Stifling a yawn, she followed Ida out of the bus.

"Why don't you have a nice bath and soak the salt from your skin? You'll feel better, I know you will." Ida's voice was overly cheerful.

"Thanks, Ida. Good suggestion."

The sun had set and the air was slightly cooler, though the night still felt sultry. Adding to the dense summer air, Taylor felt an uncomfortable heaviness that threatened to deepen her blue mood. Convinced that a cool bath and a clean body would at least interrupt her inclination to dwell on the negative turn of events, she climbed the stairs to her room, undressed, and put on the red silk robe.

In the bathroom, Taylor filled the tub, adding just enough water from the stove to make it lukewarm. Before she stepped into the water, Taylor reached to the shelf above the tub for one of the vials of scented oils. She recognized the bottle that Jackson had used when he'd taken his bath. It seemed like an eternity ago that she had peeked at him through the knothole in the wall. Her heart squeezed in anguish as she evoked the pain of their final conversation at the beach.

As Taylor pulled the cork from the bottle, she closed her eyes and breathed in the delicate fragrance of roses. Instantly, a picture of Jackson's face appeared in her mind. The smile in his bright, clear blue eyes contained a sensuous flame, and his dark eyebrows arched mischievously. Jackson's mouth widened in approval. Taylor felt gooseflesh on her skin, and a sense of pleasurable anticipation. She noticed his lips moving, but heard no sound from the vision. A probing query came into his eyes as he seemed to study her with a curious intensity. As Taylor strained to interpret the picture, Jackson's face faded to black.

Taylor blinked her eyes open, struggling to reconnect with reality. The vision had seemed so real, so painfully real. And though the swell of misery she felt was thankfully beyond tears, the effect of her sadness was shattering. Taylor breathed deeply, telling herself just to get into the tub, take a bath, and clear her head so she could decide what to do.

After pouring a bit of rosewater into the tub, Taylor gingerly returned the bottle to its place on the shelf.

As she soaked in the tub, her neck resting on its edge, she found the tepid water calmed her. What had she been thinking when she'd revealed her knowledge of Jackson's assassination plot? It had been a mistake, she realized, but there had to be a way out.

Energized by the feeling she was gaining control of her emotions, Taylor quickly finished washing her body and hair. She was suddenly anxious to be out of the tub. She intended to do some yardwork in the cooler evening air, knowing the distraction would do her good.

A sharp knock at the door confirmed her notion to finish her bath.

"Rose, are you about finished in there?"

"Audrey?" Taylor called back.

"Yes, it's me. I need to clean up a bit if you're almost through in there. Guess what? The bus driver—Corey's his name—he asked me to dinner. Can you believe it? He says he wants to court me." Audrey spoke with an even voice at first, but her giddiness surfaced in an excited, high-pitched giggle as she knocked on the door again.

"Hold on, Audrey . . . give me a minute and I'll get out and open the door." Taylor stepped out of the tub and wrapped herself in a towel. When she opened the door, Audrey walked in, nervous as a cat. Joy shone in her eyes, though, and a dazzling smile found its way through.

"I hope I didn't rush you—it's just that he'll be here in a few minutes." Audrey stripped down to her camisole and bloomers, and proceeded with her basin bath.

Taylor sat on the stool next to the tub, watching Audrey. She wished with all her heart and soul that it was she who was preparing for a date that evening, a date with Jackson.

"Rose, what if he doesn't like me?"

"He already likes you or he wouldn't have invited you to dinner, right? Come here, let me braid the sides of your hair back. Did you bring a ribbon with you?"

Audrey nodded, staring at her reflection in the mirror. "Rose, do you think I'm pretty? Pretty enough to make him forget . . . what I am?" There was a sob behind Audrey's soft voice.

Determined to boost Audrey's lowered self-esteem before it plummeted any further, Taylor replied, "What if you and Lizabeth go talk to Ida right now. Tell her your business idea, get her blessing . . . and quit working for Ida right now—tonight. Then you could answer Corey honestly if he asks you any questions about what you do."

Audrey's face glowed with her newly awakened sense of life, an expression of satisfaction gleaming in her eyes. "I'll do it. By gosh, this day starts a new life for us. Rose, hurry and finish with my hair, so Lizzie and I have time to see Ida before he gets here."

Taylor braided Audrey's long golden hair, securing it at the back of her head with a pale pink ribbon. She gave her a playful push, saying, "Go, silly. Ida should be in the kitchen. I'll tell Lizabeth to meet you down there."

Audrey slipped back into her dress, then gave Taylor a quick hug before she dashed out the door and down the back stairs.

"Lizabeth?" Taylor met her halfway down the hall and quickly described Audrey's plans, and the young woman ran down the stairs two at a time to join her friend.

The joy in seeing Audrey and Lizabeth's newborn happiness served to offset some of the devastating ache of her own heart. She would hold on to her own improved mood, while she dressed and cut fresh flowers for the house.

Dressed in a clean pair of cotton trousers and tunic, Taylor walked through the kitchen and out the back door. She could hear the enthusiastic voices of the girls, and definite sounds of encouragement from Ida. It sounded successful. It sounded right.

In that instant, she had no doubts it had been the right thing.

She scanned the garden, then walked to the shed and removed some garden pruners. The roses needed some obvious attention, and she began filling a basket with fragrant blooms.

As the voices inside the house faded, she had a strange feeling that her simple intervention had dramatically changed Audrey and Lizabeth's young lives. Perhaps Audrey and Corey would fall in love, she thought. A perfectly happy ending.

And Lizabeth, she contemplated, did have the knowledge to actually be a photographer, so why not? She was glad for them both. They each deserved happiness and success, she thought as she worked contentedly cutting roses.

Taylor sat on the grass beside one of the largest rose-bushes in the garden. Each bloom was the deep red color of blood.

"I'm listening, child."

Taylor inhaled sharply, her thoughts returning to the scene on the beach. *What about me, Dad? I don't know what to do—what if I do the wrong thing again?*

"It'll be fine. You're supposed to be here."

Taylor sighed and shook her head in frustration. She wasn't getting much from her father, but at least he confirmed that some sort of path existed—and the possibility of a solution.

Dad? Though she wasn't sure she wanted to know, Taylor was too tempted to pass up the opportunity to explore the unknown. *Dad, were you . . . was that really Mom at the séance?*

"Yes."

But how could it be? In the light of day, her instincts told her it had to be a combination of wishful thinking and the eerie atmosphere

"It's hard to explain—all our spirits blend. Yours, mine, your mother's. We belong together. That's why you can hear me."

But why was she the one chosen to be there, she wondered?

"Because you believe, Taylor Rose."

Taylor became acutely aware of the moment her father's spirit vanished. She shuddered at the contrast. Even with only his voice in her mind, she felt safe. Now she felt alone, and weakened by the emotional day that was finally ending. Craving the thought of peaceful slumber, she carried the basket of flowers into the kitchen.

Wordlessly, Taylor handed the blooms to Ida and declared her intention to get a good night's sleep. She had some investigating to do tomorrow, and knew she'd need her wits about her. Time was running out, and she felt the seeds of courage and determination beginning.

"Rose, wait. . . ." Ida put the basket of flowers on the table. She reached into her pocket and pulled out an envelope.

"What is it?"

"This just came for you by messenger."

Taylor searched Ida's face, hoping to see more than the question in her eyes. With slightly trembling fingers, she managed to break the wax seal, open the envelope, and pull out the folded linen paper.

Chapter 20

"DO YOU WANT me to stay with you?" Ida's voice overflowed with maternal concern. She prayed that the letter did not bring bad news for her mysterious Rose. She suddenly realized how fond she was of the young woman, and how accustomed she'd become to having her around. Though she was truly a different sort, Rose was definitely special.

Ida cleared her throat. "Maybe you should sit down," she suggested as she pulled out a chair. The sound of the chair scraping on the wooden floor set her teeth on edge. She had a bad feeling about the letter, and she wished Rose would get it over with and read the darn thing.

"Okay." Rose nodded, then sat at the table. She blinked her eyes a few times, focusing on the neat handwriting. Quickly her eyes scanned the few words written on the top half of the paper:

Remember my words. I meant what I said.

Ida leaned toward Taylor, to read over her shoulder. As Taylor ran her fingers across the scrawled signature,

Jackson's signature, she felt as though it would be the only part of him she would ever touch again. A hot tear rolled down her cheek.

"What does he mean, Rose?" Ida asked. "What did he say to you at the beach? Did he threaten you?"

Taylor swallowed the despair in her throat, determined to regain her composure. She didn't want Ida to be frightened, nor did she feel ready to reveal the letter's implication. She felt the sting of Jackson's resolve within the few, carefully chosen words.

"Rose, answer me. . . ."

"Ida, it's okay. He said lots of things at the beach. Some good, some not so good. We'll work it out." Taylor smiled at Ida. She felt a strange numbed comfort in knowing that perhaps it was for the best. Without the distraction of her passionate feelings for Jackson, perhaps the search for solutions would be more manageable.

"I still don't like the feel of this," Ida grumbled. "You would tell me if you were in trouble, wouldn't you? You know I'd do anything in my power to keep you safe, Rose. Believe that."

Taylor stood and put her arms around Ida. "Yes, Ida. I do believe that. And you must believe that I'll ask for any help that I need."

"Let's have a cup of tea, then. I think chamomile would be best to soothe and calm us for the rest of the night. I'll just have to trust that good head on your shoulders, Rose."

Taylor nodded. She stared at the words that still caused her to shudder. Carefully, she folded the paper and slipped it into her pocket.

Out of sight, out of mind.

Jackson waited anxiously in the reading room of the Acme Saloon for Will and Dean McLaurey. The moment he'd gotten back into town from the beach, Jackson had made his way to the City of Paris store. Charlie had handed him the package he had hoped was waiting for him. Outside, in

the shadows of the dark alley, Jackson had peeked into the
bundle to see the small revolver that would fit neatly into
his vest pocket. The note inside had told him to meet the
McLaureys that night at the Acme Saloon to finalize their
plans.

Jackson shook his head in disbelief. How could Rose
know? He had sent the messenger with his carefully worded
note to her, praying she would heed its meaning. Otherwise
. . . well, he preferred not to think in that direction. He just
knew that he couldn't . . . *wouldn't* let her interfere.

The heavy stomp of boots interrupted his thoughts as
Dean and Will entered the room carrying a bottle of whiskey and three shot glasses.

Will stared at Jackson, sniffing the air like a wolf suspicious of another predator nearby. And he didn't like what
he sensed.

"Well now, Dean, it sure looks like our boy got the message, don't it? On time, and lookin' pretty darn serious,
though." Will slammed the bottle down hard on the table
in front of Jackson, watching him flinch.

Dean set the three shot glasses next to the bottle. Sitting
next to Jackson, he licked his lips and smiled. "Looks like
we won't have to wait much longer. I can't wait to get my
hands on some o' that money—"

"You got everything under control, Jackson?" Will interrupted Dean's overeager reference to Pete Spence's reward money. That's all we need, he thought, this kid'll
want some of that money for sure. It had been a stroke of
luck finding Jackson right after they'd heard Pete was of-
fering a pretty hefty reward for Earp's life to be snuffed
out. He glared a warning to his mouthy brother, hoping his
message was clear. Dean looked down at the table, hiding
his eyes from the scowl of his older brother.

"Everything's fine. Let's just get on with it. The sooner
the better." Jackson's eyes narrowed.

"Let's have a drink on it, then." Will splashed the amber-
colored liquor into the glasses on the table. His skin still

prickled with apprehension. Jackson was in too much of a hurry, he decided. Or maybe he was starting to change his mind. Either way, he just didn't quite trust him—the kid had too much emotion attached to the whole thing, he decided. Maybe he was more trouble than he was worth.

Jackson picked up the glass of cheap whiskey and held it out to Will and Dean. "To success," he offered.

Will observed the subtle change in Jackson's eyes. Now they looked cold, without feeling. That's more like it, he thought, and smiled, relaxing at the sign that perhaps his doubts were unfounded. He tossed back the shot, relishing the sudden burn in his throat, and quickly refilled the glasses.

"The sooner the better, huh? Well then, this Saturday night'll be that bastard's last night on God's earth." Will raised his glass.

Dean clinked the bottom edge of his glass against Will's. "To Saturday night," he echoed.

Jackson nodded curtly. He drank his second shot of whiskey in a quick gulp, wiping his mouth with the back of his hand.

Both Will and Dean drank another quick shot, seemingly enjoying the excuse to finish off the bottle as quickly as possible. They both continued with more crude toasts, each one addressing their shared mission of killing the notorious Wyatt Earp. They attempted to refill Jackson's glass with each round, but he refused.

"I have to go," Jackson finally said.

"Jackson, Jackson . . . stay and drink with us. Where are you off to when we're right here with a half-full bottle?" A noisy belch escaped from Will, punctuating his question, his words slurring.

Jackson waved off their protests, shaking his head as he pushed his chair back from the table. Watching Dean and Will get drunk was more than he could handle. He hated the fact that he needed them. Whenever they were around, the hairs on the back of his neck would rise in response.

But, he admitted, having them as part of the conspiracy had at least prevented him from having to be a lone assassin, something he was pretty sure he hadn't the stomach for. With them, he acknowledged, at least the plan was plausible.

Jackson finally stood, quickly making his way out of the reading room into the main part of the saloon. The noise level in the smoky room was high enough to at least partially distract him from his own thoughts. How would he make it until Saturday night? After ten years, he reminded himself, a few days should be tolerable. Keep busy.

And stay away from Rose.

The trouble was, he couldn't stop thinking about her—and his body craved her.

As he pushed his way through the rank crowd of drifters and sailors, Jackson felt his stomach sour and threaten to eject its contents. Hungry for fresh air and eager to put some distance between himself and the saloon, he roughly shouldered his way to the door and out into the night.

Jackson gulped the cool air like water, hoping it would clear his head and relieve his nausea. Instead, an acrid taste filled his mouth. Ducking to the alley, he violently lost the contents of his stomach. "Damn cheap whiskey," he cursed, wiping his mouth on the back of his sleeve. At least he'd feel better with an empty stomach.

Church bells reminded Jackson that he would be late for work if he didn't hurry. Taking a deep breath, he left the alley to return to the street and walked briskly away from the Acme Saloon, leaving Will and Dean McLaurey behind.

"So, wha'd'ya think, Will?"

"I think you're a stupid idiot, for one thing, Dean." Will cuffed his younger brother's ear with a sharp slap.

"Owwwww . . . wha'dja do that for?" Dean rubbed his ear, cowering in his chair, trying to create a smaller target.

"Wha'dja mention the reward money for, huh? Jeez, you almost ruined the whole thing with your big mouth. I'm warnin' ya . . . any more mistakes and yer outta this plan. I don't need yer stupid mouth shootin' off in front of that fool Jackson. I could send ya right back to Arizona, quick as that." Will clumsily snapped his big, thick fingers.

"Aw, Will, I didn't mean to say nothin'. C'mon, don't get all mad. I'll be careful, you'll see." Dean's lower lip trembled.

Drunk and barely eighteen, Dean, Will knew, was more boy than man at that moment. "Quit yer whimperin'. Just work at keepin' your trap shut, okay? All we have to do now is get some horses to have waitin' for us outside the saloon Saturday night, and count the days 'til Pete Spence pays us for the job. It's gonna be easy—if you can keep your damn trap shut, that is." Will glared at Dean. He hoped his little brother wouldn't prove to be a handicap he couldn't offset.

Dean grinned at Will, his eyes glazed with alcoholic good humor. "Wha'cha gonna do with yer money, Will? I'm sure gonna have me a good time."

Will returned his grin with a menacing half-smile. "Well, little brother, I'm sure I'll come up with somethin'."

Chapter 21

JACKSON WATCHED THROUGH half-closed eyes as the satiny red robe slipped slowly off Taylor's shoulders, baring them seductively. She moistened her lips with her tongue and he found himself mesmerized by the simple act. His eyes focused on the pink tip of her tongue, watching it glide along her lips in slow motion. All he could think about was the feel of her full lips on his own. He longed to taste her again.

As she took a step closer to the bathtub, where he was submerged to his neck, she let the robe fall away in one smooth movement. She lifted her arms, then ran both hands through her slicked back mahogany brown hair. Again he was mesmerized by her simple actions. In the light of the dozen candles that surrounded the porcelain tub, her hair glowed with fiery highlights and her skin looked like fresh cream, liquid and silky.

His gaze caressed her from head to toe. For a long time he lingered deliciously at her breasts, each pink nipple rosy-peaked. Slowly, he dropped his gaze to the dark triangle of wispy curls that seemingly called out to his own body, which painfully throbbed with desire.

Licking his lips, he tried to speak. He struggled, forcing his lips to form the words that he longed to say. As hard as he tried, no sound came from his mouth. She reached out to him, her face frozen with worry. Silent words formed on her lips and he squinted his eyes, trying to understand what she was telling him. He sat up in the tub, his own arms reaching to her.

Again, he fought for words. Only silence. He stared as her eyes filled with tears, then she took a step backward. The candlelight dimmed and her image faded into nothingness; the red robe lay rumpled on the floor where she had once stood. . . .

Finally able to speak, Jackson called to Taylor, "No! Wait! I need you!"

The frantic sound of his own voice forced Jackson to open his eyes. He was sitting upright on his cot in the back room at Wyatt Earp's gambling house, his arms still extended. The dream had been the same for the past four nights, yet each time he woke, he could barely hold on to reality. The dream was so real.

And all he knew was that he wanted with all his soul to be back in that dream.

Slowly he dropped his arms and lay back on the cot. He kicked off the light blanket and clasped his hands behind his head. He was angry at his body's betrayal, that he ached for her. The dream aroused him to a hardness that remained even after he woke, and he was amazed at the effect the dream image had on him.

Was she dangerous? he wondered. And why couldn't he get her out of his mind? He felt ridiculous.

Jackson stared at the ceiling for a long time before he finally rolled over, trying to get comfortable on the board-thin mattress of the tiny cot. He missed his twice weekly break at Sherman House, and especially the luxurious mattress of his favorite room. But he knew he couldn't take the chance of seeing Rose again. Not now. The dawn's first light was shining through the dirty window when he at last dozed.

Taylor sighed. "I've never had insomnia, Ida. What's wrong with me?"

Ida finished pouring tea in two of her best china cups and carried them to the table. She was deeply troubled by Taylor's recent inability to sleep through the night. The sound of Taylor's footsteps in the hall had brought her down to the kitchen, and now she was determined to help her tormented houseguest.

At first, both women silently sipped their tea. Both were completely lost in their own thoughts.

Taylor sighed again, this time more heavily, and rubbed at her temples. Her massaging fingers stopped at the pressure points that she often used to provide headache relief. She had spent the last four days literally retracing her steps, looking for clues—for answers to why she was there and exactly what "truth" she was supposed to find.

The train station held no obvious clues. When she'd asked about Henry, the drunk she'd met that first night, no one knew where he might be. People told her that he often disappeared for weeks at a time. Great, she thought, what if he held the clue she was supposed to find?

Each day she'd visited the City of Paris store, wondering if there was some kind of mysterious information there that she'd missed. The fourth time she'd stopped in, Charlie had stared suspiciously at her, finally asking if there was something in particular she *couldn't* find. She had smiled at the double meaning of his words as she'd assured him that she was simply browsing.

One clearly missing link was the family she'd met at the café. When she'd spoken with Mrs. Reed, she'd learned that the family had taken a few days off to take the children to the back country. Mr. Johnson had heard of a doctor there that offered treatments for asthmatics, an affliction his youngest son suffered from. Mrs. Reed had told her they'd be back by noon the next day.

"How's your tea, dear?" Ida studied Taylor's expression for clues to her despondency. Well-cultivated instincts told her the problem was a certain Jackson Hoyt. Add to that the fact that he hadn't been by the house since their beach excursion, plus all conversation about him had caused Taylor to quickly change the subject.

"Your chamomile tea is always perfect, Ida. Thanks for your company. I just can't seem to quiet my brain long enough to get to sleep. It's so frustrating. Everything's so frustrating. . . ."

"Rose, I haven't pried into your affairs since you've been here," Ida began, "and you can believe it's been a struggle for me to keep my questions to myself."

Taylor looked up from her tea into Ida's concerned eyes. "You've been so kind to me, Ida. I can't thank you enough, but—"

"Now, I'm not asking you to tell me everything that's going on, child. I just want to make sure that you can handle everything that's piled on your plate. Sometimes I get the feeling that things are a bit foreign to you, and I just want you to know that you should ask for help if you need it. That's all."

"I know, I know. It's just too complicated. I have to find out something, and I don't exactly know what it is that I have to find, and time is running out, and I'm afraid I'm not going about it the right way, and—"

"Whoa, girl, slow down a bit. You're not making any sense. And what's this about running out of time, anyway? I told you, you're welcome here as long as you like. Are you telling me you're getting ready to leave us? Where will you go?"

Taylor bit her lip, sorry she'd blurted out her words. The last time she'd done just that, she remembered, was with Jackson. Very poor judgment, and not to be repeated here, she decided.

"Rose, answer me. Are you leaving soon?"

"I may have to. I'm honestly not sure. Don't worry, though, and I promise to let you know more as soon as it's clear to me." Taylor smiled weakly. She could sense Ida's worry and she hated to give her friend reason to be concerned.

Ida finished her tea and put her cup gently into the wash-basin, being extra careful of her best china. Shaking her head, she gazed at Taylor's slumped shoulders. It was obvious that the girl was carrying a burden, but it was also plain that it was a private matter.

"I'm off to bed, then," Ida said, forcing the cheer in her voice, "if you'll be all right alone." Ida walked behind Taylor's chair and stopped to give her shoulder a comforting squeeze. "You try to get some rest, and come get me if you need me."

"Thanks, Ida. I'm just going to walk in the garden for a few minutes, then I'll try to sleep. I feel more relaxed—the tea really helped."

Ida gave Taylor one last motherly look before she made her way up the back stairs.

The kitchen became still and instantly lacked the warmth of Ida's presence—so much so that Taylor felt a shiver run down her spine. Eager to leave the room, she walked out the back door, careful to keep it from banging shut. Stars flickered in the moonless night sky, and Taylor gazed to the heavens as she walked to the middle of the yard.

For the first time, Taylor felt truly alone, isolated and ill at ease. She also realized that until that solitary moment, there had not been much reason for her to measure time at all. Now there was the painful reality of an unknown dead-line, and the heaviness of it made her feel sluggish and dull.

"Taylor Rose, I'm worried about you, and . . ."

Where had he been? An unexpected tear made its way down Taylor's cheek, its hot trail ending at the corner of her mouth.

"... *time is running out.*"

That she knew, and the urgency in her father's voice confirmed her feeling that time was probably shorter than she hoped. She shook her head—she'd retraced most of her steps, but still none of it made any sense to her.

She closed her eyes to listen more carefully, hearing only soft night sounds. She tried to remember what her father had always told her when she was confused—when he was alive, he'd always counseled her to have a little more faith in her own abilities, and that everything was possible. Anything was possible.

But she'd gone over every step since she'd arrived. Maybe that's it, she thought. She hadn't considered anything from *before* her arrival.

"*Remember the Tarot cards.*"

Taylor concentrated, visualizing her encounter with the fortune-teller until bits of dialogue began to surface in her memory. First, she remembered, there was the dangerous journey, and then the false friend. What else?

She tried to picture the cards as they appeared on the table. Then, it was something about love—no, *trusting* the love. The last was still fuzzy.

Her head was beginning to throb. What was it? Look within ... look within for strength.

Think, she commanded herself, rubbing her temples again. Then the last card interpretation came to her, simple and whole—she could almost hear the old woman's voice.

The last card had been the Stars, she'd said, and the Stars promised hope. All Taylor had to do was believe in her own power to create a positive outcome.

Sounded simple, but somehow she knew this would be deceiving.

"*Believe, Taylor.*"

Oh, Dad. She interrupted his voice, a sob caught in her throat.

"*Yes, it is that simple.*"

Barely audible, a female voice whispered in Taylor's

mind like a delicate summer breeze blows through a field of tall grass, sending a rippling wave of green that seems more mirage than movement.

"I promise—everything will look brighter in the new day's light. . . ."

Taylor's eyelids flew open, and her breathing abruptly ceased. She strained to hear, concentrating on the lilting echo of the voice . . . her mother's voice.

Willing herself to listen with every cell of her body, Taylor waited for more words, for the slightest sound. After long, silent moments, Taylor gasped for air, feeling light-headed and dizzy.

Surprisingly, she felt relieved and calm. *Tomorrow.* Just thinking the word provided the first warmth of renewed trust, and the feeling of confidence she had so painfully lacked since her bitter confrontation with Jackson.

Taylor was sure with all her heart and soul that, somehow, tomorrow would bring the breakthrough she needed. Even if she had to retrace her steps from beginning to end a dozen times, she knew the key was there. She would find it. Somewhere deep in the center of her, the tension that had been building was released.

To her surprise, Taylor felt a yawn building in the back of her throat. She quietly returned to her room and fell instantly into restful slumber, eager for the better day tomorrow would bring.

Chapter 22

"MR. JOHNSON, THERE'S someone asking for you," Mrs. Reed called out the back door, where the sounds of children's laughter all but drowned her words.

Taylor sat at a table near the window, waiting for Mr. Johnson to join her, hoping she would find the right words, hoping she wouldn't sound like a total lunatic. She took three deep breaths and let them out slowly.

"Well, hello. It's Miss Martin, isn't it? What can I do for you?" Mr. Johnson extended a friendly hand to Taylor. "I have five loaves of bread cooling on the sill. If you want to wait a few minutes, I'd be glad to sell you one."

"That would be wonderful," Taylor began, "but could you join me for a few minutes while we wait?"

"Why, sure, that'd be fine. I think I'll pour me a cup of coffee first, if you don't mind."

Mr. Johnson went to the kitchen and returned with a steaming cup of coffee. He sat down opposite Taylor, his back to the window.

"Mr. Johnson . . ." Taylor's suddenly dry mouth choked off the rest of the sentence she had started. She felt awkward, still uncertain of her words. "I'm not exactly sure what I want to say, but I wanted to talk with you about something. I don't know how to describe it, but it's like there's some kind of connection between us."

Mr. Johnson returned her gaze calmly, as though her words were half-expected. No look of surprise. No expression of astonishment. He simply nodded, and took a sip of coffee.

"I felt it too, when we met at the store, and since then too. Every time you've been in the café, I've felt it. I thought maybe you reminded me of someone back home or . . . I can't quite put my finger on it." Mr. Johnson leaned closer to Taylor, resting his elbows on the table, staring at her face as though searching for some kind of clue.

Relieved, Taylor smiled. Maybe this was it. If he felt the same connection, maybe he was the key. At least it was a good sign.

With narrowed eyes and a thoughtful expression, Mr. Johnson put his coffee cup down on the table. "Well, tell me this," he began, "have you ever been in Kansas? That's where we're from. Maybe that's it."

"No. It's more likely to be something that happened to you. Or something you know or did . . . something like that. I know it sounds strange, but it's important that we figure it out."

Rubbing his chin, Mr. Johnson continued, "Well, let's see. My life story isn't that interesting. Nothing important ever happened to me, that I can recall."

"Well, tell me about coming west. What brought you to San Diego? Where in Kansas are you from?"

"Well, we lived in Wichita, mostly. It was pretty wild 'til they sent for Wyatt Earp back in '74. He was the deputy marshal, you know. Inside of two years, Wichita was a peaceful town. It was a nice place to raise a family, you know?"

Taylor's eyes widened. Wyatt Earp. A connection. "Go on," she encouraged.

"Well, we lived in town. My wife did bookkeeping for the dry goods store and for the restaurant where I worked. Then in '78 we moved. My wife's boss was openin' up another store and he wanted her to manage it and keep the books," he said proudly.

"Where was this?" Taylor asked.

"Dodge City."

Taylor's heart skipped a beat. She felt her skin goose-bump; a shiver quivered up her spine. Dodge City was where Jackson met his two ugly conspirators. Another connection.

"And even though we'd heard Dodge was pretty wild, we knew that Wyatt Earp was there, so—"

"Wyatt Earp was there too?" It was beginning to feel right to her. Pieces of a puzzle falling into place. "Sorry, go on. . . ."

"Well, we got the business started and had a little place above the store, right on the main street. Let's see, my daughter Annabelle was four, Frank was two, and little John wasn't even born yet."

"Did you live anywhere else?"

"Nope. Stayed in Dodge 'til we came out here."

"And what brought you here, exactly?"

"Well, you know, it's kind of a funny thing, actually." Mr. Johnson folded his hands around his mug of steaming coffee.

Taylor waited, wishing desperately that Mr. Johnson's story contained the final key to the mystery of Jackson's involvement in the plot to assassinate Earp. She knew the connection had to be specific. In Dodge City there was a definite connection between Jackson and Mr. Johnson. The fact that Wyatt Earp had been in both cities where the Johnsons lived was another connection. But there must be more. There had to be more.

Mr. Johnson continued. "It was actually in the summer of '78 that a promise I made opened up the idea of moving. It didn't make any sense 'til a lot later, though."

Taylor was confused by Mr. Johnson's words. "So you stayed in Dodge City for ten years before you decided to head west? Why so long?"

"Let me start over. . . . Back in '78, Dodge City was still wild. Even with Marshal Earp there, plus his brothers Virgil and Morgan as deputies—there still was trouble in the street sometimes. There was talk all the time about there bein' a reward for killing him—Marshal Earp, I mean. Only two tried, that I know of. Clay Allison and a stranger, named George Hoyt."

"Hoyt? George Hoyt? Mr. Johnson, that's it! That's the connection! Tell me what happened—everything!" Taylor's heartbeat thudded in her ears painfully. This was it. She knew she had found the key: George Hoyt had to be Jackson's father.

"It was summer . . . July, I think, and I was walkin' back to the store from the bank. This Hoyt fella came flyin' past me on his horse, shootin' his gun like a crazy man. It didn't seem like he was really aiming at anything—just shootin' blind. I remember thinkin' he was makin' a darn fool target for Marshal Earp like that."

"So, he was there to kill the marshal?"

"You know, I don't think so. It was more like he wanted to get killed *by* the marshal. When he started shootin' in the windows, everyone hit the boardwalk or ducked in the alleys, myself included. I guess the marshal heard the shots, because when I looked up, I saw him. It kinda felt like time stopped, or changed, or somethin'. Everything happened slow, kinda dreamlike. Do you know what I mean?"

Taylor nodded. *Oh, Mr. Johnson, if you only knew how well I know that feeling.*

"All I could hear was gunshots and the sound of the horse running. Hoyt had that poor horse running up and down the street, back and forth as fast as that creature could run. He was makin' an awful obvious target, like I said before."

Taylor pictured the scene in her mind as she listened to

Mr. Johnson's recollection. George Hoyt's behavior sounded more like a suicide ride, not an assassination attempt to gun down the famous Wyatt Earp.

"Then I saw the marshal watching. I swear, I don't think he blinked the whole time. It was like he was fightin' himself—like he was mad about having to go ahead and shoot the crazy guy. He had to, though. When Hoyt started shootin' the windows, there was nothin' else to do. The marshal was protecting the town."

"So he shot him, then?"

"I saw Hoyt fall from his horse. One shot. He landed about twenty feet from me. The marshal must have been almost a block away, I figure." Mr. Johnson ran his hands through his hair, pausing a moment to stretch his neck.

"Was he dead?"

"No, he wasn't dead when I got to him. But I could tell he was dyin'. I lifted his head and was surprised when his eyes opened. Then he smiled. I couldn't believe he smiled at me. It . . . it was like he'd planned on dyin' that day or something. He looked sort of happy. Relieved."

"Do you think he planned the whole thing? That he really wanted to get shot?"

"Yes, I do. That's the strange thing. And the other strange thing is what he said to me. He asked me if I had a family, and I told him that I had a boy and a girl. Then he told me he'd just found out that he had a boy himself. I could tell that he was really happy about it, too. He stared at me and said that it was his biggest regret—not knowing his own boy, and not marryin' the boy's mother. He said she was the only woman who'd ever seen the good in him."

Taylor looked down at her clenched hands, white-knuckled in her concern to absorb every word. "Was that all he said?"

"No. He also made me promise something. He's dyin' in the streets of Dodge City, and he uses the last of his strength to make me promise to cherish any family I was lucky enough to have." Mr. Johnson shook his head in amazement at the tender words spoken by a crazed gunman.

Taylor tore her gaze from her hands and looked up at Mr. Johnson's face, his eyes brimmed with unshed tears.

"And I promised him. That day, I promised him that I would cherish my family. My youngest boy, John, was born a couple years after that. He was sick a lot—had trouble breathing. He had the asthma, the doctors told us. Then we heard about San Diego having the kind of weather that was perfect for getting John well. The air was good. And there was talk about healing springwater, too. I kept remembering my promise to George Hoyt and we decided to come out west—for my son's sake."

"I saw you in the café your first day here," Taylor whispered.

"You were here? In the café? Was it you that sent us the breakfast?" Mr. Johnson shook his head in disbelief.

"Yes. You all looked so hungry, and I had the extra money. It wasn't any trouble."

"Well, I'll be . . . I guess all I can say is thank you. Because of stayin' and eatin' that morning, our luck changed completely—but then you probably know all that, don't you?"

Taylor smiled at Mr. Johnson's sincerity, pleased that everything had worked out so well for him and his family. She was even more pleased, though, about the precious information he'd divulged about Jackson's father.

At last she had the key. Now she had to figure out how to get Jackson to sit and listen to reason. Another problem to solve . . . and she had a feeling there was very little time left.

"So, what do you think all this means, anyway?" Mr. Johnson gazed at Taylor. Slowly, he reached out a hand and patted hers in a fatherly way.

Taylor looked deep into his eyes. "I need your help," she began.

"Anything. Whatever I can do for you would be my pleasure. My family and I owe you a lot. Just ask."

Taylor dropped her gaze to Mr. Johnson's large ham of a hand. Should she just tell him? she wondered, trying to predict his reaction.

"Mr. Johnson. The story you just told me about George Hoyt is the information I needed to stop the murder of Wyatt Earp. I needed that information more than you could ever realize."

"Murder? Who wants to murder Wyatt Earp?" He pushed his empty cup aside and scooted his chair closer to the table. "I didn't expect to hear talk of murder," he whispered, glancing around the café.

"Can you promise me that this conversation stays between us, at least for now?"

"Yes," he answered quietly. "Tell me what you know, and how I can help."

"You said George Hoyt had a son, right? Well, his son is here. He's here in San Diego. And he thinks his father was murdered by Wyatt Earp—gunned down in cold blood. He plans to take revenge for his father's death by killing Mr. Earp. And two men are helping him; two men he met in Dodge City before he came out here."

Mr. Johnson met her words with a low whistle. "How did you get messed up in all this? How do you know about this plan?"

Taylor hesitated, then spoke in a voice that she hoped would hide her anxiety, about both Jackson and the quick-approaching deadline.

"George Hoyt's son is Jackson Hoyt. He's the bartender at the saloon across the street. It's owned by Wyatt Earp. I overheard a couple of conversations between him and two other men—it was all pretty specific. The worst part, though, is I think something's going to happen very soon. I need to get Jackson to listen to what really happened to his father. I think it's the only way he might change his mind about going through with the killing. That's why I'm here. That's why I had to find the connection—the information you had is the key to stopping all of this from happening."

Belief and heartfelt concern shone from Mr. Johnson's eyes. "Well, I believe you. I can't think of a reason why you'd concoct such a story. What can I do to help you?" he asked.

"I'm not really sure. I need to get Jackson to meet with me. That will be the hardest part—keeping him in the room long enough to hear me out. I truly believe that once he knows the facts, he won't go through with killing Mr. Earp." Taylor sighed. It sounded easy. But how would she convince Jackson to see her?

"My goodness . . . it is a bit complicated. How well do you know this Jackson?"

An unwelcome blush crept into Taylor's cheeks. She stiffened, angry at herself for being embarrassed.

"You care for him, don't you?"

Was it that obvious? Taylor thought carefully about Mr. Johnson's question. She knew he deserved the truth from her—at least about Jackson. But she wasn't even sure what the truth was.

"You love him, don't you, Miss Martin?" Mr. Johnson tenderly presented Taylor with the only valid answer.

Taylor's face softened, transformed in the moment of recognition. She realized that it was her love for Jackson that had given her the determination to find the key. She must believe that her love for him would help her find the way to stop him from completing his mission to commit murder.

Taylor finally answered Mr. Johnson. "Yes, I do love him. And I think he loves me—though at the moment, I'm sure he would disagree passionately."

Grinning at her newfound confidant and friend, Taylor felt renewed hope, which brought a comforting blanket of pleasure to her troubled mind.

Mr. Johnson grinned back. "Well, now, that's better. Now we need to figure out how to get you two together—at least long enough to make him hear you out. Where are you staying? Can we get him to come there, maybe?"

Taylor told Mr. Johnson about the note the messenger had brought to her at Sherman House. She shared that the message meant for her to stay away from Jackson and not to interfere with his plans, that was apparent. Mr. Johnson's wide-eyed response to her living at a brothel caused her to immediately reassure him that her job at Ida's was as her gardener, nothing more.

"Jackson hasn't been there since I told him that I knew about the murder plot," she continued.

"Where does he stay, normally?"

"As far as I know, he sleeps in a back room at the saloon. Other than that, I don't know."

Mr. Johnson paused for a moment, then a devilish look came into his eyes. "I have an idea. . . ."

Chapter 23

"THE WAY I figure," Mr. Johnson began, "Jackson won't come to Sherman House if you're there, right? But it is a pretty good place to get him alone. What do you say we send him a message that you're gone? What are the chances that he would come on over—return to his pattern of staying there?"

Taylor smiled at the simplistic plan. "Pretty good, I'd say, especially knowing that I was gone. It's perfect. If I can get him alone, and if he'll listen to me, I think I can convince him."

"That's a lot of ifs, Miss Martin."

"Don't worry." Every fiber of her being told her the plan could work. It would work. It had to work.

"I'll get some paper and a pen from my wife's desk. We might as well get things started."

Taylor watched Mr. Johnson disappear through the doorway. What a strange sequence of events, she thought. One father so affected by another father's dying words that he uproots his entire family. She had to make Jackson see the big picture. Convince him that his reasons were no longer valid for killing Wyatt Earp. That he was no longer responsible for avenging his father's death. He would just have to believe her.

There was an eagerness in Mr. Johnson's eyes when he returned to the table, carefully setting paper and pen in front of Taylor.

"Make sure you say something convincing. He's bound to be a little suspicious," he said with quiet emphasis. "When you're finished, bring the paper to me in the kitchen. Then you go back, empty your room of your things—get rid of any sign of yourself at Sherman House. I'll wait an hour, and then I'll deliver the envelope myself."

"Right." Taylor stared at the blank page. She heard Mr. Johnson's footsteps as he made his way back to the kitchen. Right. What could she say that would convince Jackson she was gone? She should just get to the point—that she was going away somewhere. San Francisco? she considered.

She hated to lie to him, even in the note. She could be vague, let him draw his own conclusions.

Deliberately omitting the customary "dear" at the beginning of the note, Taylor wrote:

Jackson,

By the time you read this note, I will no longer be staying in my room at Ida's. Your secret is safe with me.

Taylor silently reread the words. Vague enough to maintain her desire not to lie, but, with any luck, leading enough to make him think she was gone?

It would have to do.

Relieved, Taylor signed "Rose" at the bottom of the letter and waited a few moments for the ink to dry. Carefully she folded the paper and inserted it into the square envelope, then wrote Jackson's name on the front.

As she handed the envelope to Mr. Johnson, she smiled and they hugged each other for luck.

"Don't worry, Miss Martin. I have a good feeling about this. You head on back, now, and hide any trace of you in that house. And try to be patient. He might not come over tonight, you know."

Taylor nodded. "I know. And thank you for listening to my story. I'm so glad we at least came up with something to try. Now it's up to me to convince Jackson to see things differently."

"Somehow, I have a feeling you can be pretty convincing." Mr. Johnson chuckled. "And besides, you've got a level head on them shoulders. You'll do just fine."

"I'd better go," she said, "but I'd like to take a couple loaves of bread back with me, if they're cool enough."

"Got two already wrapped and waitin' for ya." Mr. Johnson handed Taylor two loaves wrapped in brown paper. "Now you scoot on back home."

Both glanced at the clock. In an hour, Mr. Johnson would deliver the envelope and Jackson would read her note. Taylor said a silent prayer for success. Perhaps a certain guardian angel would tip the scales, she thought, and nudge Jackson into believing she had truly gone away.

Jackson stood behind the bar drying the seemingly endless stack of freshly washed beer mugs. Glad to have mindless tasks to fill the afternoon, he was content to straighten row upon row of glasses and polish the bar's surface until it gleamed like the mirrors he had cleaned that morning.

With the next two nights off, Jackson wondered how he would spend his time. Since final plans were in place with the McLaurey brothers, there was nothing to do but wait for Saturday night.

After placing the last mug on the shelf, Jackson paused in his work to reach in his pocket and pull out the envelope that held the message Mr. Johnson had delivered. His eyes scanned the few words on the paper for the fifth time.

She was gone.

Jackson was feeling increasingly anxious, tormented by confusing emotions: emotions carefully held in check while he worked for the man who'd murdered his father, and carefully repressed unfamiliar—*unwanted*—emotions that had to do with the mysterious Rose.

The message of her departure had given him a tremendous sense of relief. At least he wouldn't have to deal with her again. He couldn't have tolerated her interference so late in the game.

Even so, Jackson felt his body tingle when he ran his forefinger over Rose's signature. He'd even brought the paper close to his face, hoping for a whiff of her fragrance. Catching himself, he frowned, his expression a mask of stone. She was dangerous, and he knew he should be jubilant that she was gone.

If only she hadn't known, hadn't tried to interfere. . . .

Jackson turned to catch a glimpse of his glum expression in the mirror behind the bar. He smiled blandly. It was almost time. Soon he would have the satisfaction of seeing his father's murderer dead. It was all that really mattered.

The envelope returned securely to his pocket, Jackson walked into the back room, gathered some clothes, and packed a bag. Confident that no one was close by, he retrieved the tiny .32-caliber Harrington & Richardson's revolver from underneath a loose floorboard and placed it in the specially designed pocket of his vest.

Perfect.

Even when he ran his hands over the surface of the vest, there was no indication of the gun's existence. No one would notice it. No one would suspect him. It was a perfect plan.

Afternoon sunlight filtered through the window, casting an unwelcome, cheerful glow. His quarters had been adequate for the short term, fine for late nights cleaning up the bar after the usual mob of drinkers and gamblers Earp's saloon attracted. Even so, he was glad to leave the sparse room and the cot's thin mattress for the comfort of one of Ida's feather beds.

With Rose gone, Jackson mused, at least he'd have the luxury of a couple of good nights' sleep and a hot soak before Saturday night. The painful realization came to him that it would indeed be his last chance to have the luxury.

After Saturday night, Jackson knew he'd either be dead, a fugitive, or in jail.

In one long series of swallows, Taylor gulped down the cool peppermint tea Ida offered. She had really worked up quite a sweat. After leaving Mr. Johnson at the café, she had hurried home to Sherman House. And now all her things were safely stowed in the utility room off the kitchen.

There was no trace of her anywhere in the house. Ida had retrieved the dresses and other items she'd lent Taylor, and then suggested she put her things into a trunk that was being used to store kitchen linens.

Now all Taylor had to do was wait.

Ida had listened suspiciously to Taylor's weak explanations, about how she needed Jackson to believe she had left town in order for something *else* to happen. Taylor had pleaded for her patience, just one last time, and of course Ida had agreed—but only after Taylor had promised to explain everything later.

"You'll choke! Slow down—there's plenty of tea for another glass as soon as you've emptied that one."

The cool tea soothed Taylor's stomach, already clenched in nervous anticipation. She realized it was not going to be easy to just wait for Jackson to show up.

Ida's hand flew up. There was the unmistakable heavy sound of footsteps on the front porch. Even before the door's bell sounded, she had reached up to smooth her hair and straighten her gown. "Stay here, I'll see who's come in."

Taylor put her glass on the table. Somehow she knew it

was Jackson. She could almost feel him . . . feel his presence in the house. Forcing herself to breathe deeply and evenly, Taylor soundlessly rose from her chair and crept to the door, hoping to snatch a bit of conversation.

"Well, hello, Jackson. Where've you been so long? We've missed seein' you." Ida presented Jackson with her warmest smile.

Jackson's eyes darted around the room, then narrowed suspiciously. How could he be sure she was gone?

"Well, sir, are you here for a room or bit of fun, perhaps? I'd be happy to ask any of my girls to spend some time with you. . . . The blond gal with the bright blue eyes was especially taken with you the last time you visited my parlor, remember?"

Jackson's eyes softened at Ida's playful banter. She hadn't even mentioned Rose, he thought. She must be gone.

"Well, Jackson, what'll it be?" Ida smiled, her arms crossed against her chest.

"Maybe next time, Ida. Is the corner room available for the next two nights?"

Ida nodded her reply. "Would you like me to bring you an early dinner tray later?"

"That would be splendid, Ida. After a long, hot soak in the tub, I know I'll be famished. You are too kind to me."

For a long moment, Ida looked back at Jackson. "You look tired, Jackson. Everything all right with you?"

Jackson forced a grin. "Tired and hungry." Certainly a true statement, he thought.

"Well, then . . . follow me, m'lord." Ida laughed good-naturedly.

Jackson shifted his bag and obediently followed Ida up the front stairs.

Taylor leaned against the doorjamb in the kitchen, encouraged by the knowledge that she had the rest of the afternoon and evening to work on Jackson. A sudden blush crept to her cheeks as she realized the twin meaning of her own thoughts. Stick to business, she scolded herself. Quietly, she returned to her chair at the table and waited for Ida's return.

Ida walked into the kitchen shaking her head, muttering to herself. She didn't care for the feeling of tension and turmoil that was building. She'd felt it from Taylor during their scurry to move her things, and she felt it now from Jackson. He just wasn't his normal self. Something was very, very wrong.

"Looks like we secured your things just in time, eh?" Ida joined Taylor at the table.

Taylor returned Ida's smile.

"I'm going to have Maylee prepare a dinner tray to take to Jackson's room. I wouldn't suppose you would like to take it to him, now, would you?"

Ida watched as a faint light twinkled in the languid depths of Taylor's green eyes. Just as quickly, though, they lost their glint of promise.

"If I walk in there, Ida, he'll just leave and then I'll never—"

Ida grinned and pulled a key from her pocket and placed it on the table between them. "Already thought of that. He'll think it's me bringing the tray in. Just wait until he's started his bath, then take in the tray, lock the door behind you, and hide the key. Simple."

"Simple," echoed Taylor as she picked up the long brass key and considered Ida's words. Holding the key in her palm, it felt solid and strong. She hoped she could find the strength she'd need to confront Jackson with the truth.

Having already freshened up while Ida went to Maylee's for the dinner tray, Taylor passed the time pacing in the parlor. Ida had insisted that Taylor change her clothes, and had brought her a scoop-necked, pink cotton dress that hugged her slim torso and flared demurely at her hipline. Instead of attaching the fall of curled locks, though, Taylor had simply fluffed her hair and feathered a few wispy curls toward her cheeks.

After all, she thought, this was business. She wasn't there to entice or seduce. She was there to convince.

At last Ida returned from Maylee's kitchen at the Gaslamp Quarter Hotel with an enormous food tray. She poked her head into the parlor to whisper to Taylor that she was back.

When Taylor joined Ida in the kitchen, she peeked under the cloth that covered the tray to find a platter of roast beef and baking powder biscuits, two bowls of grated carrots and cabbage, and two large squares of Maylee's apple spice cake, still warm from the oven. Eating utensils were neatly rolled up in two yellow-and-white-checkered cloth napkins.

With one eyebrow raised, Taylor glanced at Ida with a half-smile twitching on her lips.

"Well, Maylee insisted that you would end up staying with Jackson and you would be hungry too. I agreed, so go on up and straighten whatever it is that you have to straighten out." Ida placed the heavy tray in Taylor's arms and held the door open for her.

Taylor took a deep breath and began to climb the stairs.

"And I was right about the dress too," Ida whispered. "You look lovely." She smiled as the serious look in Taylor's eyes was temporarily replaced with one of mild irritation. "Good luck, dear."

"Thanks," Taylor whispered. "I'm afraid I'll need it."

Chapter 24

JACKSON LEANED WEARILY against the door for a few moments after Ida let him into the room. Alone and inside the four walls he had come to know so well, he felt instantly calm and safe. The world outside was unimportant, at least for the next two nights. He would allow himself to enjoy the comfort of the room and all it offered. It was a sanctuary, a safe haven from the harsh reality of the impending completion of his plan.

Breathing deeply, Jackson filled his lungs with the floral scent of the room. Roses of every color from Ida's garden filled vases in the room. He counted them—ten large vases bursting with blooms. Roses everywhere, but the mysterious *Rose* was gone.

Jackson closed his eyes, and instantly his mind re-created a blurred image of Taylor in the garden wearing her red silk robe. A few seconds passed, and the image faded to black.

"Damn," he cursed softly. If things had gone differently, he realized, she might have shared this room with him, making his last two days as a free man much more pleasurable.

Slowly Jackson opened his eyes. They rested on the room's large tub, which sat in the far corner. A bath was what he needed. Placing his bag on the floor near the carved mahogany wardrobe, Jackson began methodically to undress.

He took the tiny revolver from the inside pocket of his vest and placed it on a low table next to the wardrobe. Then he hung his shirt and vest on the brass hooks inside and sat down to remove his boots. On the stove, water was ready and waiting for the bath he craved, and he hurriedly removed the rest of his clothing.

Jackson filled the tub with about six inches of water, mixing hot with cold. When he was finally satisfied with the temperature, he climbed in. He noticed the room's previous occupants had left a dozen or so small candles on several end tables that bordered the tub on one side. Also, a crystal clear bowl held a single perfect blossom, floating in water. A perfect blood-red rose.

Jackson stared at the rose for a long moment before he began the task of scrupulously washing the grime from his body. The water darkened as he rinsed the soap away. With the plug pulled, he stood and watched the water drain away. He wanted a soak, but not in soiled water.

Air-dried and clean, Jackson stepped from the tub and repeated the ritual of mixing hot water from the stove and cold water from the sink pump. This time he filled the tub close to the rim.

As Jackson was ready to step into the steaming tub, a cobalt blue bottle on the nightstand by the bed caught his eye. He walked over to the table, then removed the cork. The subtle fragrance of roses drifted to his nostrils. More roses, he mused. Always roses.

He tipped the bottle to capture some liquid on his fingertip. It was rose-scented oil. Impulsively, he poured some into the bathwater, then placed the bottle on one of the tables by the tub and climbed in.

Hotter this time, the water soothed his jangled nerves

quickly. The comforting fragrance of the room filled every breath and he soon found himself dozing, his neck resting on the rim of the tub.

In his relaxed haze, Jackson barely recognized the sound of a soft knock at the door.

"It's open, Ida," he murmured, eyes still closed.

The door opened without a sound as Taylor entered Jackson's room, the heavy food tray balanced precariously on one arm, the key to the lock clenched between her lips. She saw Jackson in the tub, thankfully positioned so he was facing away from the door.

"Just put the tray on the table, would you?"

"Mm-hmmm," Taylor mumbled at the moment the key turned in the lock of the door. She waited for any reaction to the clicking sound. Nothing.

Glancing around the room, Taylor searched for a hiding place for the key, and at last settled on the large Boston fern sitting on a table next to the door. She pushed the key into the soil of the plant. There, that's done, she thought.

Quietly, Taylor walked to the small dining table by the window and deposited the tray. Her stomach tightened in anticipation of Jackson's first sight of her. He'd been so angry when they'd argued at the beach, and she honestly wondered if she should be afraid of him.

"Thanks, Ida," Jackson whispered.

His voice sounded very relaxed, almost drugged. From the water, she thought, breathing deeply in an effort to calm herself. The air in the room was humid and, she noticed, filled with the almost overwhelming scent of flowers.

Taylor looked around the room. It was beautiful. The large brass bed was the focal point, practically in the center of the room. It was heaped with downy pillows and covered with a hand-stitched quilt of intertwining pastel-colored circles; a traditional wedding ring design. Lace curtains hung at the six tall windows that overlooked the garden. They fluttered in the early evening breeze, delivering rose-scented perfume from the garden below.

As her gaze nervously roamed the room, a glimmer caught her attention. Next to the wardrobe on a low table was a tiny silver revolver, glistening in the last rays of sunlight let in by the random flutter of the curtains. She hadn't noticed it when she'd entered the room, but could see it clearly from her position by the table.

Walking slowly toward the wardrobe, Taylor kept her eyes on the back of Jackson's head.

When she reached the wardrobe, she stooped slowly toward the gun. It was so small, she thought, for a murder weapon. She held it in her hand, her finger on the trigger.

The revolver felt icy cold . . . and foreign to her. Taylor's hands shook slightly as she held it. Perhaps it was the leverage she needed. Turning it over in the palm of her hand, Taylor assumed that the gun was loaded. If not, she thought, Jackson would certainly not take her seriously if she actually threatened him with it.

Slowly Taylor turned and walked to the oversized porcelain tub in the far corner of the room. Jackson still hadn't moved. She listened to his deep breaths and unconsciously tried to match their rhythm. Finally, Taylor positioned herself at the foot of the tub, with Jackson in full view.

Staring at his face, fearing Jackson would open his eyes at any moment, Taylor lowered herself into a chair. Her right arm was close to her body, elbow bent, the tiny barrel of the gun pointing at the devastatingly handsome man submerged in the still-steaming water.

She waited.

Jackson's hair had partially dried. Inky black curls caressed his forehead, and long strands curved behind and below his ears to curve along his neck. Slightly tilted to one side, his head rested on the rim of the tub so that his chin jutted upward, his lips parted slightly. He looked so peaceful . . . and desirable.

Sitting straighter in the chair, Taylor found if she extended her neck a little and leaned forward, she could gaze fully along Jackson's magnificent body. She allowed her eyes to drift downward, first to the mass of silky chest hair that waved in the water just beneath the surface.

Even though his well-toned muscles were now relaxed in the hot water, they were defined. Taylor blinked and dropped her gaze to the source of her desire. The tingling in the pit of her stomach dwarfed her fear. At the sight of him, her body instantly ached for his touch.

Now, she realized, she would never again have the magical feeling of their union. He hated her. That was clear.

As she sat back in the chair, Jackson's lower body was once more out of view. Taylor swallowed hard, then loudly cleared her throat.

Jackson stiffened at the sound and he became instantly wide awake. Anger and shock at seeing Taylor sitting demurely in a chair at the end of the tub quickly transformed to puzzlement, then fear, at the sight of his own gun pointed at him.

He felt the blood drain from his face as he stared in astonishment.

"You . . . you . . . liar! You tricked me!" Jackson spat out the words scornfully.

"Don't move . . . you just stay where you are. . . ." Taylor drew her lips into a thin line, trying her best to appear dauntless.

"What do you want? What are you doing here?" The words barely escaped from behind Jackson's clenched teeth.

"All I want, Jackson Hoyt, is your full attention." Taylor spoke with quiet, albeit desperate, firmness. "And the chance to explain."

Jackson chuckled nastily, interrupting her. "Explain what, exactly? More crazy talk about you being sent here to stop me? Is that why you have a gun pointed at me?" His voice was cold and lashing.

Taylor replied in a low voice, taut with anger, "Be quiet and listen to me." She shot him a cold look.

Jackson's blue eyes darkened like angry thunderclouds,

and he returned a hostile stare. "I'm listening," he growled.

Feeling suddenly weak and vulnerable in the face of his anger, Taylor took a deep breath. She hoped Jackson was at least a fraction as afraid as he was angry.

"I'm here, Taylor Rose."

Greatly relieved to hear her father's voice, Taylor's confidence spiraled. His presence filled her with a feeling of reassurance and control. An expression of authority gleamed in her eyes as she kept her gaze on Jackson.

Jackson narrowed his eyes as he stared at Taylor. "Did you say something?"

"Actually, that was my father."

Jackson turned his head to look behind him, quickly confirming there was no one else in the room. "Your father's dead. Or was that a lie, too?"

"My father is dead, but he's been . . . helping me. Now hear me out, Jackson—no more interruptions. Agreed?"

Jackson nodded. Something was different, he thought. Her voice had changed. Her face had changed. Examining it, he saw that now it was shining with strength and determination.

"You were right," she began, "I have been keeping things from you. I'm actually from San Diego."

At least she was admitting her lies, he thought.

"The only thing is," she continued, "I'm not from this time. I came here . . . from the future."

More mystical babble, Jackson thought. He sucked on the inside of his lower lip to keep from speaking the words aloud.

"I know it sounds crazy. I thought I was crazy. It was quite a shock, actually." After a long pause, Taylor continued, "My first night here, I ended up with Henry at the gambling house—we met there, remember? Oh, I looked different then—I was wearing pants and a vest. He introduced me to you as Taylor . . . my hat fell on the floor and you picked it up."

Jackson's eyes widened. *The stranger.* That's why she had looked familiar. More lies.

Taylor moistened her lips before she continued. "I overheard a conversation that night. I heard the tapping at the window and what you talked about with that man. And then later, after I met you again at Ida's—this time as Rose—I followed you to the Acme Saloon. I heard you talk about avenging your father's death by killing Wyatt Earp."

Taylor inhaled deeply. She had rattled off the information in one breath, wanting desperately for everything to be said as quickly as possible.

"Tell him about me."

She considered her father's words carefully. Jackson would certainly think her crazy if he didn't think so already. But something in the tone of her father's voice pulled against her own instincts.

"When things get difficult, sometimes I hear my father's voice." Taylor paused for a moment. "He's been sort of . . . protecting me . . . and providing moral support. He told me I was sent here to stop you from going through with the assassination, but in order to do so I had to solve a puzzle, a mystery. . . ." Her words faded. Even to herself, the words sounded foolish.

Jackson continued to gaze back at her with an unfriendly stare.

"So that's what I did," she said softly. "I solved the puzzle, and I came here today to tell you why you don't have to kill Wyatt Earp."

Jackson's stare turned into a scowl, his jaw clenching, his mouth stretching into a thin-lipped sneer.

"I found a man who was with your father when he died."

Jackson sat upright in the tub. "What?"

Taylor straightened the arm that was holding Jackson's gun, sharpening her aim. "Lie back down in the water . . . now."

Jackson slid back into the water with a grimace, at least

giving the appearance that he was taking her threat seriously.

"Listen to me, Jackson. There's a man here in San Diego who witnessed your father's death. He described your father as taking what sounded to me like a suicide ride through town—riding up and down the street, shooting into windows and—"

"He had a gun?" Jackson asked in a hoarse whisper.

"Wyatt Earp was the marshal and yes, he shot your father—but he was just doing his job. He was protecting the people of Dodge City. He didn't murder your father. That's what I needed to tell you." Taylor stared into Jackson's eyes, which were now filled with questions and doubt. "Do you believe me?" she asked.

Slowly, Jackson shook his head from side to side. "How would I know you're not just making this up? All I have is the word of . . . a liar."

Taylor sighed. "You're right. I probably sound like a lunatic, but I don't know how else to say it. . . ."

"Tell him I'm here."

Taylor clearly heard her father's voice next to her, as though he were standing just inches from her left arm.

"Jackson, my father is here."

"And I suppose you'll ask him to appear before me as proof? Is that it?" he murmured cynically.

Taylor's eyebrows drew together in a frown. Could her father materialize?

"You must keep your eyes on Jackson the entire time."

Taylor stared into Jackson's eyes, and waited. "He's here, Jackson, right beside me . . . just look."

Jackson returned her stare. The tenderness he now saw in Taylor's eyes surprised and amazed him, and he suddenly found it difficult to sever his gaze from her.

"Please, Jackson," she whispered, "look beside me."

Obediently, Jackson stared at the space next to Taylor. Within seconds, the air began to shimmer and quiver like a heat wave over a parched, unplanted field.

He stared, waiting.

A long moment passed, and finally an outline appeared of . . . something. There was a distinct thickening of the air, and he realized that the shape was taking substance, filling in. Now he could see the silhouette of . . . a man.

"Jackson, tell me what you see." Taylor wanted with all her heart to spin in her chair and witness the materialization of her father. Instead, she was resigned to seeing her father through the eyes of the man she loved.

"I see . . . something . . . in the shape of a man," he whispered. "I can't believe this is happening."

"Describe him to me . . . please, Jackson," she pleaded.

Jackson squinted, his forehead wrinkling in concentration. "He has his hand on your shoulder . . . he's just standing there. . . . His face isn't really clear . . . it's all kind of blurry. . . ."

Unconsciously, Taylor reached up with her left hand, hoping to feel her father's hand on her shoulder. All she felt was a kind of coolness in the air.

"This is amazing . . . either I'm seeing a ghost or you are one hell of a magician." Jackson continue to stare wide-eyed.

"Is he still there?" Taylor asked, her voice silky.

Jackson nodded. "He seems . . . tall . . . and rather thin. . . . Now he's stepping back . . . back behind you. . . ."

Taylor held her gaze steady as she felt a cool breeze in back of her.

Jackson's luminous blue eyes widened in astonishment. "Now he's moving toward the bed. . . . He's taking a rose out of the vase."

One perfect red bloom began to rise in the air.

"Jackson, what's happening?"

"He's . . . he's bringing a rose to you. This is impossible."

Taylor's father returned to his position next to Taylor, then he slowly extended the flower to Jackson.

In her peripheral vision, Taylor sensed the movement of

the flower as it floated through the air beside her. She watched in wonder as the rose came into view.

Jackson stared, then cautiously sat up to reach for the rose. His eyes softened and his tight expression relaxed into a smile as he carefully took the stem from the ghostly hand.

The moment he did, the ghostly figure vanished.

Taylor felt her father's absence immediately and abruptly turned in her chair, hoping to catch a last glimpse of her father's spirit. "He's gone, isn't he?" she whispered.

Staring in astonishment at the rose, Jackson nodded wordlessly.

Her shoulder aching with tension, Taylor lowered her arm and placed the tiny revolver on a nearby table. It was over.

If Jackson didn't believe her now, he never would.

Chapter 25

SLOWLY, JACKSON RAISED his eyes to meet Taylor's questioning gaze. "I believe you," he said, and offered her a sudden, arresting grin. An incredible peace and satisfaction filled Jackson, and he was strangely elated by the unearthly experience they had just shared.

Taylor smiled tentatively. "Really? Do you believe everything?"

Jackson nodded. "This man that you said was with my father when he died, can I meet him? Talk to him myself? I need to hear it with my own ears, I guess. I can't believe I was ready to kill someone—"

"My father kept insisting that you weren't a killer," Taylor interrupted, "and that was why it was so important that I find the catalyst to turn things in a different direction."

"Tell me more . . . about you. The truth, this time."

"What do you want to know?" Taylor smiled. The knot of fear continued to relax, her trepidation replaced by a surge of hope. It was going to be all right.

"The truth, right? No matter what?" His voice was calm, his gaze steady.

Taylor nodded. "The truth, no matter what."

"Start from the beginning. Who are you . . . really?"

Taylor exhaled a long sigh of contentment. It would feel so good to talk freely to Jackson, even though she suspected her words would still sound strange to him.

Jackson straightened a little in the tub.

"My name really is Taylor—Taylor Rose Martin. I was with Henry when I met you the first time at Wyatt Earp's gambling house. I used my name, remember? Then when I met Ida; she insisted I use my middle name, Rose, because it was more . . . feminine. My father used to call me Rose, so it felt nice—something familiar."

"And how did you get here?"

"I was traveling by train on my way back from a week-end up the coast and when I got off the train, I got off here . . . in 1888." Taylor observed a subtle change in Jackson's eyes, ranging from surprise to disbelief to curiosity.

"So, what kind of person are you . . . where you're from."

Taylor smiled. It felt peculiar to be getting the third degree from Jackson, and a bit backward. It felt like the getting-to-know-you chatter of a first date, but this chatter was with someone who knew her intimately—at least physically.

"I'm a nurse for the school system in San Diego. After my father died, I finished college to get my nursing degree," she explained.

"Ida thought you were some kind of healer."

"Well, I don't know about being a healer. I mostly lend a sympathetic ear to barely sick schoolchildren and patch up skinned knees once in a while."

"Is there anyone . . . at home . . . that might be worried, wondering what has happened to you?"

"What I told you about my father and mother was true," Taylor said, a gentle softness in her voice. "My mother died when I was a baby, and my father died five years ago. I don't have much family—some friends, but they're used to me sort of disappearing for weeks at a time. There is . . . no one else," she emphasized.

Jackson closed his eyes. He was suddenly weary from trying to comprehend all that Taylor explained. She'd spent so much time and effort to deceive him and yet, he thought, he had done the same. He hadn't been honest with her, or anyone, for that matter. He had been living a lie since he'd arrived in San Diego. How could he hold on to an anger that had no foundation?

The mysterious Rose had shared her secrets. And, more importantly, she had delivered the truth to him about the death of his father.

A stillness fell on the room as the late-day breeze ceased to blow, and both Taylor and Jackson sat quietly, alone with their thoughts. The only sound in the room was their slow, steady breathing. Their rhythms eventually synchronized so that only one sound disturbed the silence.

With eyes still closed, Jackson moistened his lips. "Taylor."

"Yes?"

"It suits you, I suppose."

"I don't mind if you call me Rose. It's your choice."

There was an underlying sensuality in the sound of her words and, with great effort, Jackson finally opened his eyes. He felt dazed at both the phenomenon he'd experienced and the marvel of the true story of his father's death.

As his gaze fell on Taylor's face, Jackson blinked with wonder. The final rays of the afternoon sunlight had formed a radiant halo behind her head, and her mahogany hair glowed with a gentle, warm fire. Her emerald eyes gleamed like cat's eyes, cautious but willing to trust.

"Rose?"

"Yes?"

No longer plagued with the seriousness of his mission of revenge, Jackson allowed his feelings for her to resurface. In a rush, the deep, lonely ache disappeared, replaced with a feeling of hope.

The faint possibility of joy crept back into his conscious-
ness, and a staggering weight ascended, leaving him feeling
buoyant with freedom. In an instant, he realized his life
was forever changed. Forever changed by his lovely Rose.

"Do you want me to leave?" Taylor asked, her tone apol-
ogetic.

Instead, Jackson sat up in the tub, a boyish grin on his
face. "Actually, I was thinking about adding a pail of hot
water to the tub and inviting you to join me."

Gladness bubbled in Taylor's laugh and shone in her
eyes. She rose from her chair and knelt next to the tub,
leaning her face close to him.

Reaching out with one hand, Jackson cupped her chin to
draw her closer to him. As his lips pressed to hers, he
caressed her mouth, coaxing the sweetness from them and
drinking deeply.

Taylor felt her knees weaken at his tender touch and soon
found her fingers entwined in his damp curls. Her senses
reeled as she felt her passions roused. Gently, she pulled
away, breathless with desire.

"What's wrong?" he whispered.

"Nothing. I just wasn't prepared to . . . I was afraid to
hope that everything would be all right between us."

Jackson smiled. "I wasn't prepared either. All I know is
how I feel—how you make me feel." Firmly, he clutched
both Taylor's hands in his.

As she stared deeply into his azure eyes, now as calm as
the sea on a windless summer day, she whispered, "Jackson." Then dropped her head, closing her eyes.

"Tell me what's wrong." The sudden apprehension he
felt in her intruded on the tender moment, and he watched
her face lose its brightness and grow serious.

Two deep lines of worry appeared between her eyes as
she struggled with whatever she was thinking about. "The
other problem with my being here," she began, "is that I'm
not at all sure if I'm going back to my own time . . . or if
I'll be staying here."

"I see."

"Every time I've asked my father if he knows, I never get a straight answer."

"And what do you want to happen?"

"I really hadn't allowed myself to wish one way or the other, but now . . . now, I want to stay." Taylor's voice was velvet-edged and strong.

"Then stay," he responded matter-of-factly, "as long as you can. The one thing I think we've both experienced is the power of determination, right? Well, we have this moment, this night. And you're here now."

Taylor nodded, her fingers tightening against his hands.

His voice smooth, but insistent, he continued. "I've spent the last few years on a mission of revenge, only looking to the end result of that mission. I never allowed myself to enjoy any particular day—just to forget what my life was about and relax, stop worrying. Never, at least, until we shared that afternoon at the beach."

Taylor's cheeks colored.

"It was the first time in a very long time." Jackson's voice grew quiet. "I took a chance and let myself feel what it was actually like to truly experience the day, truly experience being with someone. I want to feel that again. And I want to feel it with you—whether this is meant to be the last time we're together . . . or the beginning of a lifetime together. That's how I feel."

A soft and loving curve touched Taylor's lips as she returned his loving gaze. She released his hands and stood slowly. "I'll bring the water. Make room for one more."

Chapter 26

JACKSON DREW HIS knees to his chest to make room for her, as Taylor brought over a bucket of water from the wood stove and poured it in the tub. Waves of hot water soon sent fresh clouds of steam into the early evening coolness.

Taylor sat on a chair at the foot of the tub and slipped off her shoes. She watched Jackson's left eyebrow rise a fraction of an inch, and his eyes glowed with an inner fire.

"Shall I light some candles? It'll be getting dark soon." Taylor blushed at her own excitement, anticipating the delight of feeling Jackson's skin next to hers in the warm water.

Jackson nodded.

Taylor's hand trembled as she fumbled with the box of matches on the table. She took out a thick kitchen match and after three tries, finally succeeded in striking it into a flame.

First she lit a thin, hand-rolled wax candle, then used it to light the other candles scattered on the tables next to the tub.

The light from each flame bathed her profile in an ethereal glow, and her eyes shimmered with reflected candlelight.

"That's nice," Jackson murmured, "but you should hurry. The water's cooling."

Taylor reached behind her back and unbuttoned her dress. In one smooth movement, she let it fall to the floor and stood before him wearing only a pair of delicate pink silk French-cut bikini panties.

Jackson's gaze was riveted on her face. He breathed in sharply at the sight of her, then allowed his gaze to move slowly down her body. The candlelight cast just a hint of a glow that made Taylor's skin look like peach-tinted cream. His gaze stopped lovingly at her small, high-perched breasts, each nipple already taut. His fingers flexed eagerly at the thought of touching them again.

Taylor returned his smile, then shuddered with pleasure and slid off her panties, leaving them on the floor. Then she quickly stepped into the tub. The water was hot enough to send goosebumps up her legs, and her nipples hardened even more with the flush of contrasting temperature. She eased into the water facing him, and pulled her knees to her chest. The water felt delicious and she closed her eyes, breathing the soothing, fragrant vapors rising from the bath.

"No wonder you looked so comfortable; this is heaven," she murmured.

Jackson grinned. "It is now."

Taylor's mouth curved into a secretive smile. "I agree."

Jackson reached for a bar of soap and slowly began lathering a washcloth. "Since I've already bathed, why don't you turn around and I will very generously wash your back, my dear."

Taylor obeyed, her shoulders relaxing at the touch of the soaped cloth on her back. In sensuous circles, he rubbed her skin, then draped the cloth over the side of the tub. His hands massaged her soapy shoulders and neck.

"Lean back a little. Let me wash your hair."

Taylor purred an affirmative reply, straightened her elbows for support, and leaned back.

With great care and gentleness, Jackson dipped a cup into the bathwater to pour water on her short hair until it glistened like polished cherrywood. He meticulously soaped and massaged her locks, fascinated by the silkiness of her hair and how easily his hands slipped through its short layers. Supporting her neck, he carefully rinsed the soap away.

Moaning with contentment, Taylor muttered huskily, "That felt wonderful; you have such a gentle touch." Sitting up, she smoothed her hair back and squeezed out the excess moisture, then stretched like a contented cat.

Jackson extended his legs along her hips and gently pulled her back against him, wrapping his arms around her protectively.

"And this feels even more wonderful," she said softly.

Jackson sighed in agreement. He affectionately hugged Taylor snugly and then slightly shifted his position so that her body was cradled between his legs, his chin resting on the top of her head.

She felt so secure in his embrace. Heaven indeed, she thought.

In the warmth of the water, it was difficult to feel the distinction between their bodies. Skin melted into skin. Their bodies molded against each other as each curve nestled against a corresponding curve.

Jackson lay his cheek against Taylor's head and loosened his hold, freeing his right hand. Soon she felt his fingers run deliciously up and down her forearm, causing shivers of delight.

Her pulse quickened as his hand abandoned her arm to fondle first one breast, and then the other. Gently, his hand outlined the circle of her breasts, then squeezed and massaged each, caressing each nipple until both were swollen and sensitive. His touch was light and painfully teasing, and Taylor let out a long, audible breath.

Shifting their position so he rested on one hip, he eased

her more deeply into the water, allowing greater freedom for his sensuous exploration. Curled against the curve of his body, Taylor rested her cheek against Jackson's shoulder, permitting herself to relax totally.

Jackson ignored his own aching hardness to search further for pleasure points on the silken body of his beautiful Rose. His hand slid down her taut stomach to her thigh, gently moving down the length of her leg as far as he could reach.

He stroked her leg, kneading his fingers along the back of her thigh, massaging and teasing until Taylor moaned. Returning again to her belly, Jackson paused there, gently rubbing in a circular motion, slowly expanding the circle until his fingertips touched the silky mound of dark hair at the juncture of her thighs.

Taylor gasped, then bit her bottom lip in anticipation of his touch. She knew she was already slick with wanting him. Currents of desire radiated from between her legs and the focus of her world narrowed to include only her own ache for his intimate touch. She focused on the all-encompassing sensation of true, passionate desire. A delicious quiver signaled the ecstatic eruption to come.

Jackson's fingers rested at the top of the silky mound of hair, and he waited. She beckoned his touch by gently guiding his hand to the core of her desire, instantly causing her to gasp with pleasure. Intimately, she directed his eager fingers to massage the essence of her passion in soft, kneading circles.

Taylor's body squirmed, writhing gently with the movement of the sensuous massage, her arousal growing quickly. She moaned as Jackson's tongue found her ear and nibbled its edge hungrily.

"I need you, Rose," Jackson whispered.

Before she could respond, Jackson increased the pressure of his massage, causing Taylor to gasp in surprise. Fully aroused and in divine agony, she felt the swell of ecstasy build to a pinnacle of overwhelming intensity. Deep within, an erotic throbbing began its runaway journey. Eagerly she followed it over the edge until the flames of passion consumed her, sending wave upon wave of rapture through her. She rocked against Jackson's hand with each delicious spasm, hoping to clench it forever between her thighs.

The physical satisfaction of her release was more than Taylor could handle, and a tear of happiness found its way down her moist cheek. She wiped it away with a wrinkled fingertip and rolled over in the water so that her body lay on Jackson's, his hardness nestled in the soft of her belly.

With her hands on his shoulders, slowly Taylor pulled herself up to claim his lips. She gave herself to the passion of the kiss, sending echoing spirals of ecstasy through her.

Jackson moaned. He was burning with desire and devoured her lips with reckless abandon. When Taylor parted her lips he eagerly explored the recesses of her mouth, tasting her sweetness.

Breathlessly, they finally parted.

"Please . . . let's move to the bed. I want to make you feel what I feel," she pleaded.

Jackson reached for a towel. As they both stood and stepped out of the tub, he ached for her touch and, as though she could read his thoughts, Taylor reached for him. He draped a towel over her shoulders, moaning at her loving stroke, feeling as though he would explode any moment. He hugged her close and dried her back.

Taylor gently pushed away and took the towel from her shoulders, putting it between them. "Let me dry you a little," she said huskily.

Looking deeply into Jackson's heavily lidded eyes, Taylor toweled his chest and stomach, then dropped to her knees. Quickly she dried his feet, legs, and thighs. To Jackson's surprise, Taylor cradled his erection with the towel, then grasped him and drew him fully into her hot, moist mouth.

Taylor felt Jackson's knees quiver as she pulled her mouth away to tease the tip of him with her lips. When he was fully engorged, she left his shaft and kissed her way up Jackson's flat stomach, making her way through his inky black chest curls to his swollen and hungry mouth. The passion of his kiss sent the pit of her stomach into a wild swirl.

Again he moaned, this time a deep, primal sound. A brief shiver rippled through Jackson and his flesh prickled pleasurably wherever her skin touched his. Effortlessly, he slipped his arm under her legs and carried her to the feather bed. Without releasing her, he turned back the quilt and sheet, then gently placed her in the bed. She lay back, desire blazing in her eyes.

Loose tendrils of chestnut brown fringed her face, making her look younger than her years. Her eyes glowed with emerald fire, urging him to join her. Jackson climbed into the bed and gathered her into his arms, holding her snugly. Taylor buried her face against his neck, exploring its curve with her tongue, quickly stoking the fire of their passion.

Taylor looked deeply into Jackson's eyes. Her body tingled from the contact of his skin against hers, deliciously conscious of where his warm, damp flesh touched her. Nudging Jackson onto his back, she lay on top and reclaimed his lips. Divine ecstasy, simultaneously sweet and smoldering, and her lips burned with his fiery possession. While they kissed, she rubbed her body against his hardness until they both groaned with wanting.

When at last they parted, Taylor swiftly slid upward to straddle him, briefly rising to her knees to position him between her molten legs. She sank against his arousal, moaning aloud with pleasure. His hardness electrified her, and she ground her hips against his in immediate, uncontrolled desire.

A bright flame sprang into Jackson's eyes as he grasped Taylor's narrow hips to lessen her movements. "Please," he begged, "slow down . . . I want to enjoy you for a while."

Taylor controlled her thrusting hips and slowed to a more bearable rhythm. Seductively, she leaned forward, bringing her swollen breasts within tongue's reach, longing for his touch.

He eagerly kissed her taut nipples, then drew one bud into his mouth, softly sucking and drawing on it until she moaned. He withdrew his mouth gently and turned his attention to the other swollen nipple. Drawing the bud into his mouth, he lavished it lovingly, rhythmically sucking.

Groaning, she pulled away and once more sank against him until he disappeared within her. Again, she ground her hips against his. This time, he grasped her waist, encouraging her rhythm to take him to a higher level of ecstasy. Their bodies were in exquisite harmony; the tempo of their lovemaking spun their world in sweet agony.

A moan escaped Jackson's lips as he hurtled beyond the point of no return, embracing the hot tide of passion that raged between them.

As Taylor felt the liquid honey of Jackson's seed fill her, she joined him in the shared moment of uncontrolled, shuddering ecstasy. Stars exploded in a universe that transcended time and space.

Jackson's whole being flooded with joy, and he savored the feeling of a lover's satisfaction. As Taylor slumped against his chest, he held her tightly against him. They lay for a long moment before either dared speak.

Jackson swallowed hard and cleared his throat. "I've never felt like this before," he began, "it's never been like this."

Taylor smiled against the soft hairs of his chest. "It almost felt . . . dangerous . . . didn't it?"

"Too good to be true, perhaps. I've just never felt so . . . strongly before, Rose. Did you feel it, too?"

"Yes. Like we were meant to be together. There were times when I couldn't tell us apart. Our bodies were so joined—it felt like we would never be apart again."

"And I don't want us to be apart. You'll stay with me tonight, won't you?" Jackson didn't attempt to hide the apprehension in his voice.

"Of course," Taylor replied. "There's nowhere I'd rather be than with you—right here, right now." Burying her face in his neck, she breathed a kiss there, sighing with contentment.

Jackson drew Taylor closer and wrapped his arms snugly around her. She still grasped his spent manhood inside her, and he felt a oneness, a belonging that he'd stopped dreaming he'd ever find. He knew things would never be the same now . . . now that he had fallen in love.

Chapter 27

T AYLOR'S EYES BLINKED open, immediately confused—not quite sure where she was. A split second later,
though, she realized she was snuggled against Jackson,
whose own eyes slowly blinked open. A lazy smile curved
his lips upward and he pulled her close in an affectionate
squeeze.

"You're still here," he murmured and kissed her forehead.

Before she could reply, Taylor's stomach rumbled noisily, sending them both into fits of laughter.

"Well, I can't help it," she explained, "I'm hungry."

"And, hopefully, I'm partly responsible for giving you a
good appetite," Jackson added.

Taylor turned her head and glanced at the food tray on
the table. "Well, I did bring a dinner tray last night."

"All right, my hungry one, let's have a snack and rebuild
our strength." Jackson's smile changed to a wicked grin as
he dramatically threw the covers back.

Taylor playfully jumped out of bed and raced to the table
where she had placed the dinner tray. Jackson followed,

pausing to pull on his trousers and grab his shirt for her to wear.

"Here you go, put this on so you won't catch a chill."

She slipped her arms into the sleeves of his shirt and turned to face him. With unexpected delicacy, he fastened each button while she stood silently, captivated by his dainty movements.

Answering her quizzical expression, Jackson smiled and said, "Toward the end of my mother's illness, I had to help her a lot. I dressed her and fed her; took care of her as best I could." Jackson's voice reflected his loss and a look of tired sadness passed over his features.

Taylor wrapped her arms around Jackson's waist and pulled him to her in a long embrace. She could actually feel the grief in his body—his muscles felt tense, restrained, tired.

She held him until she felt his body relax—years of stress and worry eased just a little. It was a beginning.

"She was lucky to have you there with her. You were a good son."

"I don't know . . . it just seems like she shouldn't have died, you know? Such a horrible sickness, a horrible way to die."

Silently, Taylor agreed. And, she thought, if his mother had been living in *Taylor's* time, she probably wouldn't have died of tuberculosis at all.

"Come on," Taylor said, hoping to shake away the lingering gloom, "let's have a bite to eat. Dinner should taste just as good for breakfast—and, besides, we need to keep our strength up, right?"

"Yes, we do," Jackson answered. He gave Taylor a squeeze before he released her and sat at the table.

Taylor busied herself fixing two heaping plates of food from the feast that Maylee had prepared, and soon both were happily enjoying roast beef and cabbage salad.

Jackson watched with amusement as Taylor eagerly consumed all the food on her plate and reached for a piece of cake. "No wonder your stomach was growling—you look like you haven't eaten in a week." Jackson laughed as Taylor's cheeks reddened.

Gracefully, Taylor wiped the crumbs from the corners of her mouth. "Well, I've been a bit preoccupied lately solving mysteries—so who had time to eat, anyway? Now," Taylor asked teasingly, "are you gonna eat that piece of cake or what?"

"Touch my cake and lose your hand," Jackson said as he grabbed the plate and moved his dessert out of Taylor's reach. It felt good to have a meal like this, he thought. Having fun, good company, feeling at ease with life. He realized he hadn't felt this way since he'd been a child . . . long before his mother's illness had taken hold. The food tasted wonderful. He felt happy. He wasn't worrying about anything. This must be what life was supposed to feel like, he mused.

Taylor moved her empty plate out of the way and watched Jackson finish his meal. Positioning her elbows on the table, she held her chin in her hands and stared at the devastatingly handsome man sitting across from her. His wavy black hair was messy from being in bed, and she wanted to bury her fingers in the silky curls. A dark shadow of whiskers had formed on his face. His eyes were the turquoise blue of tropical ocean water, still and deep. She wanted to look into those eyes forever, but she knew she'd better enjoy the chance she had right now . . . just in case.

Jackson lifted his eyes from his plate and stared back at Taylor. Her emerald eyes seemed filled with questions and he readied himself.

"Go ahead," he said.

"What?"

"Ask me whatever it is that you're thinking about," he replied, pushing his plate away. "It's all right."

Taylor blinked, as though trying to isolate one thought, one question. "Well, I was really just enjoying being with you and hoping it wouldn't end."

"And?"

"And," she continued, "I guess I was sort of memorizing your face. I'm feeling just a little insecure, I suppose, because I'm not sure where we stand . . . with each other. . . ." Taylor's voice faded to a whisper. She hadn't realized how fearful she had become in the face of the fact that she might not be with Jackson forever.

"And there's no way your father can tell you if you're staying, right? So there's really nothing we can do to change whatever is going to happen. I may be simplifying things a little, but I was raised to believe that if it's something you can do something about, do it. If it's something you can't, then live with it."

Taylor nodded. She was beginning to understand the comfort in the simplistic conventions of the era. And it really wasn't that much different from many people's philosophies in her own time, she thought. Jackson's drive to avenge what he had perceived as the wrongful death of his father was plainly a matter of seeing that consequences were paid.

"Shit!" Jackson slapped his hand on the table, causing Taylor to gasp in surprise. "I've got to go talk to Mr. Earp and warn him about the McLaurey brothers! Now that should be one interesting conversation. . . ." Jackson closed his eyes, shaking his head.

He was right, Taylor thought. There was more explaining to do.

Eyes now wide with worry, Jackson scooted his chair back and began pacing the floor. "He'll probably have me thrown in jail before I can even get the whole story out. What'll I tell him to make him understand?"

"Well, Jackson, what are you doing here on your day off?" Wyatt Earp was behind the bar when Jackson and Taylor walked in the door of the saloon. He had a soft spot in his heart for the young man, and he had been devastated when his wife had come to him with some crazy story about his bartender getting involved with the McLaurey boys. He had reassured her that he would confront Jackson with her accusations and get to the bottom of things at the next opportunity.

And it looked like opportunity had just walked through the door.

"Mr. Earp, this is Rose Martin. Could we have a few words with you?"

Wyatt stepped out from behind the bar to extend his hand to Taylor. "Pleased to meet you, Miss Martin." Wyatt gazed into Taylor's eyes and squinted at their familiarity. "Have we met somewhere before, ma'am?"

Taylor smiled, grasping the marshal's hand firmly. "Well, sort of. . . ." She pointed at one of the tables toward the back of the gambling area. "Shall we sit?"

Jackson followed Taylor's lead and walked toward the table. When they were all seated, he cleared his throat and hoped that he would choose the right words to convince Earp that he was no longer interested in killing him. As he began, he felt Taylor's hand on his knee, squeezing it with encouragement.

When Wyatt had heard the entire outlandish story of the murderous plot, he leaned back in his chair and placed his hands behind his neck. "Well, I'll be," he began, "I guess Josie was right about you being up to something with the McLaurey boys."

Jackson looked at Taylor in surprise, then brought his gaze back to Wyatt. "How did she know?"

"She said she followed you one night over to the Acme Saloon. I guess she heard you talkin' to them and finally came to tell me about it."

"So, *she* followed me that night too. I was so sure that someone was following me, but I thought Rose was the only one."

"Well, I promised Josie I'd get to the bottom of it, and I guess we just did, didn't we? I thought San Diego might be different," Wyatt said. "I thought I might have gotten away from all the darn fools with crazy plans to gun me down."

Taylor examined Earp's face for hints of his real reaction to the murder plot. His expression had hardly changed during the entire conversation, making his mood difficult to peg.

"So, I guess we ought to either find the two scoundrels or come up with a plan to stop them." Wyatt glanced first at Jackson and then at Taylor. "Any ideas, you two?"

"Well," Jackson began, "there's no way for me to contact them at this point. That's the problem. We're set for this Saturday night."

"But I can't have them arrested just for coming in the place," Wyatt muttered, "and I sure don't want to give them another chance, even if I do scare 'em off."

"This is probably not what you had in mind," said Taylor, "but have you considered allowing them to come in, let them just get to the point where they are arguing and Jackson is supposed to pull his gun . . . and *then* have them arrested for conspiracy to murder? Jackson, you'd have to testify—"

"Not a problem. I'd be happy to."

Wyatt rubbed his chin thoughtfully. Not the best idea in the world, he thought, but it would be the only real way to foil the plan and send a clear message to the McLaurey boys. "And you think we can pull this off safely?"

Jackson and Taylor exchanged serious looks, then both nodded their answer.

"Well, so be it," declared Wyatt. His face erupted into a warm smile as Josie suddenly appeared in the doorway next to the end of the bar.

"And I agree," Josie confirmed as she walked toward the threesome at the table, her face radiating relief and determination.

"Ah, Sadie," Wyatt said, using his pet name for her, "won't you join us?" He rose from his chair and pulled another out for his wife. "You've been eavesdropping, have you?"

"Well, what do you expect? Someone around here has to be concerned about fools wanting to gun you down right and left."

"And you exaggerate, my darling." Wyatt scowled good-naturedly at Josie. He longed to escape the notoriety his past had created, and had hoped that San Diego would be a place where he could settle down. Now he was unsure. The city was getting too big. Too many people. Perhaps they would stay long enough to cash in on his real estate investments and move on, he thought, and find a quiet place out in the desert somewhere.

Taylor regarded the affectionate arguing between Wyatt and Josie. Their love for each other was indisputable, evident in the sparkle in their eyes and the electricity they produced together.

Finally taking her attention away from Wyatt, Josie turned to Rose and extended her hand. "It's good to see you again, Rose, and I'm certainly glad the circumstances are positive. I was a bit worried about your connection to all of this, you know."

Taylor took Josie's hand in hers and replied, "And I'm glad that all the pieces fell into place before something dreadful happened . . . believe me."

Josie patted Taylor's hand in an almost motherly way.

Though both women were close to the same age, Josie's twenty-four had seen the rough and ragged days of the real Wild West. She had aged emotionally due to her experiences, but her exterior portrayed a young, exotic temptress in love with a legendary lawman.

"I have a feeling everything will work out just fine," Josie said. She suddenly felt a connection to Taylor—for some unexplained reason, she sensed that the woman sitting next to her was somehow very important—important in an obscure way.

Another mystery.

Chapter 28

Wᴵˡˡ MᶜLᴀᴜʀᴇʏ ʟᴇᴀɴᴇᴅ casually against the corner of the building across the street from Wyatt Earp's gambling saloon, then pulled out his pocket watch to check the time. He'd sent Dean into the saloon fifteen minutes ago to help add to the illusion that they didn't know one another.

Will shook his head in frustration, and his stomach tightened nervously as he walked to the back of the building to check the getaway horses for the fifth and final time. All three horses were still tied securely to the rail, though, just to be safe, he inspected each of them one last time.

No detail too small, he thought. He still had regrets about bringing Dean into the plan. He was too young, too jumpy. He'd be glad when they were on their horses and leaving San Diego in their dust.

Then he would relax, and not until then.

Satisfied that the horses were secure, he made his way back to the street. With his shoulders square and his head held high, he entered the noisy saloon. The smell of cigar smoke and whiskey assaulted his nostrils as he shouldered his way through the crowd to the bar.

Though much more sedate in comparison to the raucous mob at the Acme Saloon, the bar was still boisterous and filled to capacity, with every gambling table engaged.

Jackson, busy behind the bar with customers, glanced up just in time to meet Will's stare. He nodded to Will and watched him make his way to the faro table in the back of the room. Next, Jackson looked to the end of the bar and met the stare of Wyatt Earp.

Wyatt stood nonchalantly at the opposite end of the bar, a perfect vantage point from which to observe the activity in the room.

From Jackson's descriptions of the McLaurey brothers, Wyatt had recognized young Dean the moment he'd entered the saloon. He'd watched him order a beer at the bar and quickly get settled at the faro table, just as planned. He seemed awfully green to be involved in such a murderous plot, Wyatt thought. But he was a McLaurey, he reminded himself.

When Will came in, Wyatt felt his skin crawl. It would be a pleasure indeed to see his ugly face behind bars, he thought. He hoped to God things would go smoothly. Will McLaurey was a dangerous man.

"Excuse me, sir." Taylor's cheerful voice interrupted Wyatt's serious thoughts.

Taylor was dressed in a red satin dress she'd borrowed from Josie, and she had transformed herself into the stereotypical "Wild West waitress." Setting down a tray full of glasses on a table nearby, she too saw that both McLaurey brothers had arrived. *God, I hope this goes well.*

Wyatt gave Taylor a slight grin and a wink of acknowledgment. He hoped the young woman had the sense to stay on this side of the room when things erupted. Though he had been dead against having Taylor so close to a potentially dangerous situation, he had decided to follow his hunch that, for some reason, this stranger was supposed to be there. At least Josie was safe in the back, he thought, as far away from the action as possible.

Wyatt began to make his way toward the back of the room, where Dean and Will sat next to each other at the faro table. A half dozen men were seated at the card table, while onlookers watched the game and cheered on the winners of each hand.

Wyatt flinched at the sound of a gunshot in the distance, a forewarning of what might be happening within the next few moments.

As he paused at the end of the bar, Wyatt slid the door of a hidden panel built into the face of the gleaming mahogany wood. Tucked inside was his Buntline Special. He hadn't had to retrieve it until now. With one smooth movement, Wyatt tucked the gun inside his coat and closed the panel to the hidden shelf.

At the same moment that Wyatt retrieved the hidden weapon, Jackson felt his stomach lurch.

Time to get ready.

Taking his place at the end of the bar closest to the card tables, he waited for Dean and Will to begin their staged fight—his signal to join them.

Taylor felt a sudden chill as she watched Wyatt tuck his gun into his coat. It was really happening, she realized. Maybe this wasn't such a great idea after all. . . .

"I'm here, and don't you try anything heroic."

Comforted by her father's response and parental concern, Taylor breathed a sigh of relief. She wondered if everything would turn out all right. She wondered if her father knew.

Dad—what if . . . ? As soon as Taylor began the thought, she felt her father's presence disappear. Believe in a positive outcome. Believe in a positive outcome. In her mind, the phrase repeated itself like a mantra as Taylor looked for a safe place to wait, hopefully out of harm's way.

"Hey, keep your stinkin' hands away from my chips!" Dean bellowed, his voice rough with anxiety.

It was time.

"Shut up and place your bet," Will growled. He had noticed Wyatt move closer to them and he could see that Jackson was watching from the end of the bar. So far, so good, he thought.

At that moment, Dean gave him a shove, knocking him off his chair to the floor. The crowd around the table took a step away from the scuffle, sensing the confrontation was about to escalate into a brawl.

Will gave Dean's chair leg a swift kick, sending him scrambling to his feet.

"I'll teach you—" Dean sputtered, dropping to the floor to fake a choke hold on Will.

Taylor watched the scene as if it were happening in slow motion. Both of the McLaurey brothers were on the floor fighting as Jackson made his way out from behind the bar. He had pulled the small revolver out from his vest pocket, just as the McLaureys expected.

When Wyatt arrived at the faro table, he pulled his Buntline Special from beneath his coat. And Dean turned his head to stare at the legendary lawman, just as planned.

Will could see Jackson standing directly behind Wyatt, his revolver drawn and pointed at the back of the marshal's head. *By God, the kid was going to do it.* Maybe he'd misjudged him after all.

"Kill him, Jackson!" Dean shouted. "Kill the murdering bastard!"

Will winced as he heard his brother's words. "Shut up, you idiot!" With Dean's hands still clenched around his throat, Will pushed himself up onto his elbows. Suddenly, he sensed an unexpected movement. Stars exploded and his head filled with the searing pain of metal against his skull as he realized the marshal had brought a gun butt against the side of his head.

The blow knocked Will out cold.

With a frightened gasp, Dean released his hold on his brother's neck and watched helplessly as Will's head hit the floor with a sickening thud. *Something was wrong!* Why hadn't Jackson shot the marshal when he'd had the chance? He looked up in time to see Jackson lower his revolver and grin at Earp. *Double-crossed,* Dean's mind roared.

With the fury of a cornered rat, Dean flung himself toward Wyatt, knocking him off-balance just long enough to make a leap toward the doorway to the back room.

Dean McLaurey disappeared into the hallway—the hallway where Josie was watching the events through a peephole.

Simultaneously, Jackson and Wyatt turned to follow Dean. Each having the same thought, each hoping that Josie had moved from the hallway in time.

With a painful smack, Dean ran directly into Josie Earp. Her piercing scream sent a shot of adrenaline through him and he angrily clapped his hand over her mouth.

"Shut up!"

"Let her go!" Wyatt shouted from the end of the hall.

With surprising grace, Dean ducked behind Josie and swung her around so that she faced Wyatt. She became an instant shield to Wyatt's pointed gun. With one arm around Josie's waist and the other tightly around her neck, Dean began to back away slowly.

"Stay away from me," he warned, his voice cracking with the strain of his growing panic. Pointing at the crowd gathering in the hallway, Dean sputtered, "No-nobody comes near me. Get them away from me!"

Wyatt motioned for the curious onlookers to move out of the hall and back into the saloon. "I'll handle this," he assured them. "Get back inside."

With his gaze locked on his love, Wyatt waited helplessly while Jackson and Taylor stood silently behind him.

The three of them watched as Dean backed his way into an open room, slamming the door closed.

Slowly, Wyatt dropped his gun. *How had this happened? This wasn't supposed to happen.*

"What do we do?" Taylor whispered.

Wyatt brought a finger to his lips, and motioned for Taylor to stay put while he and Jackson inched their way down the hall. Floorboards creaked ominously as they walked slowly toward the closed door.

Wyatt hoped he could talk some sense into the boy, desperately searching for the words that would convince him to let Josie go.

Jackson took his position on one side of the door, while Wyatt stood almost directly in front of the door.

They waited, heads cocked, listening.

Inside the dimly lit storeroom, Dean stood in the center of the room, his arm still tight around Josie's neck.

"Just let me go . . . please." Josie's voice was a hoarse whisper as she struggled to speak. As she felt Dean's hold tighten around her neck, the room seemed to darken a little.

"Shut up! Shut up! Shut up!" Dean fought the feeling of rancid beer threatening to erupt from his throat. He felt sick to his stomach and the terror of the moment threatened to overwhelm him.

"You just shut up! I can't think!" He tightened his hold on Josie's neck even more. From the other side of the door, Dean heard a soft knock, then Wyatt's voice.

"Just let her go, son. You're in over your head. There's not much you can do, now, is there? Be smart and open the door. Let her come out . . . then we'll have us a talk." Wyatt's voice sounded firm and fearless. His body betrayed him, though, and he wiped the sweat from his forehead.

He glanced at Jackson, who nodded his reassurance.

Josie whimpered softly, her hands clutching at Dean's arm at her throat.

"Shut *up!*" Dean's adrenaline shot out of control as he squeezed his arm against Josie's neck. Moments passed before he realized that he was supporting her dead weight in his arms.

In a sickening moment of panic, he let Josie's lifeless body slide to the floor.

A low moan escaped from his clenched lips as he real--ized that Josie was no longer breathing. Sweat poured down his face as he whirled around, looking for anything he might use as a weapon. He felt completely defenseless as he searched the room.

Seconds later, his gaze stopped at the window at the far end of the room. He sensed movement. Sliding himself along the wall, Dean made his way closer to investigate.

Outside, three horses stood calmly waiting. The getaway horses.

Without hesitation, Dean dove through the glass of the window just as Wyatt and Jackson burst into the room, guns drawn.

Chapter 29

AT THE SOUND of the breaking glass, Taylor ran full tilt down the hall to the room, ignoring Wyatt's instructions to stay put. She followed the men into the room, calling Josie's name.

Jackson ran to the window, just as Dean jumped onto one of the horses and rode furiously down the street. There had been no time to get reinforcements, so Dean made a clean getaway.

Wyatt dropped to his knees next to the lifeless body of his wife. "Oh, my God . . . *no!*" The pain in his voice was heartwrenching.

Taylor rushed to Josie's body, quickly assessing her condition as critical. "Jackson, turn up the lamp! I need more light here."

Jackson quickly obliged, bringing the oil lamp to Taylor, startled at the command in her voice.

With Wyatt and Jackson looking on in astonishment, Taylor checked Josie's airway, tilted her head back, and placed her ear over Josie's mouth. Quickly she pinched Josie's nose shut and blew into her mouth twice. Next, she felt for a pulse. Nothing.

"Josie's not breathing, I need to start CPR—"

"What are you talking about?" Wyatt interrupted.

"Please, you've got to trust me," Taylor explained in a low, composed voice. "I might be able to . . . bring Josie back—start her breathing again."

Wyatt and Jackson exchanged confused looks.

"Let her try," Jackson said. "She's a trained healer . . . a nurse . . . she knows things."

Wyatt nodded. Then he moved out of Taylor's way as he watched her place the heel of her hand on his wife's chest, place the other hand on top, and interlace her fingers.

With her arms straight and her shoulders directly over her hands, Taylor began pushing on Josie's chest.

A cracking sound disturbed the tense silence and Wyatt lunged at Taylor.

"You're hurting her!"

Jackson grabbed Wyatt as Taylor continued her compressions.

"I have to push this hard. Her ribs might be cracked but it's the only way," she explained.

Wyatt watched as Taylor again tilted Josie's head, pinched her nose, and breathed into her mouth. The glow of the lamplight cast a halo around Taylor and Josie, and suddenly Wyatt was convinced that this stranger was actually breathing the life back into his lovely wife.

He relaxed against Jackson's arms and watched with amazement as Taylor continued to push on Josie's chest.

After four cycles of compressions and rescue breaths, Taylor checked Josie's pulse.

Nothing.

Her own heart was beating hard against her chest and she had begun to perspire. Only once in her nursing career had she administered CPR, but she had been relieved within moments by paramedics.

This time, she realized, there was no one else to assist her.

"Come on, Josie . . . *breathe*," Taylor pleaded as she completed another cycle of compressions.

Wyatt stared as Taylor placed her fingers on the side of Josie's neck. He mimicked her position, placing his fingers on his own neck and felt his panicked heartbeat pounding out of control. "Sadie," he whispered, "come back to me."

At the same instant, in her mind Taylor heard the soothing sound of her mother's voice.

"She's coming back. It's not her time."

All at once, there was a pulse under Taylor's fingers.

Josie's eyes blinked open and her chest rose triumphantly with her first breath.

"Josie!" Wyatt called out, afraid to believe his eyes. Though only moments had passed, it had felt to him like a lifetime. It was a miracle. His Josie was alive.

Wide-eyed, Josie reached out to Wyatt and he gingerly embraced her. Even his gentle touch caused her to gasp in pain, and tears flowed down her cheeks.

With a hoarse voice, she asked, "What happened? My chest hurts. What happened to me?"

"Your ribs are probably cracked," Taylor confirmed. "They should heal fine. You can bind them if you like . . . then just rest." Taylor helped Wyatt scoop Josie up into his arms, wincing in empathy at Josie's pain.

Wyatt's eyes brimmed with unshed tears and gratitude. "I am forever indebted to you, Rose. How can I ever repay you for bringing my Sadie back to me?"

Taylor beamed, her own eyes filling with happy tears. "You belong together . . . and you deserve the miracle. Go home and make her rest. She'll be sore for several days, but other than that, she should be just fine."

Wyatt looked at Jackson, unable to speak.

"I'll look after things here," Jackson offered. "Take Josie home—do as Rose says. She knows what's best."

Wyatt nodded. "Close the place down for tonight and tomorrow. Then come talk to me . . . I'm thinking you'd make a pretty good partner, Jackson. And besides, I'm ready to find a smaller town to live in anyway. Someplace where it's harder for these fools to find me." Wyatt smiled at Josie, limp in his arms.

"Let's go home," Josie whispered, a weak smile on her pale face.

"This is the last of them," Taylor declared as she brought a tray of dirty glasses to Jackson.

After Wyatt had taken Josie home to recuperate, Jackson had closed the saloon down. Grumbling, the crowd had hoped for at least drinks on the house to top off their exciting evening.

Instead, Jackson had directed them to carry the still-unconscious Will McLaurey off to jail and keep on going to the next saloon. He and Taylor had plenty of work to do before they too could go home.

Taylor sighed. Even busily washing and drying glasses behind the bar Jackson looked devastatingly handsome. His black curls fell lusciously onto his damp forehead, and his arm muscles flexed with the mundane movement of rubbing each glass dry. The night was warm and Jackson had unbuttoned his shirt to the waist. Silky black chest hair threatened to make Taylor melt with desire.

Jackson met Taylor's dreamy gaze. Her eyes were heavy-lidded and seductive, and he felt his arousal stir instantly at the intensity of her gaze.

Taylor's smile indicated that she was well aware of the effect her gaze had on him. "Can we go soon?"

Nodding his approval, Jackson abruptly stopped his cleaning. It had been a long night. Glasses could wait until tomorrow, he decided.

Taylor raced through the saloon and blew out all the lamps while Jackson grabbed the set of keys from behind the bar, then smoothly locked up the cash drawer and the expensive liquor cabinet.

Taking Taylor's hand in his, he said, "Let's go home."

Arm in arm, Taylor and Jackson strolled along the boardwalk to Ida's. The night air was cool and refreshing. Summer aromas drifted around them, signaling fertile ground and lush flowers.

Nearing the Gaslamp Quarter Hotel, Taylor tugged at Jackson's arm to direct him to Ida's via the alley that passed by Maylee's kitchen door.

"I want to stop a minute and see if Maylee is still up," she explained. "I don't know about you, but a midnight snack sounds good."

Jackson laughed good-naturedly. "Well, at least I don't have to worry about your appetite," he said. He was a little surprised at Taylor's revelry about eating, but he'd decided it was an improvement over the typical finicky style of most women he'd known.

Taylor's peculiarities, once he got used to them, had begun to feel rather comfortable, and he wondered if she were as comfortable with the ways of 1888. Looking forward to talking more with her about what things were like in her time, Jackson smiled at his ravenous beauty as Taylor knocked softly at the kitchen door of the hotel.

The door opened just a crack and Maylee peeked out at them. "Rose, is that you? Well, my goodness, you're out awfully late this evening. Is that Jackson with you there?"

"We didn't wake you, did we?" Taylor asked.

"Heavens, no. In fact, I was just having a bite to eat before I headed off to bed. I'm spending the night here— lucky for you." Maylee chuckled as she opened the door for her late-night visitors.

The kitchen table was already laid out with thick slices of bread, cheese, and pieces of chicken. A raspberry pie and ginger cookies completed the choices.

Taylor's stomach rumbled loudly.

"Well, come in, you two, and keep me company. Let me take the kettle off the stove for tea. Will you have some with me?" Maylee bustled about the spotless kitchen, grabbing more plates and teacups as she waved Taylor and Jackson to have a seat.

Taylor grinned. "We just had a small snack in mind, but this spread looks too good to pass up. Jackson?"

Reaching for a slice of bread, Jackson nodded his approval and began to fill a plate.

"Oh, dig in," Maylee directed. "And here's your tea."

Silent moments passed as all three filled their plates with food and enjoyed their midnight meal.

Maylee caught Taylor's eye and nodded toward the teacup in front of her.

Taylor smiled and spun the cup three times clockwise and scooted it toward Maylee.

As Maylee gazed at the remaining remnants of leaves, a frown formed on her face.

"What's she doing?" whispered Jackson.

"Shhhhh . . . Maylee reads tea leaves. Drink yours," she directed, "you're next."

Jackson obeyed, spinning his cup as Taylor had done.

Maylee looked up from Taylor's cup, still frowning. "Let me see yours, Jackson."

He pushed his cup toward Maylee.

"What is it, Maylee? Is it different when you look at them together?" Taylor asked.

"Interesting . . ." Maylee began. "With the two cups together, there is a definite scene. I haven't seen this very often. Both cups show half an arch, so together, the arch is complete, see?"

Taylor stood up to peek over Maylee's shoulder. "What does an arch mean?"

"Like this, it means a journey together. But it's confusing, because the arches apart mean separate journeys. Are you two planning a trip?"

Jackson shook his head after he and Taylor exchanged glances.

"Anything else, Maylee?" Taylor asked, taking her place again at the table.

Maylee remained silent. Usually the signs were so clear and numerous that she normally interpreted several symbols within the tea leaves. The messages in Taylor's and Jackson's cups were confusing. Much different from what she'd ever seen.

As she stared at the tea leaves, Maylee resisted the urge to elaborate on several of the confusing signs she saw in both teacups and instead focused on one of the more positive symbols.

"Ah," she said, smiling broadly, "the wheel appears in both your cups too. Fulfillment of desire awaits you."

Taylor blushed as she sent Jackson a sidelong glance.

"On that note," Jackson said, "I think it's time for us to go."

Maylee laughed and nudged them both toward the door. "Off to bed, you two. I'll take care of the kitchen. Shoo!"

Taylor paused in the doorway and turned. She wrapped her arms around Maylee and hugged her tightly before she joined Jackson. "Good night, Maylee, and thank you . . . for everything," she whispered.

Maylee returned the hug, then gently pushed Taylor away. She watched as the couple started down the alley, waving when Taylor looked over her shoulder.

She watched until they disappeared through Ida's garden gate, then closed and latched the door. With a heavy sigh, she sat once again at the table and returned her attention to the two teacups before her.

Jackson's cup had been the most disturbing, and she stared at the remaining bits of tea leaves more carefully. No matter how she squinted, it still resembled a clock sitting on top of a cross.

"I don't like this," Maylee grumbled. The combination indicated death. But how did that figure in with the definite signs of a journey? Frustrated, she spun Jackson's cup to destroy the layout of the leaves.

Then she stared again into Taylor's cup. Under the half arch she saw the shape of a moon, a bouquet of flowers, and a knife. All the symbols conflicted with each other—

the moon meant happiness and the flowers meant happy
love, but the knife meant parted lovers.

Shaking her head in frustration, Maylee gathered all the
cups and put them into the soak pan. Quickly storing the
leftover food in the icebox, she blew out the lamp and shuffled off to bed.

Perhaps the messages would be more clear in the morning.

$\mathcal{C}hapter$ 30

CAREFUL TO KEEP the back door from slamming shut, Taylor and Jackson entered Sherman House through the kitchen and made their way up the back stairs. The sound of music and laughter filled the parlor, typical of a busy Saturday night.

As Taylor and Jackson stepped onto the stairs, Ida peeked through the door from the parlor, a smile painted on her face. When she saw that her friends had returned, her smile instantly became genuine. "Oh, you're back," she whispered. "Your room is waiting for you—have a good night. Will I see you in the morning for tea?"

Taylor nodded. There would be much to share with Ida, and advice to solicit. With the murder plot no longer an issue, it was time to think about more permanent living arrangements, and Taylor was sure that Ida would be of help.

"Good night, Ida," Taylor whispered as the madame returned her attention to the crowd in the parlor.

Jackson took Taylor's hand in his, covering a yawn with his other hand. "It's been a long night, Rose."

"Yes, it has," Taylor agreed. It felt so comfortable and so right to be climbing the stairs to bed with Jackson. She squeezed his hand affectionately.

As they reached the doorway, Jackson impulsively swept Rose up into his arms and carried her into the room. He nudged the door closed and, with great care, he placed Taylor on the bed and dropped to one knee.

"Jackson—"

"Hush, Rose. Let me say what I need to say."

Taylor brought her trembling fingers to her lips.

"Taylor Rose Martin," he began, "I want us to be married. I feel married already, but I want to make things legal. I've never felt like I do when I'm with you, and I want to feel that way forever. Shall we find a preacher tomorrow? We could have a ceremony down in the garden—something quick and simple. What do you think?"

Every inch of her wanted to shout a resounding yes to Jackson's question. Her heart was almost bursting with joy, but her brain began questioning the logic of commitment when she had no idea how time would affect their union. She wished she knew what the future held.

"What is it?" Jackson asked softly.

As she stared into the depths of Jackson's sea blue eyes, all fear suddenly washed away as one thought stood out in her troubled mind. The thought screamed at her: *Live in the moment.* Relief flowed through her as she dropped her hands from her lips and leaned forward to kiss her love.

When they finally parted, Taylor whispered, "Yes. Yes, I want to marry you. Yes, I want to make a home with you. Yes, Jackson, yes."

"You're worried about the future, aren't you?"

"Not anymore. I can't control the future. I can only control what we have right now. And right now I feel so . . . connected . . . to you. . . . That has to be what being married is supposed to feel like."

"I know," Jackson answered. "I always wondered how I

would know when love was real. But it's just . . . there. Unmistakable."

Taylor nodded. At last she had found the magic—the same magic her parents must have had. And it had been well worth the wait.

"I love you, Rose."

"And I love you, Jackson. Now . . . come to bed." Taylor stood, already beginning to unbutton her dress.

Jackson remained on the floor, gently pulling Taylor's dress down her slim hips until a puddle of crimson satin was heaped at her feet. Petticoat soon followed and Jackson drew Taylor to him, snuggling his cheek against her soft belly.

His hands worked their way up the back of Taylor's thighs until they reached her silky bikini panties. Deftly, he pulled them down to her ankles so that Taylor stood before him, her naked body gleaming in the moonlight.

"You are so beautiful. I love everything about you." Turning his head, Jackson traced a sensuous downward path, kissing his way to the silky triangle between Taylor's legs. Then he lovingly continued his exploration there with his tongue.

Taylor groaned in pleasure and surprise as Jackson tenderly lavished her with the most intimate attention. As he licked and suckled, his hands kneaded her behind, sending more shivers of delight to her already throbbing groin.

Waves of ecstasy pulsated through Taylor as she gasped in sweet agony, "Jackson . . . please . . . come to bed . . . now. I need you."

Jackson snuggled his cheek once again against the silky skin of Taylor's stomach, then slowly stood up. His hands caressed Taylor's back as he paused a moment to hold her tightly against him.

Taylor managed to slip a hand between them, feeling for Jackson's hardness.

He groaned as she grasped him, and he released her from his embrace. Frantically, they both attacked his shirt buttons, desire building with every beat of their hearts.

Taylor turned down the bed just as Jackson slipped out of his trousers. She shivered at the sight of him—his body glistening slightly with perspiration, his inky black chest hairs sparkling in the moonlight. She looked lower, lovingly approving of his obvious desire for her.

Between the fresh sheets of the bed, they fell into each other's arms. Jackson's mouth covered Taylor's hungrily as he eased himself on top of her. As he guided himself into her warm, moist depths, his kiss became more urgent and demanding.

Taylor returned his kiss, freely and passionately. At the moment he entered her, she instinctively grasped and squeezed him until he groaned with pleasure.

Their lovemaking was swift and intense, as though they felt in danger that time might run out. As their loving rhythm synchronized, Jackson pulled his lips from Taylor's, leaving her mouth burning with fire. They gazed into each other's eyes as they embraced the peak of passion as one.

Explosions of desire shook them as together their bodies climbed to the height of bliss, flew over its edge, and tingled with sensuous completion.

Divine exhaustion enveloped them and they fell into a deep, welcome sleep.

Chapter 31

A WARM SUMMER breeze ruffled the curtains and fanned the pages of a book on the table next to the bed. The sound of the soft rustling caused Jackson's eyes to flutter open and he blinked at the bright morning sunshine.

The thick aroma of roses drifted in with each breeze. Jackson listened to the lilting sounds of a mockingbird running through its repertoire, identifying its pattern, listening to the varied songs.

A perfect summer day.

Taylor was nestled against his chest, one arm draped around his waist. Her mahogany brown hair was tousled; wispy curls caressed her cheek.

Taylor's own eyes fluttered open, and she smiled. "Hi . . . nice night, Mr. Hoyt."

Jackson grinned. "Yeah, too bad we slept through most of it." He gave Taylor a squeeze, then playfully pulled her on top of him. Taylor relaxed against his chest, burying her face against his neck. Jackson explored the hollows of her back with his hand, massaging and squeezing the skin gently.

The mere touch of his hand on her sent a warming shiver through Taylor, causing her heart to flutter wildly. A tremor of wanting ran through her as she began to cover Jackson's neck with warm, wet kisses, and her hips began a slow, sensuous grind against him.

Her renewed passion made Jackson instantly grow hard against her belly. She could feel his heartbeat quicken as his body responded to hers. Gently, he pulled her upward so their lips could join in an intimate kiss.

The kiss sent the pit of Taylor's stomach into a wild swirl and she quivered at the sweet tenderness of it. She returned the kiss, lingering, savoring every moment. Jackson's hands moved to her bottom, deliciously kneading and caressing as she continued to move her hips against his hardness.

Breaking away from his kiss, Taylor drew her knees apart and lifted herself from him just long enough to guide him into her. She watched the ember of passion in Jackson's eyes burst into flame as he pulled her hips down against him, pushing every inch of his arousal into her.

Taylor straddled him and arched her back in sensual pleasure, moaning as Jackson began to softly fondle her breasts. She leaned forward, bringing her nipples to his lips. Soon he was tantalizing the buds with his tongue, exploring there until she felt dizzy with arousal.

Their bodies melted together as her hips moved against him until, once again, pleasure exploded in a downpour of fiery sensations—electricity seemed to arc through them. Their perfect tempo of love bound their bodies together, sending them both to an even higher level of bliss. And as their bodies finally came to rest, contentment and peace flowed between them. A happy exhaustion, a sweet agony.

Taylor sighed a deep sigh, moaning with the gratification of a contented lover. "What a wonderful way to wake up."

Jackson kissed the top of her head. "I agree."

"Shall we stay in bed forever?" she asked.

"A wonderful thought, but not so practical. . . . Besides,

you'll be hungry soon and, God knows, I have to keep you fed to keep you happy," he teased.

"You are rotten, Jackson Hoyt. I don't know why I love you at all." Taylor softly punched Jackson's shoulder as she lifted herself off him and rolled over to the edge of the bed.

"I know many that would agree with you, my dear." Jackson laughed at Taylor's scrunched nose as she pretended to be angry with him.

"Well, even though I don't like you at all, would you like to take a bath with me?" Taylor walked to the stove to check the buckets of water, hoping the fire had smoldered through the night. "It's a bit better than lukewarm," she said, pouring both buckets into the tub. "Better hurry, though, it won't be warm for long."

Jackson got out of bed to join Taylor in the tub. "I'm up for a quick bath, then I've got work to do at the saloon. Can you keep yourself busy today?"

Taylor smiled as she joined Jackson in the tub. "Sure. There's always gardening to do here. I haven't been concentrating on Ida's yard for a few days. There's plenty to keep me busy."

"And," Jackson added, "I will send a carriage this evening to pick you up and take you to the finest restaurant in San Diego for a proper meal"—Jackson paused and his eyes sparkled—"before I make you my wife. I intend to find a preacher today and make you an honest woman tomorrow."

Taylor leaned forward to press her lips to his, caressing his mouth tenderly. "Sounds like a plan, my love."

At tea, Taylor told Ida about the ordeal at Wyatt Earp's saloon and Jackson's involvement in the murder plot.

Wordlessly, Ida listened, captivated by Taylor's description of the discovery of how exactly Jackson's father had been killed by the famous lawman and, finally, how Josie had come **so close** to perishing at the hands of the younger McLaurey **brother**.

"You shouldn't have been doing all this by yourself, you know," Ida scolded. "You could have been killed."

"I know, I know. But it's all over now—don't scold me. I couldn't stand it if you were really angry with me."

Ida shook her head and smiled warmly at Taylor. "So . . . you and Jackson . . . ?"

Taylor sighed. "Jackson asked me to marry him and I said yes."

Ida squealed with delight. "Oh, you can get married in the garden. It will be perfect. The girls can get all dressed up and we'll have a party—no business for the night. Just us. Like family."

"I'd love to have all of you there," Taylor said, "and the garden will be a perfect setting. Jackson's in town finishing up some things at the saloon today and arranging for a minister. We're meeting tonight for dinner—I'll tell him then."

Ida covered Taylor's hands with her own, her eyes brimming with tears of joy. When she looked in Taylor's eyes, she could see the true love there and an immense amount of happiness shining from their emerald green depths. It warmed her heart to see Jackson and Taylor's love, and the thought of them building a life together felt like a match made in heaven.

"Now, I've got work to do in the garden. I want it to look perfect for tomorrow. Will you pick out something for me to wear tonight?"

Ida nodded and watched Taylor walk out the back door to the garden. She wore a big gardening hat and the oversized tunic and pants that she'd worn the first day she'd worked in the garden.

"Bother," Ida said to herself. "Now I've got to find a new gardener."

•   •   •

Taylor gulped down the glass of lemonade that Ida had left for her on the table in the garden. It had been a good day gardening. The rosebushes were filled with blooms, and each flower bed had been weeded and watered. She plopped down on one of the chairs, pulled her hat off her head, and wiped her brow. A perfect day.

"Congratulations."

The cheerful sound of her father's voice startled Taylor, then filled her with joy.

But dread soon replaced her joy. Again she had the distinct feeling something was going to happen, especially since the mystery had been solved.

"Are you happy, Taylor?"

She'd never been happier. She knew Jackson was what she needed. And wanted. Would she have a future with him?

Taylor listened to the silence, her stomach knotting in fear.

Dad?

"Your future belongs to you."

She didn't understand. All she wanted was to know how much time she had.

Taylor's eyes filled with tears of frustration. She felt as though she might disappear at any moment, and at the same time it felt as if she could have whatever she set her mind to have. *Which was it?*

"Rose! Come inside! I've drawn a bath so you can clean up and get dressed. Hurry or you'll be late for dinner," Ida called.

Welcoming the interruption, Taylor blinked back her tears, then deposited her tools in the shed and joined Ida inside.

"Rose, the carriage is here. Let's have a look at you."

Taylor walked into the parlor dressed in a lacy, shimmering peach dress, a satin bow at her waist accentuating her slim build. Her mahogany hair was brushed back from her face, and long curls were secured to the back of her head. Pearls at her throat completed the look of a Victorian socialite going out for the evening.

"Perfect," gushed Ida. "You look perfect. Jackson will fall in love with you all over again. Turn around, let me see the back."

Smiling at Ida's motherly attention, Taylor whirled around in a slow circle with her arms held out. She felt like a beauty contestant waiting for a judge's approval.

"I have to admit, Rose, that it's been a pleasure transforming you to the beauty that you have become. And I know Jackson would agree."

"Oh, Ida. You are a miracle worker. Thank you for lending me so many of your pretty things." Taylor wrapped her arms around Ida in a long hug.

Ida held Taylor at arm's length for another look. "I'm so glad that you're happy, Rose. You deserve it."

"Thanks, Ida. And so do you. . . . Always remember that."

"Off with you, now—the driver's waiting. Have a wonderful dinner."

Taylor blew a kiss to Ida from the carriage as the driver urged the horses forward. As she settled back in the coach, she covered a yawn with her gloved hand. Working in the yard had been more tiring than she had realized.

Her eyelids felt strangely heavy and she soon found that she couldn't keep them open. If she could just close her eyes for a few minutes, she'd be fine. . . .

Jackson slid the final bottle of brandy onto the shelf. The saloon was clean again, everything in its place, the bar lovingly polished to a brilliant luster. He looked around the room, amazed that a few short days ago, he'd thought that today he'd be either dead, in jail, or on the run from a murder. Now he was looking at a possible partnership with Wyatt Earp and marriage to a beautiful stranger named Rose.

The thought of her filled him with a rush of joy and happiness. He closed his eyes and her face filled his mind. *Rose.*

The creak of a floorboard disturbed Jackson's thoughts. He turned toward the door. "Sorry, we're closed—"

With a shock, he felt blinding pain in his chest, followed by an eerie feeling that he had stepped outside himself as he looked at Dean McLaurey, standing ten feet away, his gun smoking.

Jackson's head snapped at the sound of another shot.

The thunderous noise filled the room, along with the ear-splitting sound of glass breaking. Jackson looked toward the window in time to see Mr. Johnson, his gun drawn.

Then he watched as Dean McLaurey's body fell to the floor with a heavy thud.

Then total blackness . . . he was falling into the blackness. . . .

Chapter 32

THE RHYTHM OF the carriage had lulled Taylor into a peaceful sleep. Her eyes still felt heavy as she tried desperately to rouse herself, tried so desperately to wake up.

I need to wake up. Jackson is not going to be very impressed with a sleeping bride-to-be.

The blaring sound of a car horn made Taylor's eyes pop open in alarm. Her heart at her throat, she sat up in her seat and blinked painfully at car lights in the oncoming lane.

Eyes filling with stinging tears, Taylor covered her mouth, holding in the sob that threatened to escape. *Jackson. Oh, Jackson.*

Stunned, Taylor looked down.

She was still dressed in Ida's lacy peach dress, and she was still riding in a carriage.

But soon she saw that she had made the journey home to modern San Diego, evident with one look at her surroundings. How had it happened?

Tears overflowed onto her cheeks as she closed her eyes, grief overwhelming her. Her heart felt like it was breaking. *How will I survive without him?*

Another car horn blared and the carriage pulled to a stop at the curb with a lurch. Taylor massaged her ears at the pain of the modern noises and slowly opened her eyes. She was home. Her apartment windows were dark, and she could see mail overflowing from her postal box.

She had indeed come back. Alone.

"Sorry about the rough stop. That guy in the truck was determined to get past us. I have a feeling he's not overly fond of sharing the road with a horse and buggy."

The driver made his way over to the side door to help Taylor out of the carriage. He opened the door and extended his hand to her.

As their fingers touched, she felt an unexpected surge of energy shoot up her forearm. It tingled all the way to her shoulder. Her eyes widened as she recognized the feeling.

The driver pulled his hand away quickly and stepped back.

"Did you feel that?" he asked. "Must have been static electricity or something."

Taylor stared into the driver's sea blue eyes. *The same eyes.* Her gaze dropped to his mouth. *The same lips.*

Her eyes searched his for any sign of recognition, logic battling the urge she felt to leap into his arms.

"Yes, I felt it too," she whispered.

"Oh, I almost forgot. While you were sleeping, an elderly man gave this to me . . . and said to give it to you when you woke up. He said you'd understand. He seemed harmless . . . a nice old guy, actually."

Taylor watched as the driver reached into the front seat and presented her with a perfect, long-stemmed red rose.

Dad?

Only silence.

"Are you all right?" the driver asked.

"I'm fine . . . really." Taylor brought the rose to her lips, feeling its softness.

"Do you think you know the old guy that gave this to me to give to you?"

"Yes, I think I do." Taylor smiled at the carriage driver and breathed in the aroma of the rose. "Mmmmmmm . . . wonderful. Smell?"

The driver leaned over to inhale the fragrance, closing his eyes for just an instant. When he opened them again, their faces were only inches apart.

Taylor looked again into his eyes and, as she held his gaze, she heard—as though from a great distance—first a female voice singing, *"He's the one,"* followed by a male voice singing, *"She's the one."*

Probably just a car stereo, she reasoned. A popular song lyric at best.

As though he too had heard the ghostly voices, the driver jolted and stepped back, falling hard onto the sidewalk.

Taylor hurried out of the carriage to see if he had seriously hurt himself. She knelt on the sidewalk next to him.

"Are you hurt? Are you all right?"

"Embarrassed, but fine, thanks." Again the driver gazed into Taylor's eyes, bringing his face closer to hers.

Taylor said a silent prayer, asking for a sign that this man was who he appeared to be. Who she desperately wanted him to be.

"The man . . . said something else," he said.

Taylor waited, catching her breath.

"It's weird."

"Tell me."

"He said to believe in the voices." The driver grinned. "Did you just hear something a minute ago?"

"Wise man," Taylor answered.

"I know this is going to sound crazy . . ."

"Go ahead," Taylor urged.

"Have we met before? I feel like we . . . know each other. I promise you, this is not some kind of line."

Taylor nodded.

"What's your name?"

"Taylor Rose Martin. But you can call me Rose. It's your choice." Taylor extended her hand to the driver.

When their hands touched, the warmth traveled up both their arms, ending at their hearts.

"Nice to meet you, Rose. I'm Jack Hoyt. My friends call me Jackson."

"Well, Jackson, why don't you come inside and let me check your ankle," she said, returning his smile. "Maybe we can figure out this déjà vu thing if we try hard enough."

Author's Note

I HOPE YOU ENJOYED reading *Forever Rose* as much as I enjoyed researching and writing about this particular time in history. Although this is certainly a work of fiction, I have tried to present as many historical facts as possible.

The setting for Taylor's adventure back in time is known as the Gaslamp Quarter, which covered a large portion of an area called the Stingaree District. Many claimed the Stingaree was as wild and dangerous as the Barbary Coast in San Francisco. By the late 1880s, the city of San Diego had grown from a dusty Western town to a bustling, exciting city with over 40,000 residents.

Wyatt Berry Stapp Earp had already gained folk hero status (from the 1881 shoot-out with the Clanton gang near the O.K. Corral) when he and his wife, Josie, came to San Diego with plans to capitalize on the land boom of 1887. Over the years, Earp owned or leased at least four saloons and gambling halls, which offered such games as faro, roulette, poker, blackjack, and keno.

Ida Bailey also arrived in San Diego during the big real estate boom of the late 1880s. A *San Diego Union* journalist wrote in February 1888, "In the midst of these low hovels on the corner of Third and 'I' looms up the notorious Sherman House, which assumes the proportions and pretensions of a maison de joie. Here are thirteen girls presided over by Ida Bailey, 'Redheaded Ida,' who is always such a conspicuous figure in the front rows of the Opera House." She remained a businesswoman until her retirement in 1909.

One of the most enigmatic and creative figures who resided in San Diego during this exciting era was internationally celebrated author, spiritualist, and musician Jesse Shepard. He lived for two years in the Villa Montezuma, a house designed by the architectural firm of Comstock and Trotsche. Painstakingly restored under the leadership of the San Diego Historical Society, this imaginatively designed Victorian still stands at 1925 K Street.

George Hoyt was the first known man Wyatt Earp killed in the line of duty. Though not much is known about him, it was reported by a cowhand that Hoyt was "wanted by Texas police." Descriptions say that in 1878, Hoyt rode wildly through the streets of Dodge City, recklessly firing a gun.

Some researchers claim Pete Spencer participated in the murder of Wyatt Earp's brother, Morgan, and eventually ended up in jail. Frank and Tom McLowrey were both killed in the famous gun battle near the O.K. Corral.

All other characters depicted throughout the pages of *Forever Rose,* though modeled after the people of this fascinating era, are completely fictitious.

I love to hear from my readers.

> Janet Wellington
> P.O. Box 1864
> Spring Valley, CA 91979
> mail@janetwellington.com

And I invite you to visit my website:
> www.janetwellington.com

Author Bio

Janet Wellington grew up in the Midwest spending wonderful childhood summers checking out ten books at a time every week from the neighborhood library. Her lifelong dream of becoming a published author is one of those special wishes that has come true with much hard work, perseverance, positive thinking, and a great deal of assistance from Romance Writers of America.

She now lives in southern California with her own full-time hero, Jim, and a very persnickety feline named Grease Spot. Readers are welcome to write her at P.O. Box 1864, Spring Valley, CA 91979 or e-mail to: mail@janetwellington.com.

FRIENDS ROMANCE

Can a man come between friends?

❏ **A TASTE OF HONEY**
by DeWanna Pace   0-515-12387-0

❏ **WHERE THE HEART IS**
by Sheridon Smythe   0-515-12412-5

❏ **LONG WAY HOME**
by Wendy Corsi Staub   0-515-12440-0

All books $5.99

DO YOU BELIEVE IN MAGIC?

MAGICAL LOVE

The enchanting series from Jove will make you a believer!

With a sprinkling of faerie dust and the wave of a wand, magical things can happen—but nothing is more magical than the power of love.

❏ *SEA SPELL* by Tess Farraday　　　0-515-12289-0/$5.99

A mysterious man from the sea haunts a woman's dreams—and desires...

❏ *ONCE UPON A KISS* by Claire Cross

0-515-12300-5/$5.99

A businessman learns there's only one way to awaken a slumbering beauty...

❏ *A FAERIE TALE* by Ginny Reyes　　　0-515-12338-2/$5.99

A faerie and a leprechaun play matchmaker—to a mismatched pair of mortals...

❏ *ONE WISH* by C.J. Card　　　0-515-12354-4/$5.99

For years a beautiful bottle lay concealed in a forgotten trunk—holding a powerful spirit, waiting for someone to come along and make one wish. .

VISIT PENGUIN PUTNAM ONLINE ON THE INTERNET:
http://www.penguinputnam.com